THE CHINESE LAKE MURDERS

THE
CHINESE LAKE MURDERS

ROBERT VAN GULIK

With an Introduction
by
DONALD F. LACH

THE UNIVERSITY OF CHICAGO PRESS
Chicago and London

The University of Chicago Press, Chicago 60637
The University of Chicago Press, Ltd., London

83   5432

ISBN: 0-226-84865-5
LCN: 79-1537

The Chinese Lake Murders *is published by arrangement
with Harper & Row, Publishers, Inc.*

CONTENTS

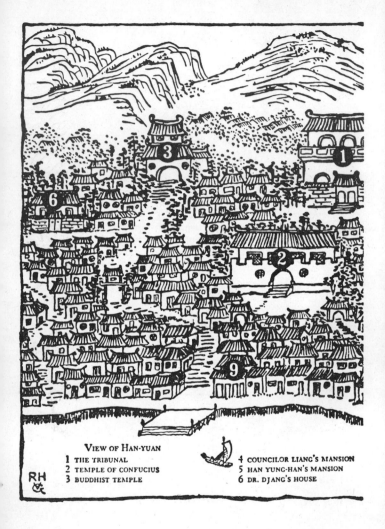

VIEW OF HAN-YUAN

1 THE TRIBUNAL
2 TEMPLE OF CONFUCIUS
3 BUDDHIST TEMPLE

4 COUNCILOR LIANG'S MANSION
5 HAN YUNG-HAN'S MANSION
6 DR. DJANG'S HOUSE

RH

漢源全景

7 LIU FEI-PO'S VILLA
8 WILLOW QUARTER
9 FISH MARKET

PREFACE

The Chinese Lake Murders describes how Judge Dee solved three difficult cases in A.D. 666, shortly after he had been appointed magistrate of Han-yuan.

Han-yuan was a small old town, only sixty miles northwest of the imperial capital; but hidden among high mountains, it had always remained an isolated place and few people from outside had settled there. It lay on the shore of a mountain lake, the mysterious lake of Han-yuan, about which since olden times people told strange stories. The bodies of persons drowned there were never found, but their ghosts were said to have been seen walking among the living. At the same time, however, the lake was famous for its "flower boats," floating houses of assignation where the guests could feast with beautiful courtesans and stay overnight on the water.

In this strange old town Judge Dee is confronted with a cruel murder. Just when his investigation of that crime is getting under way, he is faced with two new baffling puzzles, and soon he finds himself in a maze of political intrigue, sordid greed and dark, forbidden passion.

At the beginning of this volume the reader will find a view of Han-yuan, and in the middle a picture of the flower boat. The latter plate, and also the plan of that boat were kindly drawn for me by my friend Hilary Waddington, former Superintendent of Monuments of the Archaeological Service, New Delhi, India.

ROBERT VAN GULIK

INTRODUCTION

YEARS ago when looking for English materials on life in traditional China, I found the novels, commentaries, and reflections of Lin Yu-tang, Pearl Buck, and Alice Tisdale Hobart very enlightening. Their perceptions, written in charming prose, gently introduced the readers of the 1930s to Chinese society, with its gentry, peasants, and businessmen of the port cities. These writers also translated sensitively certain pieces of popular Chinese literature. Materials of such caliber and character became exceedingly difficult to find in the years following the Second World War, since most Western observers of China, as well as the Chinese themselves, had become obsessed with efforts to explain the decline and fall of the Nationalist government and the rise of the Communists to power. So it was with a sense of relief and satisfaction that readers of the 1950s welcomed the appearance of Robert Hans van Gulik's Judge Dee detective novels, in which imperial China is depicted as a living, identifiable culture rather than as a characterless pawn in the international power game. Because it is no longer possible to recapture the old China by visiting the new, the Dee stories continue to be one of the best available means of recovering a bit of the everyday life of the past.

The career of Van Gulik was a varicolored tapestry woven of threads from the skeins of scholarship, diplomacy, and art. The son of a medical officer of the Netherlands army of Indonesia, he was born in 1910 in Zutphen in Holland's province of Gelderland. Between the ages of three to twelve he lived as a colonial in Indonesia. Upon his family's return to Holland in 1922, young Robert was enrolled in the classical gymnasium (secondary school) at Nijmegen, where his considerable talents for language were quickly recognized. Through C. C. Uhlenbeck, a linguist of Amsterdam University, he was introduced at this early age to the study of Sanskrit and to the language of the Blackfoot Indians of America. In his spare time, he took private lessons in Chinese, his first tutor being a Chinese student of agriculture in Wageningen.

In 1934 Van Gulik attended the University of Leyden, one of Europe's major centers for East Asian studies. Here he worked at Chinese and Japanese systematically but without relinquishing his earlier interest in other Asian languages and literatures. For example, in 1932 he published a Dutch translation of an ancient Indian play written by Kālidāsā (ca. A.D. 400). His doctoral dissertation on the horse cult of China, Japan, India, and Tibet, defended at Utrecht in 1934, was published in 1935 by Brill, the publisher of Leyden who specializes in Asian materials. In the meantime Van Gulik also wrote articles for Dutch periodicals on Chinese, Indian, and Indonesian topics; in these articles he first displayed his love for the ancient ways of Asia and his resigned acceptance of the changes taking place.

With his university studies behind him, Van Gulik entered the foreign service of the Netherlands in 1935. His first assignment took him to the legation at Tokyo, where he had an opportunity in off hours to pursue his private scholarly studies. Most of his subjects of inquiry were chosen with reference to the preoccupations of the traditional Chinese literati. His investigations were limited in scope, though rarely in depth, by the time restrictions under which he worked. Like a traditional Chinese gentleman, he himself collected rare books, small objets d'art, scroll paintings, and musical instruments. He also scrutinized his treasures with a scholarship and a connoisseurship that won the respect of leading Oriental collectors. He translated a famous Chinese text by Mi Fu on ink stones, the valued objects on which the calligrapher prepares his ink for writing. He was himself a talented calligrapher, a rare achievement for a Westerner. He played the ancient Chinese lute (ch'in) and wrote two monographs about it based on Chinese sources. Most of his publications in these peaceful and seminal years were issued in

Peking and Tokyo and won appreciation from both Asian and European scholars.

The holocaust of the Second World War brought an abrupt end to Van Gulik's first Tokyo sojourn. Evacuated in 1942 with other Allied diplomats, he was sent to Chungking as secretary of the Netherlands mission to China. At this remote post he published in 1944 an edition of a rare Chinese work about the Ch'an master Tung-kao, a Buddhist monk who was loyal to the Ming cause in the days of its defeat. He remained in China until the end of the European war in 1945, then returned to The Hague until 1947. The following two years he spent as Councillor of the Dutch embassy in Washington, but in 1949 he finally returned to Japan for a four-year tour of duty.

In 1940 Van Gulik had run across an anonymous eighteenth-century Chinese detective novel that entranced him. Thereafter the vagaries of war and its aftermath cut him off from many of his sources and deprived him of much of his leisure, but he managed to spend odds and ends of free time in studying Chinese popular literature, especially detective and courtroom stories. He prepared an English translation of a traditional detective tale which he published at Tokyo in a limited edition in 1949 under the title *Dee Goong An*. This story in three episodes was the first of the publications through which the Western world learned of the exploits of Judge Dee, one of China's traditional detective heroes.

Van Gulik's fascination with Judge Dee, an exemplar of the imperial magistrate and of the Confucian scholar, led him to further investigations of Chinese jurisprudence and detection. In 1956 he published his English translation of a thirteenth-century case manual called *T'ang-yin pi-shih*.

Van Gulik's engrossment with detective literature was soon paralleled by an interest in Chinese erotic literature and art, especially in that of the Ming dynasty (1368–1644). Dalliances with courtesans and concubines were often as much a part of

3

the Chinese gentleman's life as the collecting of ink stones or the playing of the *ch'in*. To demonstrate this point, Van Gulik, always a connoisseur of Chinese pictorial art, published at Tokyo in 1951 a private edition in fifty copies of erotic color prints of the Ming era along with a handwritten essay on the history of Chinese sex life from 206 B.C. to A.D. 1644. While extramarital sex and the popular novel were generally considered off-limits for the Confucian scholar-gentleman, it is clear that many such men relished illicit sex and enjoyed and wrote novels surreptitiously. Through a number of works Van Gulik showed that although the gentlemen of traditional China often gave lip-service to high moral standards, they displayed in their personal lives the moral weakness of people everywhere.

While the erotica published by Van Gulik circulated only to a select audience, his numerous translations and adaptations of Chinese detective stories made Judge Dee famous in the West, especially during the 1950s. Whether posted in New Delhi, The Hague, or Kuala Lumpur, Van Gulik continued to turn out the Judge Dee stories, to a total of at least seventeen. His final diplomatic appointment brought him back to Tokyo in 1965 as the ambassador of the Netherlands to Japan, a post that he had long coveted. Two years later, while on home leave, Van Gulik put down his writing-brush for the last time.

Throughout his relatively short life, Van Gulik found time in the midst of his busy diplomatic career to inquire into an amazing variety of esoteric subjects and to publish his findings. He did not focus upon the great political, social, or economic problems of China, though he was certainly aware of their significance, in touch with the latest scholarly debates, and cognizant of contemporary political events. He did not specialize in a particular period, or even in literature alone, but ranged in his quests from Chinese classical antiquity (ca. 1200 B.C.–A.D. 200) to the end of the Ch'ing dynasty (A.D. 1644–1911). His interest was limited to traditional China rather than

4

to the twentieth-century country with its postimperial and revolutionary struggles. He sought out the "little topics" usually favored by dilettantes and amateurs of arts and letters. To the investigation of these previously unstudied byways he brought his considerable talents as linguist, historian, and connoisseur. While many of his scholarly works appealed to a limited public, his researches into the novel, jurisprudence and crime detection, and erotica were brought to Western popular audiences through his stories about the exploits of Judge Dee, the Sherlock Holmes of China.

Until the present century, the popular Chinese novel was not studied seriously by scholars either in China or in the West. It was in the era between the two world wars that intensive study of Chinese popular literature began. In the aftermath of the Chinese revolution of 1911-12 and of the disruptions brought on by the First World War, the new literati of Republican China sought to establish the spoken language (*pai-hua*) as the general language in order to help modernize the country. The leaders of this radical literary renaissance—Hu Shih, Lu Hsün, and Ts'ai Yüan-p'ei—began to revive the popular literature of the past in the hope of showing that the spoken language had been, and so might be to a greater extent in the future, a sturdy vehicle of literary expression. Because they were also eager to provide new reading matter for the masses, they looked to the past for appealing tales, intricate plots, and moral examples which could be reissued or refurbished for the public. As recently as 1975, Chinese archeologists uncovered in Hupeh Province a cache of bamboo books from the Ch'in dynasty (221-207 B.C.) which reportedly include materials on crime and detection as well as popular accounts of the magistrate as detective. Thus the search for the origins of the crime novel is being continued.

The Japanese literati, who were not as prejudiced against popular literature as their Chinese contemporaries, had long collected Chinese popular dramas and stories and had sometimes adapted them to Japanese tastes before publishing new editions. Western scholars, especially the French school of sinologues exemplified in our century by Paul Pelliot, had studied Chinese legend and story before the reforming scholars of the Chinese Republic became alert to their importance as mediums of political instruction and propaganda. In the 1930's the Chinese Communists likewise became aware of the significance of popular drama for propaganda; nor have they lost that awareness since taking over the government in 1949.

Van Gulik, a product of the European sinological school dominated by Pelliot, shared that school's enthusiasm for comparative studies and exotic subjects. For this breed of scholars, the smallest and most esoteric topics became broadly meaningful through the extraordinary linguistic, literary, and artistic analyses and perceptions of the investigator. In short, the subject was given importance, substance, and relevance by the imaginative powers and talents of the researcher. When Van Gulik first arrived in Japan in 1935, he was quick to see that its artistic collections and libraries were rich in the materials of Chinese popular culture. As an imaginative scholar with limited time at his disposal, Van Gulik immediately realized that he could produce fascinating studies of the culture of the Chinese gentry through intensive study of the objects which those privileged people collected and the customs they observed.

The Chinese crime or courtroom novel was a later form of one of the main genres of the colloquial narrative tradition—the detective story. From the time of the Sung dynasty (A.D. 960-1279), and probably much earlier, the common people delighted in listening to the tales of the storytellers who performed in the bazaars or on the streets of cities and towns. One of the popular detective heroes of the storytellers was Judge Dee (Ti Jen-chieh), a historical personage and statesman of the T'ang court who lived from A.D. 630 to 700. He and other magistrates, especially Pao Cheng (A.D. 999–1062), were celebrated by storytellers, dramatists, and novelists. In the process the historical deeds of the judge became the basis for legendary accomplishments in detection, unswervingly right conduct, and superhuman insight. The judge-detective became the central figure of a stereotype that permeated all forms of popular literature.

The hero of the traditional Chinese detective novel is normally a local magistrate. The story is usually told in colloquial language from the point of view of the working magistrate, who acts as detective, inquisitor, judge, and public avenger. It ordinarily involves a number of crimes, for the magistrate rarely had the leisure or opportunity to deal with one crime at a time. The crimes normally occur early in the story and are often interrelated. Usually the plays or stories are not didactic, and involve crimes against the person rather than misdeeds against society. The crime is always a specific infraction of statute law, ordinarily murder or rape or both. The judge acts as the instrument of the state or the emperor in establishing the facts of the case, capturing the criminal, and meting out the punishments prescribed by law. There is almost no place in the traditional stories for the judge personally to exercise discretion, extend mercy, or play favorites. The judge exemplifies courage, sagacity, honesty, impartiality, and severity; he possesses a flair for detection which is sometimes aided by superhuman insights or by knowledge conveyed to him by ghosts directly from the netherworld. Humor and lightness are rarely associated with the judge, though his subordinates sometimes become involved in clownish escapades.

The judge, always a middle-aged male of the literary class, is disdainful of luxury, protective of the weak or wronged, and above corruption and flattery. The criminal, especially the murderer, is usually cold-blooded and irredeemably evil, requires several beatings to confess, and deserves the awful punishments prescribed by law. The criminal may be of any age or class and

7

of either sex. Tartars, Mongols, Taoists, and Buddhists are almost always cast as miscreants. The victim ordinarily belongs to the artisan class, as did most of the audience.

A rudimentary theme of social justice runs through the stories. In imperial China the administration of justice aimed at retribution and the redress of wrongs; a magistrate dutifully and correctly performs these functions as he keeps the affairs of this earth in harmony with the will of Heaven. All trials were held in the courtroom and could be viewed by the public. The prosecuting judge had to question the accused in open court and never in private. While the judge himself was thought to recognize guilt or innocence intuitively and immediately, he was required to prove his case in public and had to force a confession from the accused. All the proceedings were carefully written down for the record, and the accused had to verify the accuracy of the transcript by signing it. Because criminals were often sly, the judge was sometimes confused, though never more than momentarily. Although most of the investigation was conducted by bailiffs, the judge, in the interests of efficiency or justice would sometimes make a personal investigation. The public, both in the street and in the courtroom, criticized or praised the activities and decisions of the judge. If the people suspected the judge of corruption, favoritism, or wrong-headedness, public protests and disorders were expected to follow. If a magistrate's superiors became convinced of his wrongdoing, he was dismissed and punished; if a public protest was adjudged wrong and seditious, an entire district would be punished.

When Van Gulik published his first translation of a Judge Dee story in 1949, he suggested that a modern writer of detective stories might try his hand at a novel in the Chinese mode for the day's readers. Because nobody accepted this challenge, Van Gulik decided to undertake the task himself, even though he had no previous experience in writing fiction. Originally he intended to show the reading public of Japan and China how much better the traditional stories were than those translated from Western originals then being sold in the stalls of Tokyo and Shanghai. He wrote his first two novels in English as working drafts for versions that he intended ultimately to publish in Japanese and Chinese. When his Western friends exhibited enthusiasm for this new type of detective story, he decided to continue writing in English, another foreign language in which he had become highly proficient.

The giant step from scholarly research and translation to imaginative writing was one that Van Gulik made decisively and successfully. His former involvement with unfrequented paths of scholarly research proved to be splendid preparation for his leap into the writing of atmospheric Chinese detective stories. Now it was no longer necessary to stick to precise historical facts and texts; accuracy of background and realistic portrayal of life in traditional China had become paramount. While using Judge Dee as a stock character, Van Gulik could draw freely upon the plots, stories, and data offered by the whole body of Chinese literature. And to these he could easily add fascinating and titillating embellishments from his own scholarly researches and reading. He also enlivened the novels with his own imaginary maps and with his drawings of Chinese scenes based on sixteenth-century pictorial block prints.

Van Gulik's earlier Judge Dee stories, prepared between 1950 and 1958, are closer to Chinese originals than are those he wrote subsequently. Five in number, these early novels include *The Chinese Bell Murders* and *The Chinese Nail Murders* now reproduced in new editions. Van Gulik wrote the *Bell Murders* in Tokyo during 1950 as the first of his efforts; the *Nail Murders* he wrote in Beirut in 1956. He ordinarily chose his plots and characters while relaxing from official duties, and laid out the preliminary topography as he prepared a map of an imaginary city. In the *Bell Murders* all three plots were taken directly from Chinese stories; in the other Judge Dee books Van Gulik him-

9

self supplied most of the themes and plots. Once the actual writing began, it normally took him about six weeks to complete a novel.

From the beginning Van Gulik was aware of the limitations of traditional Chinese prose fiction. Stories of murder, adultery, mystery, and violence were sure to appeal to a Western audience which never seemed to be sated by such offerings. But other features of Chinese colloquial fiction were not likely to be so well received. The criminal's identity was ordinarily revealed at the beginning of Chinese stories; out of deference to Western custom Van Gulik puts the solution near the end. Chinese materials were too often drawn from unfamiliar customs and beliefs, and Chinese authors too often content to solve a puzzling mystery by calling for supernatural knowledge or intervention. Where Westerners would expect morals to be drawn or motivations clarified, the Chinese authors rarely made these matters explicit. Character portrayal in Chinese novels was often limited to depiction of social types. Practically no effort was made to analyze or develop individual character and to evaluate the influence of environment or background upon it.

Judge Dee himself, as depicted in the Chinese stories, was a character utterly foreign to Westerners. To make him more credible Van Gulik sought to make him more human. Occasionally he smiles, becomes excited in the presence of an attractive woman, or feels unsure of himself and his decisions. Van Gulik also plays down Dee's strict Confucian view of the world, which included an unshakable faith in the superiority of everything Chinese and a disdain for all foreigners, a steadfast belief in all aspects of filial piety, a matter-of-fact attitude toward torture, and an unrelenting hostility to Buddhism and Taoism. While he could not completely ignore these traditional attributes, Van Gulik preferred to soften his Judge's attitudes and to add to his human dimension by making him a devoted family man, a connoisseur of arts and letters, and a deeply religious person. Normally the Judge also tries to solve crimes rationally and without intervention at critical moments from the netherworld.

While consciously adapting his stories to the Western audience, Van Gulik preserved extraordinarily well the way of life of imperial China. The reader will appreciate the part played in that society by family when Dee chastizes the father for not watching more closely over the virtue of his daughter. He will come to understand the role of the student, his privileges and responsibilities to society, and the relation of education to morality. He will also learn from Dee that Buddhist monks typically lust for women and are crafty in politics, that Tartars are untrustworthy and, like Taoists, given to black magic, and that southerners differ greatly from northerners in spoken language and customs. The smallest items—ink stones, nails in a Tartar shoe, the gongs of Taoist monks, door knobs—are brought into the stories at strategic points in the plot to give Van Gulik the opportunity to enlighten the Western reader about these strange objects and their functions. No foreign reader can escape a feeling for the importance in China of the written language and of written records and documents; for the prevalence of social corporations unfamiliar to Westerners, such as the Beggar's Guild; or for the exaggerated concern with proper ceremony and polite forms of address. The seamy side of life is also exposed by reference to the sale of female children into slavery and by the prevalence of prostitution. Asides on foreign trade, on the imperial salt monopoly, on "squeeze" or petty bribery, and on cooking add to the realism of the stories. The role of women is depicted as limited to homemaking, sex, handicrafts, and childrearing.

The Judge Dee stories should not be taken as completely accurate depictions of life in imperial China. For one thing, they are anachronistic. The historical Judge Dee lived in the seventh century, but most of the Chinese stories about him were written down in the sixteenth to nineteenth centuries and reflect the standards and practices current then. Van Gulik based his adaptations on these later collections. Although he was a close student of the Ming and Ch'ing dynasties, the Dutch scholar's experiences with life in China were limited to a few brief visits and to several years' stay during the Second World War. He idealizes the China which existed before the empire had been shaken by the disruptive influences of the West and Japan. He sees imperial China most often from the viewpoint of the Confucian gentry for whose way of life he had respect and affection.

Still, these stories, for all their limitations and biases, provide relatively accurate portrayals of certain aspects of everyday life in imperial China. Van Gulik's personal observations were made in a pre-Communist era when the old ways were still followed in the villages and towns and when the magistrate was still dominant in local affairs. Highly sensitive to the stuff of everyday life, Van Gulik was not an ordinary observer of the Chinese scene. From his studies and his experience with the highest echelons of government he acquired qualifications for understanding traditional China that are no longer part of the equipment of specialists. No amount of reading in classical texts, gazeteers, dynastic histories, or diplomatic documents will by itself provide depth of understanding about the basic workings of life in traditional China. For the Westerner, direct translations of Chinese popular tales are often too foreign in nature and leave references to common matters too frequently unexplained for full comprehension. The insights and elucidations offered by Van Gulik provide the Westerner with a painless and pleasant introduction to premodern China and with an understanding of how different, yet sometimes how similar, are the peoples and societies of China and the West. And, besides, these are entertaining stories and should be appreciated simply for their own sake.

DONALD F. LACH

DRAMATIS PERSONAE

It should be noted that in Chinese the surname—here printed in capitals—precedes the personal name.

Main characters

DEE Jen-djieh, Magistrate of Han-yuan, a small mountain district sixty miles west of the capital. Referred to as "Judge Dee," or "the judge."

HOONG Liang, Judge Dee's trusted adviser and sergeant of the tribunal. Referred to as "Sergeant Hoong," or "the sergeant."

MA Joong, first lieutenant of Judge Dee.

CHIAO Tai, second lieutenant of Judge Dee.

TAO Gan, third lieutenant of Judge Dee, enters in Chapter Twelve.

Persons connected with "The Case of the Drowned Courtesan"

HAN Yung-han, wealthy landowner, leading citizen of Han-yuan.

Willow Down, his daughter.

Almond Blossom ⎫
Anemone   ⎬ courtesans of the Willow Quarter in Han-yuan.
Peach Blossom ⎭

WANG, master of the Goldsmiths' Guild.

PENG, master of the Silversmiths' Guild.

SOO, master of the Jadeworkers' Guild.

KANG Po, a wealthy silk merchant.

KANG Choong, his younger brother.

Persons connected with "The Case of the Vanished Bride"

DJANG Wen-djang, a Doctor of Literature.

DJANG Hoo-piao, his son, a Candidate of Literature.

LIU Fei-po, a wealthy merchant from the capital.

Moon Fairy, his daughter.
KOONG, a tea merchant, neighbor of Dr. Djang.
MAO Yuan, a carpenter.
MAO Loo, his cousin.

*Persons connected with "The Case of the Spendthrift
Councilor"*

LIANG Meng-kwang, Imperial Councilor, living retired
in Han-yuan.
LIANG Fen, his nephew who acts as his secretary.
WAN I-fan, a promoter.

Others

MENG Kee, Grand Inquisitor.

AN AILING OFFICIAL COMPLETES A WEIRD RECORD; JUDGE DEE ATTENDS A BANQUET ON A FLOWER BOAT

Only Heaven that wrote the scroll of human life
Knows where its beginning is, and where its end—
If end there be. We mortals can not read its writ,
We even know not whether the text runs down or up.

Yet when a judge is seated behind his scarlet bench
His is the power of Heaven, over life and death—
But not Heaven's knowledge. Let him—and us!—beware
Lest passing judgment on others, we ourselves be judged.

NO ONE, I TRUST, WILL CALL TWENTY YEARS OF SERVING our illustrious Ming Emperor a poor record. My late father, it is true, served fifty years, and when he died a Councillor of State, he had just celebrated his seventieth birthday. I shall be forty, three days hence—but may Heaven grant that I shan't be then still alive.

In the ever rarer moments that my tortured brain is clear, I let my thoughts go back to the years that have passed, the only escape now left. Four years ago I was promoted to Investigator of the Metropolitan Court, a signal honor for an official of only thirty-five. People predicted a great future for me. How proud I was of this large mansion assigned to me, and how I loved to walk in the beautiful garden, hand in hand with my daughter! How small she was then, only a child, but she knew already the literary names of every flower I pointed at. Four years—but how long ago that seems now. Like memories from a previous existence.

Now you, threatening shadow, again press close to me; shrinking in terror, I must obey you. Do you grudge me even this brief respite? Didn't I do all you ordered me to do? Didn't I last month, after my return from that fey old city of Han-yuan by its sinister lake, choose at once an auspicious date for my daughter's wedding; and wasn't she married last week? What do you say now? My senses are numbed by the unbearable pain; I can't hear you

15

well. You say that . . . that my daughter must learn the truth? Almighty Heaven, have you no pity? That knowledge shall break her heart, destroy her. . . . No, don't hurt me, please. I shall do as you say, only don't hurt me. . . . Yes, I shall write.

Write, as every sleepless night I write, with you, inexorable executioner, standing over me. The others can't see you, you say. But isn't it true that when a man has been touched by death, others can see its mark on him? Every time I come upon one of my wives or concubines in the now deserted corridors, she quickly averts her face. When I look up from my papers in the office, I often catch my clerks staring at me. As they hurriedly bend again over their documents, I know that they covertly clasp the amulets they have taken to wearing of late. They must feel that after I had come back from my visit to Han-yuan I was not merely very ill. A sick man is pitied; a man possessed is shunned.

They do not understand. They need only pity me. As one pities a man condemned to the inhuman punishment of inflicting on himself with his own hand the lingering death: being forced by the executioner to cut away his own flesh, piece by piece. Every letter I wrote, every coded message I sent out these last days cut away a slice of my living flesh. Thus the threads of the ingenious web I had been weaving patiently over the entire Empire were cut, one by one. Every thread cut stands for a crushed hope, a thwarted illusion, a wasted dream. Now all traces have been swept out; no one shall ever know. I even presume that the *Imperial Gazette* shall print an obituary, mourning me as a promising young official who met an untimely death by a lingering disease. Lingering, indeed, lingering till now there is nothing left of me but this bloodstained carcass.

This is the moment that the executioner plunges his long knife in the tortured criminal's heart, giving him the merciful deathblow. Why, then, do you, fearful shadow, insist on prolonging my agony, you who call yourself by the name of a flower? Why do you want to tear my heart to pieces, by forcing me to kill the soul of my poor daughter? She never committed any crime, she never knew. . . . Yes, I hear you, terrible woman; you say that I still must write, write down everything, so that my daughter shall know. Tell her how Heaven denied me a quick, self-chosen end, and condemned me to a slow death of agony in your cruel hands. And that after having granted me one brief glance of . . . what could have been.

Yes, my daughter shall know. About meeting you on the shore of the lake, about the old tale you told me, all. But I swear that if there still be a Heaven above us, my daughter shall forgive me; a traitor and a murderer she shall forgive, I tell you. But not you! Not you, because you are only hate, hate incarnate, and you shall die together with me, die forever. No, don't pull away my hand now; you said "Write!" and write I shall. May Heaven have mercy on me and . . . yes, also on you. For now— too late—I recognize you for what you really are, and I know that you never come uninvited. You haunt and torture to death only those who have called you up by their own dark deeds.

This, then, is what happened.

The Court had directed me to Han-yuan, to investigate a complicated case of embezzlement of government funds; it was suspected that the local authorities were involved. You will remember that this year spring came early. A feeling of expectancy was vibrating in the warm air; in a reckless mood I had even thought of taking my daughter along with me on that trip to Han-yuan. But that mood passed, and I took Chrysanthemum, my youngest concubine, with me instead. I thus hoped to restore peace to my tormented soul, for Chrysanthemum had been very dear to me before. When I had arrived in Han-yuan, however, I realized that it had been an idle hope. She whom I had left behind was more than ever with me. Her image stood between us; I couldn't even bring myself to touch Chrysanthemum's poor slender hand.

Feverishly, I devoted all my efforts to the case, trying to forget. I solved it within a week; the culprit proved to be a clerk from the capital, and he confessed. On my last night in Han-yuan the grateful local authorities gave a splendid parting dinner for me, in the Willow Quarter, the abode of the singing girls, of century-old fame. They were profuse in their protestations of gratitude and admiration for my speedy solution of the vexing case. They said they only regretted that they could not have Almond Blossom dance for me. She was the most beautiful and accomplished dancer of the quarter, they said, named after a famous beauty of bygone times. Unfortunately, the girl had unaccountably disappeared, that very morning. If only I could prolong my stay in Han-yuan for a few days, they added wistfully, doubtless I would then solve for them that mystery too! Their flattery pleased me; I drank more wine than usual, and when late in the night I came back to the luxurious hostel that had been placed at my disposal, I was in an elated mood. All would be well, I felt; I would break the spell!

Chrysanthemum was waiting for me. She wore a peach-colored single dress that admirably set off her young figure. She was looking at me with her lovely eyes, and I would have folded her in my arms. Then, suddenly, the other, the forbidden one, was there, and I could not.

A violent shiver shook my frame. Muttering I know not what excuse, I ran out into the garden. I felt as if I were suffocating; I wanted air. But it was sultry and hot in the garden. I had to go out, to the lake. I tiptoed past the dozing doorman, and went out into the deserted street. When I had reached the bank of the lake, I stood still and looked out for a long time over the still water, deep despair in my heart. What would my carefully built-up scheme boot me? Who could rule men when himself not a man? At last I knew there was only one solution.

Once I had taken that decision, I felt at peace. I loosened the front of my purple robe, and pushed the high black cap back from my perspiring brow. I strolled along at a leisurely pace, looking for a place on the bank that would suit my purpose. I think I even hummed a song. Is not the best time for leaving the painted hall when the red candles are still burning and when the wine is still warm in the golden goblets? I enjoyed the charming surroundings. On my left the almond trees, laden with white blossoms whose scent hung heavily in the warm spring air. And on my right the silvery expanse of the moonlit lake.

I saw her when I turned a corner of the winding road.

She was standing on the bank, very close to the water, clad in a white silk robe with a green sash, and wearing a white water lily in her hair. As she looked round at me, the moonlight shone on her lovely face. Then I knew in a flash that here at last was the woman who would break the laming spell, the woman Heaven had destined for me.

She also knew, for when I had gone up to her there

18

was none of the usual greetings and polite inquiries. She only said:

"The almond blossoms are out very early, this spring!"

And I said:

"It is the unexpected joys that are the greatest!"

"Are they always?" she asked with a mocking smile. "Come, I shall show you where I was sitting just now."

She went among the trees, and I followed her into a small clearing just off the road. We sat down side by side among the tall grass on a low ridge. The blossom-laden branches of the almond trees hung over us like a canopy.

"How strange this is!" I said, delighted, as I took her small, cool hand in mine. "It is as if we were in another world!"

She just smiled and gave me a sidelong glance. I put my arm round her waist and pressed my mouth on her moist, red lips.

And she took away the spell that had maimed me. Her embrace healed me, our burning passion cauterized the gaping wound in my soul. I thought exultantly that all would still be well.

When I was idly tracing with my finger the shadows cast by the branches on her beautiful body, white and smooth like the finest white jade, I suddenly found myself telling her about the spell she had broken for me. She leisurely brushed away the blossoms that had fluttered down on her perfect breasts. Sitting up, she said slowly:

"One time, long ago, I heard something similar." And then, after some hesitation: "Tell me, aren't you a judge?"

I pointed at my cap where I had hung it on a low branch, the moonlight shining on its golden insignia of rank. Then I replied with a wry smile:

"Even better than that, I am a Court Investigator!"

She nodded sagely, then lay back in the grass, folding her rounded arms under her shapely head.

"That old story," she said pensively, "ought to interest you. It concerns a clever judge, who served as magistrate here in Han-yuan many centuries ago. At that time . . ."

I know not for how long I listened to her soft, compelling voice. But when she fell silent a cold fear had gripped my heart. I rose abruptly, donned my robe and wound the long sash round my waist. As I placed my cap on my head I said hoarsely:

19

"You need not try to fool me by a fanciful tale! Speak up, woman. How did you come to know my secret?"

But she only looked up at me, her charming mouth trembling in a provoking smile.

Her utter loveliness swept away my anger. Kneeling by her side, I exclaimed:

"What does it matter how you knew! I care not who you are or who you have been. For I tell you that my plans are better laid than those you told about, and I swear that you and you only shall be my queen!" Looking at her tenderly, I took up her dress and added: "A breeze is blowing in from the lake; you'll be cold!"

She slowly shook her head. But I rose and covered her naked body with the silk dress. Then I suddenly heard loud voices nearby.

Several men came into the clearing. Greatly embarrassed, I stood myself in front of the woman reclining in the grass. An elderly man, whom I recognized as the magistrate of Han-yuan, shot a quick look past me. Then he bowed deeply and said in an admiring voice:

"So you have found her, sir! When tonight we searched her room in the Willow Quarter and found her message, we came to look in this direction. For there is a current in the lake that comes into this bight. It is indeed astonishing how you succeeded in finding out all this before we did! But you needn't have troubled to get her here from the shore, sir!" Turning to his men he ordered: "Bring that stretcher here!"

I swung round and looked. The white dress, clinging to her body like a shroud, was dripping wet, and slimy water weeds tangled with her tresses stuck to her still, lifeless face.

Dusk was falling as Judge Dee sat sipping a cup of tea on the open terrace, up on the second floor of the tribunal. Sitting straight in an armchair near the low, carved marble balustrade, he surveyed the scene spread out before him.

One by one lights went on in the town below, a solid mass of roofs. Farther down there was the lake, a wide stretch of smooth, dark water. The opposite bank was hidden by a mist hovering at the foot of the mountains over on the other side.

It had been a hot and sultry day that was changing

now into an oppressive night. Not a leaf stirred in the trees in the street below.

The judge shifted his shoulders uncomfortably in his formal robe of stiff brocade. The old man who was standing silently by his side gave his master a solicitous look. That night the gentry of Han-yuan were giving a banquet in honor of Judge Dee, on a flower boat out on the lake. He reflected that unless the weather changed it would hardly be an enjoyable affair.

Slowly caressing his long black beard, the judge followed aimlessly the course of a boat, a small dot at that distance, being sculled to the pier by a belated fisherman. When it had disappeared from his view, the judge suddenly looked up and said:

"I still have to get used to living in a town that is not surrounded by a wall, Sergeant. Somehow or other it makes one feel . . . uncertain."

"Han-yuan is only about sixty miles from the capital, Your Honor," the elderly man remarked. "Thus we are here within easy reach of the Imperial Guards. Besides, the provincial garrisons are—"

"Of course, I am not referring to military problems!" the judge interrupted him impatiently. "I am talking about the situation here inside the town. I have a feeling that there is much going on in this city that we are kept ignorant of. In walled cities the gates are closed at nightfall, one then feels that the situation is in hand, so to speak. But this open city, sprawling at the foot of the mountains, and those suburbs along the bank of the lake . . . All kinds of people can leave or enter here at their own sweet will!"

The other tugged at his frayed white beard; he did not know what to say. His name was Hoong Liang. He was Judge Dee's faithful assistant. In the olden days he had been a retainer of the judge's family; he had carried the judge in his arms when he was still a child. When, three years before, Judge Dee had been appointed district magistrate of Peng-lai, his first post in the provinces, Hoong had insisted on accompanying him, despite his advanced age. The judge had then made him sergeant of the tribunal. But he did that mainly to give Hoong official status. Hoong's main task was to act as Judge Dee's confidential adviser, with whom he could discuss unreservedly all his problems.

"Two months have elapsed since we arrived here,

Hoong," Judge Dee resumed, "and not a single case of any importance has been reported to this tribunal."

"That means," the sergeant said, "that the citizens of Han-yuan are law-abiding people, Your Honor!"

The judge shook his head.

"No, Hoong," he said. "It means that they keep us ignorant of their affairs. As you just said, Han-yuan lies near to the capital. But because of its location on the shore of this mountain lake, it has always been a more or less isolated district; few people from elsewhere have settled here. If anything happens in such a closely-knit community, they'll always do their utmost to keep it hidden from the magistrate, whom they consider an outsider. I repeat, Hoong: there is more going on here than meets the eye. Further, those weird tales about this lake—"

He did not complete his sentence.

"Does Your Honor give any credit to those?" the sergeant asked quickly.

"Credit? No, I would not go as far as that. But when I hear that in the past year four persons drowned there and their bodies were never found, I—"

At that moment two stalwart men dressed in plain brown robes and wearing small black caps walked out on the terrace. These were Ma Joong and Chiao Tai, Judge Dee's other two assistants. Both were over six feet tall and had the broad shoulders and thick necks of experienced boxers. After having greeted the judge respectfully, Ma Joong said:

"The hour set for the banquet is approaching, Your Honor! The palanquin is standing ready below."

Judge Dee rose. He let his eyes rest for a moment on the two men standing in front of him. Both Ma Joong and Chiao Tai were former "brothers of the green woods" —a flattering term for highwaymen. Three years before they had once attacked the judge on a lonely road, but he had so impressed them by his fearless and forceful personality that the two had given up their violent profession and begged him to take them into his service. Judge Dee, moved by their sincerity, had granted their request. His judgment had proved right; this formidable pair had served him loyally and proved extremely useful in the catching of dangerous criminals and the execution of other difficult tasks.

"I have just told the sergeant here," Judge Dee said to

them, "that in this town much is happening that is being kept concealed from us. While the banquet on the flower boat is in progress, you two had better let the servants and the crew partake freely of wine, and make them gossip a bit!"

Ma Joong and Chiao Tai grinned broadly. Neither of them was averse to a good drinking bout.

The four men descended the broad stone staircase leading down into the central courtyard of the tribunal compound. The ceremonial palanquin of the judge was standing ready. Judge Dee ascended together with Sergeant Hoong; twelve bearers placed the poles on their calloused shoulders. Two runners took the lead, carrying large paper lanterns with the inscription "The Tribunal of Han-yuan." Ma Joong and Chiao Tai walked behind the palanquin, followed by six constables in leather jackets with red sashes, and iron helmets on their heads.

The guards opened the heavy, iron-studded gate of the tribunal, and the procession went out into the street. The sure-footed palanquin bearers trod down the steep steps leading into the city. Soon they entered the market place in front of the Temple of Confucius, where a dense crowd was milling round the oil lamps of the night stalls. The runners sounded their copper gongs and shouted:

"Make way, make way! His Excellency the Magistrate is approaching!"

The crowd drew back respectfully. Old and young gazed with awe at the procession as it filed past.

Again they descended, passing through the quarters of the poor till they arrived on the broad highway running all along the bank of the lake. After about half a mile the procession entered a lane lined by graceful willow trees. It was these that had given their name to the Willow Quarter, the abode of the courtesans and singing girls. Their houses were gaily decorated with lampions of colored silk; stray bits of song and the strumming of stringed instruments floated in the night air. Young ladies dressed in gaudy robes crowded the red-lacquered balconies; chattering animatedly, they looked down at the procession.

Ma Joong, who fancied himself as a connoisseur of wine and women, looked up eagerly and scanned that array of beauty. He succeeded in catching the eye of a plump girl with a pleasant round face who was leaning over the balustrade up on the balcony of the largest house. He sent her a laborious wink and was rewarded by an encouraging smile.

The bearers lowered Judge Dee's palanquin on the landing stage. A group of gentlemen clad in long robes of glittering brocade stood waiting there. A tall man in a violet robe with a golden flower pattern came forward and greeted the judge with a deep bow. This was the wealthy landowner Han Yung-han, the leading citizen of Han-yuan. His family had lived for centuries in the spacious mansion high upon the mountain slope, on the same level as the tribunal.

Han led the judge to a magnificent flower boat moored alongside the landing stage, its broad foredeck level with the pier. It was ablaze with the lights of hundreds of colored lamps hung all around the eaves of the main cabin. When Judge Dee and Han entered the dining room through the portal, the orchestra sitting near the entrance struck up a gay tune of welcome.

Han took the judge across the thick carpet to the place of honor, a high table placed in the back of the room, and bade him sit down on his right. The other guests sat down behind the two secondary tables standing opposite each other on either side, at right angles to that of the judge.

Judge Dee surveyed his surroundings with interest. He had often heard about the famous flower boats of Han-yuan, a kind of floating houses of assignation where the guests could feast with female companions and spend the night out on the water. The lavish appointments surpassed his expectations. The room was about thirty feet long. On either side it was closed by bamboo curtains. From the red-lacquered ceiling hung four large lanterns of painted silk; the slender wooden pillars were elaborately carved and gilded.

A slight rocking motion indicated that the boat had left the pier. When the music stopped one could hear the rhythmic splashes of the oars handled by the rowers in the hold below.

Han Yung-han briefly introduced the other guests. The table on their right was headed by a thin, elderly man with a slight stoop. He proved to be Kang Po, a wealthy silk merchant. As Kang rose and bowed three times to the judge, Dee noticed that his mouth twitched nervously and that his eyes darted left and right. The fat man with the complacent face seated next to him turned out to be

Kang Choong, his younger brother. Judge Dee idly reflected that the two brothers were most unlike both in appearance and personality. The third guest at that table was a rotund man of pompous mien, introduced as Wang, the master of the guild of the goldsmiths'.

The table opposite was headed by a tall, broad-shouldered man wearing a gold-embroidered brown robe and a square gauze cap. His heavy, darkish face bore a commanding air. This, together with his stiff, black beard and long side whiskers, made him look like an official, but Han introduced him as Liu Fei-po, a wealthy merchant from the capital. He had built a splendid villa next to the Han mansion where he used to spend the summer. The two other guests at Liu Fei-po's table were Peng and Soo, respectively masters of the guilds of the silversmiths' and of the jadeworkers'. The judge was struck by the contrast between these two guildmasters. Peng was a very thin, elderly gentleman with narrow shoulders and a long white beard. Soo, on the contrary, was a young, hefty fellow with the heavy shoulders and the thick neck of a wrestler. His rather coarse face bore a sullen expression.

Han Yung-han clapped his hands. While the orchestra started another gay tune, four servants entered through the doorway on Judge Dee's right hand, carrying trays with cold dishes and pewter jugs of warm wine. Han proposed a toast of welcome and the banquet started.

While nibbling the cold duck and chicken, Han began a polite conversation. He was evidently a man of taste and learning, but the judge detected a certain lack of cordiality in his courteous address. He seemed very reserved, and not partial to strangers. After he had emptied a few large goblets in quick succession, however, he loosened up a little and said with a smile:

"I believe that I am drinking five cups against one of Your Honor's!"

"I am fond of a cup of good wine," Judge Dee replied, "but I only drink at such pleasant occasions as the present one. This is indeed a most lavish entertainment!"

Han bowed and said:

"We hope and trust that Your Honor will enjoy his stay in our small district. We only regret that we are but simple country folk here, not fit for Your Honor's distinguished company. And I fear that Your Honor will find life rather monotonous; so little happens here!"

"I saw indeed from the files in the tribunal," Judge Dee

said, "that the people of Han-yuan are industrious and law-abiding, a most gratifying state of affairs for a magistrate! But as to a lack of eminent persons, you are much too modest. Apart from your distinguished self, didn't the famous Imperial Councilor Liang Meng-kwang choose Han-yuan as place of retirement?"

Han pledged the judge another goblet, then said:

"The Councilor's presence honors us! We deeply regret that the last six months his indifferent health has prevented us from profiting from his instruction."

He emptied his goblet in one long draught. Judge Dee thought that Han was drinking quite a lot. He said:

"Two weeks ago I applied for a courtesy visit to the old Councilor, and was then informed that he was ill. I hope it is not serious?"

Han gave the judge a searching look. Then he answered:

"He is nearly ninety, you know. But apart from attacks of rheumatism and some trouble with his eyes, he used to be in remarkable good shape. For half a year or so, however, his mind has . . . Well, Your Honor had better ask Liu Fei-po. Their gardens adjoin each other; he sees more of the Councilor than I."

"I was rather astonished to learn," the judge remarked, "that Liu Fei-po is a merchant. He has all the marks of an official to the manner born!"

"He nearly was one!" Han whispered. "Liu comes from an old family in the capital, and was educated to become an official. But he failed to pass the second literary examination, and that embittered him to such a degree that he gave up all his studies and became a merchant. In that he was so successful that now he is one of the richest men in this province and his commercial enterprises are spread over the entire realm. That is the reason why he travels about so much. But please never mention to him that I told you this, for his earlier failure still rankles!"

Judge Dee nodded. While Han went on drinking, the judge listened casually to the conversation that was going on at the side tables. Raising his wine beaker to Liu Fei-po, the jovial Kang Choong called out:

"Here is a toast to the young couple! May they live happily together till their heads have grown gray!"

All clapped their hands, but Liu Fei-po only bowed. Han Yung-han hastily explained to the judge that Liu's

26

daughter, Moon Fairy, had been married the day before to the only son of Dr. Djang, a retired professor of classical literature. The wedding, celebrated in Dr. Djang's house over on the other side of the city, had been a very boisterous affair. Then Han called out: "We miss our learned professor tonight! He had promised to come, but at the last moment asked to be excused. I presume that his own wine has proved too strong for him!"

This remark provoked general laughter. But Liu Fei-po shrugged his shoulders with a bored air. Judge Dee reflected that Liu himself was probably having a hangover from the wedding dinner. He congratulated him, and added: "I regret to have missed this opportunity of meeting the professor. His conversation would doubtless have been most instructive."

"A simple merchant like me," Liu Fei-po said sullenly, "does not pretend to understand classical literature. But I have heard it said that book learning does not always imply a high character!"

There was an awkward pause. Han quickly gave a sign to the waiters, who rolled up the bamboo curtains.

All laid down their chopsticks to admire the view. They were well out on the lake now; beyond the broad expanse of water the myriad lights of Han-yuan twinkled in the distance. The flower boat was lying still now; it rocked slowly on the rippling waves. The rowers were eating their evening rice.

Suddenly the curtain of crystal beads on Judge Dee's left was drawn aside with a tinkling sound. Six courtesans entered and made a deep bow for the guest of honor.

Han Yung-han selected two of them to keep him and the judge company; the four others went to the side tables. Han introduced the girl standing next to Judge Dee as Almond Blossom, the famous dancer. Although she kept her eyes modestly down, the judge could see that she had a very regular and handsome but slightly cold face. The other girl, called Anemone, seemed a more cheerful sort; when she was introduced to the judge she gave him a quick smile.

As Almond Blossom poured out a cup of wine for the judge, he asked her how old she was. She replied with a soft, cultured voice that she soon would be nineteen. She spoke with an accent that reminded Judge Dee of his own province. Agreeably surprised, he asked:

27

"Could it be that you hail from Shansi Province?"

She looked up and nodded gravely. Now that he saw her large, shining eyes, the judge realized that she was indeed a remarkable beauty. But he detected at the same time a certain dark, somber glow in her eyes that seemed strange in such a charming young girl.

"I myself am a member of the Dee family of Tai-yuan," he said. "Where is your native place?"

"This person hails from Ping-yang," the girl replied softly.

Judge Dee offered her a drink from his own cup. He now understood why she had those strange eyes. The women of Ping-yang, a district a few miles to the south of Tai-yuan, had since olden times been famous as experts in sorcery and witchcraft. They could cure sickness by chanting spells and incantations; some were even reputed to practice black magic. The judge wondered how she, a beautiful girl and apparently of a good family in the faraway province of Shansi, had landed in this unfortunate profession in this small district of Han-yuan. He started a conversation with her on the fine scenery and the many historical monuments of Ping-yang.

In the meantime, Han Yung-han had been engaged in a drinking game with Anemone. They recited a line from a poem in turn, and the one who could not immediately cap it had to empty a cup as fine. Han apparently had lost often; his voice had become slurred. Now he leaned back in his chair and surveyed the company with a benign smile on his large face. The judge noticed that his heavy-lidded eyes were nearly closed; he seemed to be dozing off. Anemone had come round to the front of the table; she was watching Han's efforts to stay awake with interest. Suddenly she giggled.

"I'd better get some hot wine for him!" she said across the table to Almond Blossom, who was standing between Han and the judge. Anemone turned round and tripped over to the table of the Kang brothers. She filled Han's goblet from the large wine jar that a servant had just put down there.

Judge Dee took up his wine beaker. Han was snoring softly. The judge reflected morosely that if people were getting drunk, this party would not only be boring, but also something of a strain. He must try to leave early. Just as he was taking a sip, he suddenly heard Almond

28

Blossom speak up by his side in a soft but very distinct voice.

"I must see you later, Your Honor. A dangerous conspiracy is being plotted in this town!"

Second Chapter

THE JUDGE WATCHES THE DANCE OF THE CLOUD FAIRY; HE IS SUDDENLY STARTLED BY A GRUESOME DISCOVERY

JUDGE DEE QUICKLY PUT HIS BEAKER DOWN AND TURNED round to her. But she avoided his eyes, and bent over Han's shoulder. He had stopped snoring. Anemone was approaching the table again, carrying in both hands a goblet filled to the rim with wine. Still not looking at the judge, Almond Blossom said quickly:

"I hope Your Honor plays chess, for—" She broke off, for Anemone was now standing in front of their table. Almond Blossom leaned over and took the goblet from her. She brought it to Han's lips, who hastily took a long draught. Then he said, laughing:

"Ho, ho, you forward wench! Do you think I can't hold my own wine beaker any more?" He laid his arm round Almond Blossom's waist, pulled her close and continued: "Now what about you showing His Excellency here some nice dance of hours, eh?"

Almond Blossom smiled and nodded. She expertly extricated herself from Han's embrace, made a low bow and disappeared through the crystal curtain.

Han started on a rather confused account of the various ancient dances the courtesans of Han-yuan could perform. Judge Dee nodded absentmindedly; he was thinking of what Almond Blossom had just told him. All his boredom was gone. So his intuition had been right; there was indeed some evil brewing in this town! After her dance he must try to find immediately an opportunity for talking to her alone. If a courtesan was clever, she could learn many secrets from the conversation of the guests at the banquets she attended.

The orchestra started a seductive melody punctuated by drumbeats. Two courtesans advanced to the center of the room and began to execute a sword dance. Each of them carrying a long sword, they swiftly wove in and out of various fencing positions, clanging the swords together to the accompaniment of the martial tune.

The finale of the drums was drowned in the enthusiastic applause. Judge Dee complimented Han on the performance, but he said disparagingly:

"That was nothing but an exhibition of skill, Your Honor; it has nothing to do with art! Wait till you have seen Almond Blossom dance. Look, here she comes!"

Almond Blossom went to stand in the center of the carpet. She wore only a single robe of thin white silk on her bare body, with wide, trailing sleeves, and round her waist a green sash. Round her shoulders she had a long scarf of green gauze, the ends of which hung down to the floor. Her hair was done up in a high chignon, with a white water lily as unique decoration. She shook her sleeves and gave a sign to the orchestra. The flutes began an eerie, unworldly melody.

She slowly raised her arms above her head; her feet did not move but her hips started to sway to the measure of the music. The thin robe accentuated her youthful figure; the judge thought he had seldom seen such a perfectly molded womanly shape.

"That is the dance of the Cloud Fairy!" Han whispered hoarsely at his ear.

As the castanets began to click, the dancer lowered her arms to the level of her shoulders, took the tips of the scarf between her tapering fingers and, waving her arms, made the thin gauze billow around her, the upper part of her body swaying to and fro. Then zitherns and violins took the melody over in a pulsating rhythm. Now she started to move her knees; the rippling movement spread over her entire body, but she still did not move one inch from her place.

Judge Dee had never seen such a fascinating dance. Her impassive, slightly haughty face with the downcast eyes stressed by contrast the voluptuous writhing of her lithe body that appeared to personify the flame of burning passion. The robe fell away, exposing her perfectly rounded naked breasts.

The judge perceived the intense, sensuous attraction that emanated from this woman. He turned his gaze to the guests. Old Kang Po did not look at the dancer at all; he stared in his wine cup, his thoughts elsewhere. But the eyes of his younger brother were glued to her every movement; without averting his gaze, he whispered a remark to Guildmaster Wang by his side. Both laughed surreptitiously.

31

"I don't think those two are talking about dancing!" Han Yung-han remarked dryly. Evidently his intoxication did not mar his powers of observation.

The guildmasters Peng and Soo were looking ecstatically at the dancer. Judge Dee was struck by the curious, tense attitude of Liu Fei-po. He sat perfectly still, his imperious face set, his thin lips compressed under his jet-black mustache. But the judge saw in his burning eyes a strange expression. He thought he could detect a violent hatred in it, but also something of deep despair.

The music grew softer; it changed into a tender, nearly whispering melody. Almond Blossom now walked on tiptoe in a wide circle, whirling round and round all the time so that the long sleeves and the ends of the gauze scarf flew round her. The rhythm accelerated, and quicker she turned round, quicker and quicker till her swift feet did not seem to touch the floor any more; it seemed as if she were floating among the billowing clouds of the green scarf and her fluttering white sleeves.

Suddenly there was a deafening clash of the gong and the music ceased abruptly. The dancer stood still, high on her toes, her arms raised above her head, still as a stone statue. One only saw the heaving of her naked breasts. It was absolutely quiet in the room.

Then she lowered her arms, pulled the scarf round her shoulders, and made a bow toward Judge Dee's table. While a thunderous applause burst loose she went quickly to the door and disappeared through the crystal curtain.

"That was indeed a superb performance!" the judge remarked to Han. "That girl could well perform before His Majesty!"

"Exactly what that friend of Lieu's said the other day!" Han said. "He was a high official from the capital, and saw her dance at a banquet in the Willow Quarter. He immediately offered her owner to introduce him to the duenna of the Imperial seraglio. But Almond Blossom refuses absolutely to leave Han-yuan, and we of this city are grateful to her for that!"

Judge Dee rose and stood himself in front of his table. Raising his cup, he proposed a toast to the charming courtesans of Han-yuan, which was received with great enthusiasm. Then he went over to Kang Po's table, and began a polite conversation. Han Yung-han had also risen, and had gone to the musicians to compliment their leader.

Old Mr. Kang Po had evidently drunk too much; red spots had appeared on his lean face, and his brow was covered with perspiration. But he managed to give coherent answers to Judge Dee's questions about business conditions in Han-yuan. After a while his younger brother said with a smile:

"Fortunately, my brother has now cheered up a bit! The last days he has been worrying all the time over a perfectly safe business transaction!"

"Safe?" the elder Kang said angrily. "You call a loan to that person Wan I-fan a safe transaction?"

"They say that in order to make good profits you must be prepared to take risks!" Judge Dee said soothingly.

"Wan I-fan is a scoundrel!" Kang Po muttered.

"Only fools believe the gossip of the street!" Kang Choong said sharply.

"I . . . I refuse to be called names by my own brother!" old Kang Po stuttered furiously.

"Your brother has the duty to tell you the truth!" Kang Choong retorted.

"Ho, ho!" a deep voice spoke up by Judge Dee's side. "Enough of your wrangling! What will His Excellency think of us!"

It was Liu Fei-po. He carried a wine jar in his hand, and quickly filled the cups of the two brothers. They meekly drank a toast to each other. Judge Dee asked Liu Fei-po the last news about the illness of Councilor Liang. "Mr. Han told me," he added, "that you live next door to the Councilor, and that you see him often."

"Not lately," Liu replied. "Half a year ago, yes; then His Excellency would often ask me to join him when he was walking in his garden, as our grounds are connected by a small gate. But he has grown very absentminded; his conversation became more and more confused; often he didn't even seem to recognize me. I haven't seen him for several months now. It's a sad case, Your Honor! The decline of a great mind."

The guildmasters Peng and Wang now joined the group. Han Yung-han brought a wine jar and insisted on pouring out a cup for each of them himself. Judge Dee had a talk with the guildmasters, then returned to his table. Han was sitting there already, making jokes with Anemone. As the judge sat down he asked:

"Where is Almond Blossom?"

33

"Oh, she'll be here presently!" Han replied indifferently. "Those girls always take an awful time over their powder and rouge!"

Judge Dee quickly surveyed the room. All the guests had resumed their places, and were starting on the intermediary course, a dish of stuffed fish. The four courtesans were pouring out new wine, but Almond Blossom was nowhere to be seen. Judge Dee said curtly to Anemone:

"Go the dressing room and tell Almond Blossom that we are waiting."

"Ha!" Han exclaimed. "It is a great honor for Hanyuan that the rustic charms of our girls should captivate Your Honor's favor!"

Judge Dee politely joined the general laughter.

Anemone came back and said:

"It's very strange; our mother says that Almond Blossom left the dressing room quite a while ago. I have looked into all the rooms, but I can't find her!"

The judge muttered an excuse to Han, rose and left the room by the door on his right. He walked aft on the starboard side.

In the stern a gay party was in progress. Sergeant Hoong, Ma Joong and Chiao Tai were sitting on a bench against the cabin, each with a wine jug between his knees and a cup in his hand. Half a dozen servants were sitting in a half-circle opposite them, listening intently to Ma Joong. The burly fellow hit his fist on his knee, and concluded: "And just at that moment the bedstead collapsed!"

They burst out in uproarious laughter. Judge Dee tapped Hoong on his shoulder. He looked up, and quickly nudged his two friends. They jumped up and followed the judge to the starboard deck.

There Judge Dee told them that a dancer had disappeared and that he feared she might have met with an accident. "Did any of you see a girl pass?" he asked.

Sergeant Hoong shook his head.

"No, Your Honor," he answered. "The three of us sat facing the stern, in front of the trap door that leads down into the kitchen and the hold. We only saw the waiters coming and going; there was no woman."

Two waiters carrying soup bowls came down the deck on their way to the dining room. They said they hadn't seen the dancer after she had left the room to change.

34

"And we hadn't much chance to either," the elder one added, "for the rule is that we use starboard only. The ladies have their dressing room on the port side, and that's also where the main cabin is. We aren't supposed to go to that side unless we are called."

Judge Dee nodded. He went back aft, followed by his three assistants. The servants were talking with the helmsman; they knew that something was afoot.

The judge crossed the stern to the port side. The door of the main cabin was ajar. He looked inside. Against the side wall stood a broad couch of carved rosewood, covered with a brocade quilt. Against the back wall he saw a high table, with two burning candles, in stands of worked silver. There was an elegant toilet table of rosewood on the left, and two tabourets. But no one was there.

Judge Dee hurriedly went on, and looked through the gauze curtain that covered the window of the adjoining cabin. This evidently was the dressing room of the courtesans. A portly lady clad in black silk was dozing in an armchair and a maidservant was folding up colored robes.

The last window, that of the sitting room, was open. There was no one there.

"Did Your Honor look on the upper deck?" Chiao Tai asked.

The judge shook his head. He quickly went to the companionway and ascended the steep ladder. Probably Almond Blossom had gone up there for a breath of fresh air. But one glance sufficed to show that the upper deck was completely deserted. He went down again and remained standing in the companionway, pensively stroking his beard. Anemone had already looked in the cabins on starboard. The dancer had disappeared.

"Go and have a look in all the other cabins," he ordered his three lieutenants, "and also in the bathroom!"

He walked back to the portside deck and went to stand by the railing, next to the gangway. Folding his arms in his wide sleeves, he looked out over the dark water. There was not a breath of air stirring; it was hot and oppressive. The feast in the dining room was still in full swing; he could hear the murmur of voices and a few bars of music.

35

He looked down over the railing at the reflection of the colored lamps. Suddenly he stiffened. Just under the surface of the water below a pale face was looking up at him with still, wide eyes.

Third Chapter

**THE TRIBUNAL IS SET UP IN UNUSUAL SURROUND-
INGS; A MAIDSERVANT DESCRIBES A LOATHSOME
APPARITION**

ONE GLANCE SUFFICED. HE HAD FOUND THE DANCER.

The judge was about to step down the gangway when
Ma Joong appeared round the corner. Judge Dee silently
pointed at his find.

Ma Joong cursed. He quickly went down the gangway
till he stood up to his knees in the water. He lifted the
dead body in his arms and brought it on deck. The
judge led him to the main cabin; there the body was
laid on the couch.

"The poor wench is heavier than I thought!" Ma Joong
remarked while wringing out his sleeves. "I suppose something heavy was put in her jacket."

Judge Dee had not heard him. He stood there looking
down at the dead face. The still eyes stared up at him.
She was wearing her dance costume of white silk, but
over it she had put on a jacket of green brocade. The
clinging wet robe revealed her beautiful body in a manner
that was nearly obscene. Judge Dee shivered. A few moments before she had been whirling round in her en-
chanting dance. And this was the sudden end.

He roused himself from these morbid thoughts. Stooping over the body, he examined the dark-blue bruise on
the right temple. Then he tried to close the eyes, but
the lids would not move and the dead woman's stare
remained fixed on him. He took his handkerchief from
his sleeve and spread it over the still face.

Sergeant Hoong and Chiao Tai entered the cabin. Turning to them, the judge said:

"This is the courtesan Almond Blossom. She was murdered, practically under my eyes. Ma Joong, you stand
guard outside on deck and let nobody pass. I don't want
to be disturbed. Don't say anything about this matter."

Judge Dee raised the limp right arm and felt in the
sleeve. With some difficulty he extricated from it a round
incense burner of bronze. The ashes had turned into gray

mud. He handed the burner to Hoong and went to the wall table. In between the two candlesticks he saw three small depressions in the red brocade of the tablecloth. He beckoned Hoong and let him place the incense burner on the table. The three legs fitted exactly into the depressions. Judge Dee sat down on the tabouret in front of the dressing table.

"Simple and effective!" he said bitterly to Hoong and Chiao Tai. "She was lured to this cabin; the murderer knocked her unconscious from behind. He put the heavy bronze incense burner in her sleeve, carried her outside and let her down into the water. Thus there was no splash, and she would sink straight to the bottom of the lake. But in his hurry he didn't notice that the sleeve of her jacket caught on a nail in the gangway. She still was drowned, because the weighted sleeve kept her face several inches under water." He rubbed his hand over his face in a tired gesture. Then he ordered: "See what she has in her other sleeve, Hoong!"

The sergeant turned the sleeve inside out. It contained only a wet package of Almond Blossom's small red visiting cards, and a folded sheet of paper, which he handed to the judge.

Judge Dee carefully unfolded it.

"That is a chess problem!" Hoong and Chiao Tai exclaimed at the same time.

The judge nodded. He remembered the last words of the courtesan. "Give me your handkerchief, Sergeant!" he said. He wrapped the wet sheet of paper in it, and put it in his sleeve. He rose and went out.

"You stay here and guard the cabin!" he ordered Chiao Tai. "Hoong and Ma Joong shall go back with me to the dining room. I shall there institute a preliminary investigation."

While they were walking forward Ma Joong remarked:

"At any rate we shan't need to look far, Your Honor! The murderer must be on board this ship!"

Judge Dee made no comment. He entered the dining room through the crystal curtain, followed by his two assistants.

The dinner was nearing its end and the guests were eating the traditional last bowl of rice. An animated conversation was going on. When Han saw the judge he exclaimed:

"Good! We were just planning to go up on the roof and enjoy the moon!"

Judge Dee did not answer. He rapped the table sharply with his knuckles and called out:

"Silence, please!"

All looked at him in astonishment.

"In the first place," Judge Dee said in a clear voice, "I wish, as your guest, to thank all of you sincerely for this lavish entertainment. Unfortunately, this pleasant gathering must now be broken up. You will understand that if from now on I speak to you as your magistrate and not as your guest, I do so because it is my duty to the State and to the people of this district, including yourselves." Turning to Han he added: "I must request you to leave this table, sir!"

Han rose with a dazed look. Anemone carried his chair over to Liu Fei-po's table. He sat down, rubbing his eyes.

Judge Dee shifted to the middle of the table. Ma Joong and Sergeant Hoong came to stand by his side. Then the judge said, speaking slowly:

"I, the magistrate, open the temporary tribunal convened to investigate the willful murder of the courtesan called Almond Blossom."

The judge quickly surveyed his audience. Most of them did not seem to take in the full meaning of his words but looked at him in blank astonishment. Judge Dee ordered Sergeant Hoong to fetch the master of the boat, and a set of writing implements.

Han Yung-han now took a hold of himself. He had a whispered consultation with Liu Fei-po. When the latter nodded Han rose and said:

"Your Honor, this is a most arbitrary proceeding. We, the leading citizens of Han-yuan, wish to—"

"The witness Han Yung-han," Judge Dee interrupted him coldly, "will resume his seat and be silent until he is ordered to speak!"

Han sank back in his chair with a flushed face.

Sergeant Hoong brought a man with a pock-marked face before the table. The judge ordered the master of the boat to kneel and draw a plan of the ship. As the master set to work with trembling hands, Judge Dee looked the company over with a bleak stare. The sudden transition from a happy drinking party to a criminal investigation had sobered them completely and left them in a miserable state. When the master had his sketch ready he laid it respectfully on the table. Judge Dee pushed the sheet over to Hoong and ordered him to add the position of the tables and write in the names of the guests. The sergeant beckoned to a waiter, who whispered the name of each guest as Hoong pointed at him. Then the judge addressed the company in a firm voice:

"After the courtesan Almond Blossom had finished her dance and left this room there was considerable confusion. All of you were moving about. I shall now ask each of you to describe exactly what you were doing at that particular time."

Guildmaster Wang rose. He waddled to the table and knelt down.

"This person," he said formally, "respectfully begs Your Honor to be allowed to deliver a statement."

As the judge nodded the fat man began:

"The staggering news that our famous dancer has been foully murdered has naturally greatly upset all of us. But this event, terrible as it is, should not rob us of our sense of reality.

"Now I, having for many years attended feasts on this particular flower boat, dare say that I know it like the palm of my hand. I respectfully inform Your Honor that in the hold below are eighteen oarsmen, twelve actually at the oars, and six who take their turns at intervals. Now, far be it from me to cast aspersions on my fellow citizens, but Your Honor will in any case find out sooner or later that the oarsmen of these boats are, as a rule, a bad lot, addicted to drinking and gambling. It is among them, therefore, that the murderer should be looked for. It would not be the first time that a good-looking rascal among those fellows had an affair with a courtesan and became violent when she wished to sever the relation."

Here Master Wang paused. Casting an uneasy glance at the black mass of water outside, he continued:

"Besides, there is also another aspect to be considered, Your Honor. From times immemorial mystery surrounds our lake. It is commonly believed that its waters well up from deep under the earth, and on that occasion foul creatures come up from its unfathomable deep to harm the living. Not less than four persons drowned there this year, and their bodies were never recovered. Some say that later they saw these drowned persons, hovering about among the living.

40

"I thought it my duty to draw Your Honor's attention to these two aspects of this murder, so as to place this horrible crime against its proper background, and in order to spare my friends here the unnecessary ordeal of being questioned like common criminals."

A murmur of approval rose from the audience.

Judge Dee rapped the table. Looking steadily at Wang he said:

"I am grateful for any advice brought forward in the proper manner. The possibility of the murderer having come from the hold had already occurred to me. I shall in due time question the crew. Also, I am not an impious man and I certainly don't rule out the possibility of unholy forces being concerned in this case.

"As to the expression 'common criminal' employed by the witness Wang, I wish to point out that all men are equal before this court. Until the murderer is found each and every one of you assembled here is as much under suspicion as the rowers in the hold and the cooks in the kitchen.

"Does anyone else wish to speak?"

Guildmaster Peng rose and went to kneel in front of the table.

"Would Your Honor deign to enlighten us," he asked anxiously, "as to the manner in which that unfortunate girl met her death?"

"Those details," Judge Dee said immediately, "cannot be divulged at this stage. Anyone else?" When no one spoke he continued: "Since all of you have had full opportunity for proffering your views, you will from now on hold your peace and let me deal with this case as I, the magistrate, see fit. I shall proceed as indicated. The witness Peng will return to his seat, and the witness Wang will come forward and describe his movements during the time referred to."

"After Your Honor had kindly proposed a toast to the dancers of Han-yuan," Wang said, "I left this room by the door on the left and proceeded to the sitting room. Since there was nobody there, I went through the corridor to the washroom. When I returned from there to this room, I heard that the Kang brothers were quarreling, and went over to them after Mr. Liu Fei-po had restored peace."

"Did you meet anyone in the corridor or in the washroom?" the judge asked.

41

Wang shook his head. Judge Dee waited till Sergeant Hoong had noted Wang's testimony down; then he called Han Yung-han.

"I went to say a few kind words to the orchestra leader," Han began in a surly voice, "then I suddenly felt a bit dizzy. I went out on the foredeck, and stood there for a while leaning against the right side of the portal. After I had enjoyed the view over the water I felt slightly better, and sat down on the porcelain barrel seat that is standing there. There Anemone found me when she came to fetch me. Your Honor knows the rest."

The judge called the orchestra leader, who was standing together with the musicians in the far corner of the room. He asked:

"Can you confirm that Mr. Han did not leave the foredeck all that time?"

The man looked at the musicians. When they shook their heads he replied unhappily:

"No, Your Honor. We were busy tuning our instruments; we didn't look outside till Miss Anemone came to ask after Mr. Han. Then I walked together with her out on the foredeck, and we saw Mr. Han sitting there on the barrel seat, just as he said just now."

"You can go!" Judge Dee said to Han. He had Liu Fei-po led before the table. Liu now seemed less self-possessed than before; the judge noticed that his mouth was twitching nervously. But his voice was steady when he began.

"After the dance of the courtesan I noticed that my neighbor, Guildmaster Peng, was looking unwell. Just after Wang had left this room I brought Peng through the door on the left out on the starboard deck. While he was leaning over the railing I went through the corridor to the washroom, and then rejoined Peng, without having met anybody. Peng said he felt better, and we came back here together. I saw that the Kang brothers were quarreling, and proposed that they make it up with a cup of wine. That's all."

Judge Dee nodded, and had Guildmaster Peng called. He confirmed Liu Fei-po's statement in all details. Then the judge had Guildmaster Soo brought before him.

Soo gave the judge a sullen look from under his heavy eyebrows. He shifted his broad shoulders, then began in an expressionless voice.

"This person confirms that he saw first Wang, and

42

thereafter Mr. Liu, leave this room. Left alone at our table, I talked for a while with the two courtesans who had performed the sword dance, till one of them pointed out that my left sleeve was all soiled by the fish sauce. I rose and went to the second cabin along the corridor. That cabin had been reserved for me, and my servant had placed there a bundle with clean clothes, and my toilet articles. I quickly changed. When I came out into the corridor, I saw Almond Blossom walking forward through the sitting room. I overtook her in the companion-way and complimented her on her dancing. But she seemed rather agitated and said hurriedly that she would see me presently in the dining room. Then she turned the corner on the left, on the portside. I entered this room through the starboard door. I saw that Wang, Liu and Peng were not yet back, so I continued my conversation with the two courtesans."

"How was Almond Blossom dressed when you saw her?" Judge Dee asked.

"She still had on her white dance costume, Your Honor, but over that she wore a short jacket of green brocade."

Judge Dee sent him back to his place, and ordered Ma Joong to fetch the duenna of the courtesans from the dressing room.

The portly lady declared that her husband owned the house in the Willow Quarter to which Almond Blossom and the five other courtesans belonged. When the judge asked her when she had seen Almond Blossom last, she said:

"When she came back from her dancing, Excellency, and didn't she look beautiful! I said: 'You'd better change quickly, dearie; you are all wet and you'll catch cold!' And I tell the maid to put out her nice blue robe for her. But suddenly Almond Blossom pushes the maid away, puts on her green jacket, and off she goes! That's the last I saw of her, Excellency, I swear it! How did the poor chicken get killed? That maid is telling such a queer story; she says that—"

"Thank you!" Judge Dee interrupted her. He told Ma Joong to bring the maidservant before him.

The girl came in sobbing wildly. Ma Joong patted her reassuringly on her back but without much effect. She wailed:

"The evil monster from the lake has taken her, Your Honor! Please, Your Honor, let us go back to land, before it draws this boat under! That horrible apparition; I saw it with my own eyes!"

"Where did you see that apparition?" Judge Dee asked, astonished.

"It beckoned her from outside the window, Your Honor! Just when mother had told me to lay out the blue dress. And Miss Almond Blossom saw it too! It beckoned her, Your Honor! How could she disobey that ghostly summons?"

A subdued murmur rose from the audience. Judge Dee rapped the table, then asked:

"What did it look like?"

"It was a huge, black monster, Your Honor. I saw it clearly through the gauze curtain. In one hand it waved threateningly a long knife, with the other hand . . . it beckoned!"

"Could you see what dress and cap it wore?" the judge asked.

"I said it was a monster, didn't I?" the girl said indignantly. "It had no definite shape; it was just a horrible, loathsome black shadow."

Judge Dee gave a sign to Ma Joong. He led the maidservant away.

Thereafter he heard Anemone and the four other courtesans. Except for Anemone, whom the judge had sent away himself to look for the dancer, none of them had left the dining room. They had been talking together and with Soo; they had not seen Wang, Liu or Peng leave, and they were very vague as to when Soo had come back exactly.

Judge Dee rose and announced that he would hear the waiters and the crew on the upper deck.

As he was ascending the steep ladder followed by Sergeant Hoong, Ma Joong went with the master of the boat to get the crew members.

The judge sat down on a barrel seat next to the railing. He pushed his cap back from his forehead and said: "It is as stuffy here as inside!"

Hoong quickly offered him his fan. He said dejectedly:

"That hearing didn't get us any forrader, Your Honor!"

"Oh, I don't know," Judge Dee said, vigorously fanning himself. "I think it did clarify the situation, to a certain extent. Heavens, Wang didn't lie when he said that the rowers are a bad lot! They don't look very prepossessing!"

The group of oarsmen who now appeared on deck were

44

muttering angrily amongst themselves, but some cursing from Ma Joong and the master soon made them adopt the proper respectful attitude. The waiters and cooks were made to stand opposite them. Judge Dee thought it unnecessary to hear the helmsman and the servants of the guests, for Hoong had assured him that they had been listening so intently to Ma Joong's spicy stories that none of them had thought of stirring from his place.

The judge started with the waiters, but they hadn't much to tell. When the dancing had begun they had gone to the kitchen to have a quick snack. Only one of them had gone up to have a look in the dining room to see whether anything was needed. He had seen Guildmaster Peng leaning over the railing, vomiting violently. But Liu had not been with him then.

A thorough cross-examination of the cooks and the oarsmen brought to light that none of them had left the hold. When the helmsman had shouted through the trap door that they could take a rest, the oarsmen had started gambling and no one had thought of leaving the game.

When Judge Dee rose, the master, who had been studying the sky with a worried face, said:

"I fear that we are in for a storm, Your Honor! We'd better take her back quickly. She is not easy to handle in rough weather!"

The judge nodded, and descended the ladder. He went straight to the main cabin, where Chiao Tai stood guard by the dead body of the courtesan.

Fourth Chapter

THE JUDGE HOLDS A VIGIL FOR A DEAD WOMAN; HE STUDIES POEMS AND PASSIONATE LETTERS

JUST WHEN JUDGE DEE SAT DOWN ON THE TABOURET IN front of the dressing table a peal of thunder rent the air. A torrential rain clattered down on the roof. The boat started to rock.

Chiao Tai hurried outside to fasten the shutters. The judge stared silently ahead of him, slowly caressing his side whiskers. The sergeant and Ma Joong stood looking at the still form on the couch.

When Chiao Tai had come back and bolted the door, Judge Dee looked up at his three lieutenants.

"Well," he said with a bleak smile, "only a few hours ago I complained that nothing happened here!" He shook his head, then went on gravely: "Now we are confronted with a murder, complete with all angles of doubt and suspicion, including even the supernatural element." Seeing Ma Joong giving Chiao Tai an anxious look, he continued quickly: "If during the hearings I didn't discourage the idea that a ghostly being was concerned in this crime, it was only to lull the criminal's suspicions. Don't forget that he doesn't know how and where we discovered the body. He must be greatly puzzled by the fact that it didn't sink down to the bottom of the lake. For I can assure you, my friends, that the murderer is a man of flesh and blood! And I know also why he had to murder the dancer!"

Then the judge told them about Almond Blossom's startling announcement. "As a matter of course," he concluded, "Han Yung-han is our most likely suspect, for he was the only one who, feigning to be asleep, could have overheard what she said to me. Although in that case he must be a consummate actor."

"Han also had the opportunity," Sergeant Hoong observed. "Nobody could confirm the story about his hanging around on the foredeck. Perhaps he walked aft on

46

the portside, and beckoned the dancer from outside the window to follow him."

"But what can be the meaning of that knife the maid was talking about?" Ma Joong asked.

Judge Dee shrugged his shoulders.

"Imagination played an important role there," he said. "Don't forget that the maid started telling her weird story only after she had heard that the dancer had been murdered. She saw in fact only the shadow of a man dressed in a wide, long-sleeved robe such as all of us are wearing. He beckoned, and in his other hand he held a folded-up fan. That must have been the knife she was talking about."

The boat was rocking violently now. A large wave hit its side with a resounding crash.

"Unfortunately," the judge resumed, "Han is far from being our only suspect. It is true that he is the only one who could have overheard her words, but any one of the other guests could have noticed that she whispered something to me and concluded from her secretive manner— I told you that she wasn't even looking at me—that she was giving me important information. And therefore he decided to take no chances."

"That means," Chiao Tai said, "that next to Han we have four other suspects, namely the guildmasters Wang, Peng and Soo, and Liu Fei-po. Only the Kang brothers go free, because Your Honor said that they didn't leave the room. All of the four others left the room for a shorter or longer period."

"Indeed," Judge Dee said. "Peng is probably innocent, for the simple reason that he lacks the strength for knocking down the dancer and carrying her to the gangway. It was only therefore that I questioned the crew: I thought that Peng might have an accomplice among them. But none of them has left the hold."

"Han, Liu and the guildmasters Wang and Soo seem perfectly capable of killing her," Chiao Tai remarked. "Especially Soo; he is a hefty fellow."

"After Han," the judge said, "Soo seems our best candidate. If he is the murderer, he must be a dangerous, cold-blooded criminal. For then he must have planned the murder in all detail while Almond Blossom was still dancing. He must have soiled his sleeve expressly in order to have a good excuse for leaving the dining room later, and at the same time a good excuse for changing, in case his robe would get wet while letting the body down in the

water. He must then have gone directly to the window of
the dressing room, beckoned the dancer, stunned her and
put her in the water. Only thereafter did he go to his
cabin and change his clothes. You'd better go to that
cabin now, Chiao Tai, and see whether the robe Soo took
off is wet!"

"I'll go, Your Honor!" Ma Joong said quickly. He had
noticed that Chiao Tai was getting pale; he knew that his
friend was not a very good sailor.

Judge Dee nodded. They waited in silence for Ma
Joong's return.

"Water all over the place!" Ma Joong muttered when
he came back. "Everywhere except on Soo's robe! That
was bone dry!"

"Good," Judge Dee said. "It doesn't prove that Soo is
innocent, but it is a fact to keep in mind. Our suspects
are now Han, Soo, Liu, Wang and Peng—in that order."

"Why does Your Honor put Liu before Wang?" Sergeant Hoong asked.

"Because I assume," the judge answered, "that there
was a love affair between the dancer and her murderer.
If not, she would certainly not have gone to him immediately when he called her, and she would not have
gone alone with him to the cabin here. The position of a
courtesan is quite different from that of an ordinary prostitute, who has to give herself to anyone who pays the
price. One must win the favors of a courtesan, and if
one doesn't succeed in that, there's nothing one can do
about it. Courtesans, and especially famous ones like
Almond Blossom, bring in more money by their singing
and dancing than by sleeping with the guests, so their
owners don't exercise pressure on them to grant their
favors to the customers. Now I could well imagine that
Han or Liu, both well-preserved men of the world, could
win the love of such a beautiful and talented dancer. And
also, Soo, who suggests a kind of brutal strength that
some women find attractive. But hardly the rotund Wang,
or the cadaverous Peng. Yes, I think we'd better scratch
Peng entirely from our list."

Ma Joong had not heard the last words of the judge, he
was looking at the dead woman in speechless horror. Now
he burst out:

"She's shaking her head!"

All turned to the couch. The head rolled to and fro.

48

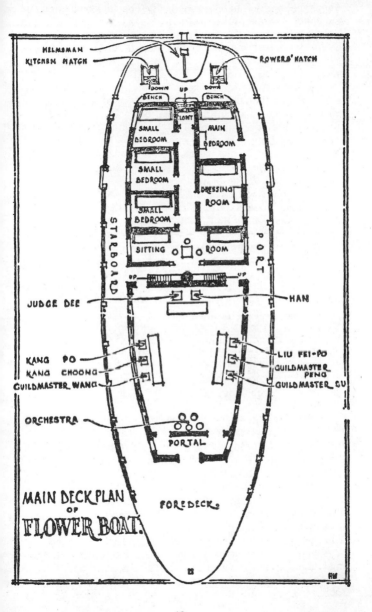

MAIN DECK PLAN
OF
FLOWER BOAT.

49

The handkerchief had dropped off. The flickering light of the candles shone on the wet hair.

Judge Dee rose hurriedly and went over to the couch. Deeply shocked, he looked at the white face. The eyes had closed. He placed a pillow on either side of the head, and quickly covered it up again with the handkerchief. He sat down and said in a calm voice:

"Thus our first task is to find out who of the three persons mentioned had intimate relations with the courtesan. The best method will probably be to question the other girls of her house; those women usually have few secrets from each other."

"But to make them tell outsiders about those things," Ma Joong said, "is quite another matter!"

The rain had stopped, the boat was going more steadily now. Chiao Tai was looking better. He said:

"I think, Your Honor, that there's an even more pressing task ahead, namely that we search the dancer's room in the house in the Willow Quarter. The murderer had to improvise his crime after he had boarded this boat and if she kept in her room letters or other proof of her relation with him, he'll hurry there as soon as we have landed in order to destroy those clues."

"You are quite right, Chiao Tai," Judge Dee said approvingly. "As soon as we have landed, Ma Joong shall run ahead to the Willow Quarter, and arrest anybody who wants to enter the dancer's house. I'll go there in my palanquin, and we shall search her room together."

There were loud shouts outside, indicating that they were nearing the landing stage. Judge Dee rose and said to Chiao Tai:

"You'll wait here for the constables. Tell them to seal this cabin, and let two of them stand guard in front of this cabin till tomorrow morning. I'll tell the owner of the dead woman's house to send an undertaker tomorrow for encoffining the body."

As they stepped out on deck they found that the moon had come out again. Its rays shone on a dismal scene. The storm had blown away all the colored lamps and torn the bamboo curtains of the dining room to shreds. The gay boat now presented a disheveled appearance.

A very subdued crowd awaited the judge on the landing stage. During the storm the guests had fled to the sitting room and the close air there, together with the rocking, had made them feel all the more miserable. As

50

soon as Judge Dee had told them that they could go home they rushed to their sedan chairs.

The judge ascended his palanquin. After they were out of earshot he told the bearers to take him to the Willow Quarter.

When the judge and Sergeant Hoong entered the first courtyard of Almond Blossom's house they heard loud laughter coming from the dining room beyond. Despite the late hour a party was still in progress there.

The manager of the house came rushing out to meet these unexpected visitors. When he recognized the judge he fell on his knees and three times knocked his head on the floor. Then he inquired in a cringing voice the magistrate's pleasure.

"I want to examine the room occupied by the courtesan Almond Blossom," he said curtly. "Take us there!"

The manager hastily led them to the broad staircase of polished wood. Upstairs they found a dimly lit corridor. The manager halted before one of the red-lacquered doors and entered first to light the candles. He cried out in terror when an iron hand closed round his arm.

"It's the manager; let him go!" Judge Dee said quickly. "How did you come here?"

Ma Joong said with a grin:

"I thought it better that nobody should see me enter, so I vaulted over the garden wall and climbed up on the balcony. I found a maid asleep in a corner and made her point out the dancer's room. I waited behind the door here but no one came."

"Good work!" the judge said. "You can go downstairs now together with the manager. Keep an eye on the entrance!"

Judge Dee sat down in front of the dressing table of carved blackwood and started to pull out the drawers. The sergeant went over to the pile of four clothes boxes of red-lacquered leather that stood beside the large couch. He opened the one on top, marked "Summer," and went through its contents.

In the upper drawer of the dressing table the judge found nothing but the usual toilet articles, but the lower one was full of cards and letters. He quickly glanced through them. A few letters were written by Almond Blossom's mother in Shansi—acknowledgments of money transmitted by the girl, and news about her small brother, who was doing well in school. The father seemed to be dead. She wrote in a polished literary style and the judge again marveled what cruel fate had compelled a girl from a good family to enter such a questionable profession. The rest were all poems and letters from admirers; leafing through them, Judge Dee found the signatures of all the guests who had been present at the banquet, including Han Yung-han. These documents were written in the customary formal style. Invitations to attend banquets, compliments about her dancing—nothing of a more intimate character. Thus it was very difficult to assess the exact relations of the courtesan with those gentlemen.

He gathered all the papers in a sheaf and put them in his sleeve for further study.

"Here are some more, Your Honor!" Sergeant Hoong suddenly exclaimed. He showed the judge a package of letters carefully wrapped up in tissue paper which he had found on the bottom of the clothes box. Judge Dee saw at a glance that these were real love letters, couched in passionate language. All were signed with the same pen name: "The Student of the Bamboo Grove."

"That man must have been her lover!" the judge said eagerly. "It shouldn't be too difficult to identify the writer. Style and handwriting are excellent; he must belong to the small group of literati in this town."

A further search produced no other clues. The judge walked out on the balcony and remained standing there for a while, looking out over the landscape garden below. The rays of the moon were reflected in the water of the small artificial lotus ponds among the flowers. How many times the dancer would have stood here, looking at this same nostalgic scene! He abruptly turned round. Apparently he had not yet served long enough as a magistrate to remain unperturbed by the sudden death of a beautiful woman.

The judge blew out the candles, and he went back downstairs followed by Sergeant Hoong.

Ma Joong was standing in the portal talking with the manager. The latter bowed deeply when he saw the judge.

Judge Dee folded his arms in his sleeves.

"You'll realize," he sternly addressed the manager, "that since this is a murder investigation, I could have had my constables turn your house upside down and question all your guests. I refrained from doing so because for the time being such measures do not seem necessary, and I never importune people without sufficient reason. You shall, however, draw up immediately a detailed report containing everything you know about the dead dancer. Her real name, her age, when and under what circumstances she entered your house, who were the guests she usually associated with, what games she could play, and so on. See to it that your report reaches me early tomorrow morning, written out in triplicate!"

The manager knelt and started upon a long tirade to express his gratitude. But Judge Dee cut him short, saying impatiently:

"Tomorrow you'll send an undertaker to the flower boat to fetch the body. And see to it that her family in Ping-yang is informed of her demise."

As he turned to the door, Ma Joong said:

"I beg to be allowed to follow Your Honor later."

Judge Dee caught his meaningful look. He nodded his assent and ascended his palanquin together with Sergeant Hoong. The constables lighted their torches. Slowly the procession went its way through the deserted streets of Han-yuan.

MA JOONG TELLS OF THE SECRET OF A DANCER; A PROFESSOR IS ACCUSED OF A HEINOUS CRIME

THE FOLLOWING MORNING, JUST AFTER DAWN, WHEN Sergeant Hoong reported for duty, he found Judge Dee sitting already fully dressed in his private office at the back of the court hall.

The judge had arranged the letters found in the courtesan's clothes box in neat piles on his desk. As the sergeant poured out a cup of tea for him, the judge said:

"I have read through all these letters carefully, Hoong. Her affair with that so-called Student of the Bamboo Grove must have started about half a year ago. The early letters refer to a gradually developing friendship; the latter ones speak of a passionate love. About two months ago, however, the passion seemed to wane. There is a marked change in tone; here and there I find some passages that could be construed as threats. That man must be found, Hoong!"

"The senior scribe of our tribunal is an amateur poet, Your Honor," Sergeant Hoong said eagerly. "In his spare time he acts as recording secretary of the local literary club. He could probably identify that pseudonym!"

"Excellent!" Judge Dee commented. "You'll presently go to the chancery and ask him. First, however, I want to show you this." He took from a drawer in his desk a thin sheet of paper and spread it out flat. The sergeant recognized the chess problem found in the dead girl's sleeve. Tapping it with his forefinger the judge said:

"Yesterday night after we had come back from the Willow Quarter I had a good look at this chess problem. The curious thing is that I can't make head or tail of it!

"I admit that I am no expert at this game, but I played it often in my student days. As you see, the square is divided by eighteen columns either way, producing 289 points where they cross each other. One player has 150 white men, his opponent the same number of black ones. These men are small round stones, all of the same value.

54

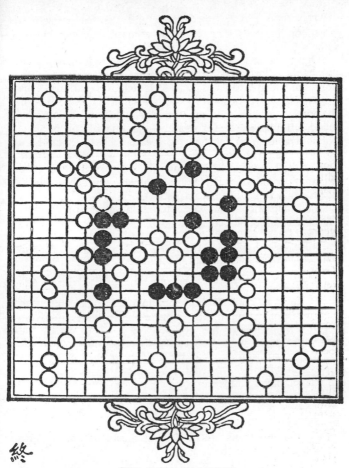

終

THE CHESS PROBLEM

Starting with a clear board, the two participants play alternately, placing one stone on a point. The aim is to take as many of the other player's men as possible by surrounding them completely, single or in groups. The men thus taken are immediately removed from the board. He wins who succeeds in occupying the greatest number of points on the board."

"That sounds quite simple!" Hoong observed.

Judge Dee answered with a smile.

"The rules are indeed simple, but the game itself is most complicated; they say that a man's lifetime hardly suffices for mastering all its intricacies!

"Our great chess masters often published manuals of the game, illustrated with diagrams of interesting positions, and also problems with detailed explanations. This sheet must have been torn from such a handbook. It is the last page, for you see the word *finis* printed in the lower left corner. Unfortunately, the title of the book is not indicated. You must try to locate a chess expert here in Han-yuan, Hoong. Such a person will doubtless be able to tell from which book this sheet was torn. The explanation of this particular problem must have been printed on the penultimate page."

Ma Joong and Chiao Tai entered and greeted the judge. When they were seated in front of his desk he said to Ma Joong:

"I suppose that last night you stayed behind in order to gather information. Tell me the result!"

Ma Joong placed his large fists on his knees. He began with a smile.

"Yesterday Your Honor mentioned the possibility of getting information on the courtesan's private life from the other inmates of her house. Now it so happened that last night when we were passing there on our way to the lake, one girl standing on the balcony rather caught my fancy. So when we visited the house later, I described her to the manager, and the obliging fellow immediately had her called away from the dinner party she was attending. Her name is Peach Blossom, a most apt appellation indeed!"

Ma Joong paused. He twirled his mustache and his grin grew broader as he continued.

"She is indeed a most charming girl and somehow or other I didn't seem to displease her either. At least she—"

"Spare me," Judge Dee interrupted peevishly, "the details of your amorous exploits! We'll take it for granted that you two got along well together. Now what did she tell you about the dead dancer?"

Ma Joong looked hurt. He heaved a sigh, then went on with resigned patience.

"Well, Your Honor, this girl Peach Blossom was a close friend of the dead courtesan. The dancer arrived in the Willow Quarter about one year ago, one of a batch of four brought by a procurer from the capital. She told

Peach Blossom that she had left her home in Shansi because of an unfortunate incident, and that she could never go back there. She was rather particular; although a number of distinguished guests tried hard to win her favor she politely refused all of them. Guildmaster Soo especially was most assiduous in his attentions and gave her many costly presents, but he never had a chance."

"That," Judge Dee interrupted, "we'll note down as a point against Soo. Scorned love is often a powerful motive."

"However," Ma Joong continued, "Peach Blossom is convinced that Almond Blossom was by no means a cold woman; the fact is that she must have had a secret lover. At least once a week she would ask the manager's permission to go out shopping. Since she was a steady and obedient girl who never had shown the slightest inclination to run away, the manager always said yes. She went alone, and her friend assumed it was to a secret rendezvous. But she never found out who it was or where she met him, though not for want of trying, I am sure!"

"How long was she gone each time?" the judge asked.

"She would leave shortly after the noon meal," Ma Joong answered, "and come back just before the evening rice was served."

"That means that she couldn't have gone outside the town," Judge Dee observed. "Go and ask the scribe about that pen name, Sergeant!"

As Hoong went out a clerk entered and handed the judge a large sealed envelope. Judge Dee opened it and spread a long letter out on his desk. It had two copies attached to it. Caressing his side-whiskers, he slowly read it through. Just as he was leaning back in his chair Sergeant Hoong came back. Shaking his head Hoong said:

"Our senior scribe is certain, Your Honor, that no scholar or writer in this district uses the sobriquet Student of the Bamboo Grove."

"That's a pity!" Judge Dee said. Then, sitting straight and pointing to the letter in front of him, he went on in a brisk voice. "Now we have here the report of the manager of the courtesan's house. Her real name was Miss Fan Ho-i, and she was bought seven months ago from a procurer of the capital, exactly as Peach Flower or whatever she's called told Ma Joong. The price was two gold bars.

"The procurer stated that he had purchased her under

57

unusual circumstances. She had approached him herself and agreed to sell herself for one gold bar and fifty silver pieces, on condition that she would be resold only in Han-yuan. The procurer thought it strange that this girl transacted the deal herself, instead of through her parents or through a middleman. But since she was good-looking and skilled in singing and dancing he saw a handsome profit and did not trouble to question her. He paid her the money and she disposed of it herself. However, since the house in the Willow Quarter was a good client, the procurer thought it wise to inform the manager of the unusual manner in which he had acquired the girl, so as to bear no responsibility if later complications should arise."

Here the judge paused, and angrily shook his head. Then he went on:

"The manager asked her a few pertinent questions but as she evaded a direct answer he let the matter go. He says that he assumed that her parents had expelled her because of an illicit love affair. The other details about her life in the house tally with what Ma Joong learned from the other girl. The manager notes here the names of the citizens who showed particular interest in Almond Blossom. The list includes nearly all the prominent citizens of Han-yuan, but not Liu Fei-po and Han Yung-han. On occasion he urged her to accept one of those as her lover, but she had steadfastly refused. Since she brought in good money by her dancing alone, the manager had never insisted.

"Now, at the end of his report he states that she liked literary games, wrote a good hand, and was a more than average painter of birds and flowers. But he says specifically that she didn't like chess!"

Judge Dee paused. Looking at his lieutenants he asked:

"Now how do you explain the remark she made to me about playing chess, and her carrying that chess problem in her sleeve?"

Ma Joong perplexedly scratched his head. Chiao Tai asked:

"Could I have a look at that problem, Your Honor? I used to be rather fond of the game."

The judge pushed the sheet over to him. Chiao Tai studied the problem for a while; then he said:

"That is quite a meaningless position, Your Honor! White occupies nearly the entire board. One might conceivably reconstruct some of the moves whereby it blocked black's progress, but in black's position there's neither rhyme nor reason!"

Judge Dee knitted his eyebrows. He remained in thought for some time.

He was roused by three beats on the large bronze gong suspended at the main gate. They reverberated through the tribunal, announcing that the morning session was to be opened.

The judge replaced the chess problem in his drawer and rose with a sigh. Sergeant Hoong assisted him in donning his official robe of dark-green brocade. As he was adjusting the black winged judge's cap on his head, he said to the three men:

"I shall first review the murder on the flower boat. Fortunately, there are no other cases pending, so we can concentrate our attention on this baffling murder."

Ma Joong drew aside the heavy curtain that separated the judge's private office from the court hall. Judge Dee passed through and ascended the dais. He sat down behind the high bench covered with scarlet brocade. Ma Joong and Chiao Tai stood themselves behind his chair, Sergeant Hoong took his customary place at Judge Dee's right hand.

The constables stood in two rows in front of the dais carrying whips, clubs, chains, handscrews and the other paraphernalia of their office. The senior scribe and his assistants were sitting at lower tables on either side of the dais, ready to note down the proceedings.

Judge Dee surveyed the court hall. He noticed that a large crowd of spectators had gathered. The news of the murder in the flower boat had spread like wildfire and the citizens of Han-yuan were eager to hear all the details. In the front row he saw Han Yung-han, the Kang brothers and the guildmasters Peng and Soo. He wondered why Liu Fei-po and Master Wang were not there; the headman of the constables had notified all of them that they would have to be present.

He rapped his gavel on the bench and declared the session open. He then commenced to call the roll.

Suddenly a group of people appeared at the entrance of the court hall. They were headed by Liu Fei-po, who shouted excitedly:

"I demand justice! A foul crime has been committed!"

Judge Dee gave a sign to the headman. He went to

meet the newcomers and led them before the dais.

Liu Fei-po knelt on the stone flags. A tall, middle-aged gentleman clad in a plain blue robe and wearing a small black skullcap knelt by his side. Four other men remained standing beyond the row of constables. Judge Dee recognized one of them as Guildmaster Wang; the other three he didn't know.

"Your Honor!" Liu cried out, "my daughter has been cruelly murdered on her wedding night!"

Judge Dee lifted his eyebrows. He said curtly:

"The complainant Liu Fei-po shall report everything in the proper sequence. I learned last night during the banquet that your daughter's wedding was celebrated the day before yesterday. Why do you come now, two days after the event, to report her death to this tribunal?"

"It's all due to the evil scheme of that wicked man here!" Liu cried out, pointing at the gentleman kneeling by his side.

"State your name and profession!" the judge ordered the middle-aged man.

"This insignificant person," the other said calmly, "is named Djang Wen-djang, a Doctor of Literature. A fearful calamity has struck my house, robbing me at the same time of my beloved only son and his young bride. As if that were not enough, this man Liu Fei-po accuses me, their father! I respectfully beg Your Honor to right this terrible wrong!"

"The impudent rascal!" Liu Fei-po shouted.

Judge Dee rapped his gavel.

"The complainant Liu Fei-po," he said sternly, "shall refrain from using invectives in this court! State your case!"

Liu Fei-po mastered himself with difficulty. He was evidently completely beside himself from grief and anger; he seemed quite a different man from the one of the evening before. After a few moments he began in a calmer voice.

"August Heaven had so willed it that I would not be granted male issue. My only child was a daughter, called Moon Fairy. It proved that I was to be compensated for the lack of a son in this one daughter. She was a charming and sweet-tempered girl. To see her develop into a beautiful and intelligent young woman was the great joy of my life; I—"

60

He broke off; a sob smothered his voice. He swallowed a few times, then continued with a trembling voice.

"Last year she asked whether she might follow a private course in classical literature which this professor was giving in his house for a group of young women. I agreed, for till then she had been interested mainly in riding and hunting, and I was glad that now she also felt attracted by the arts and letters. How could I have foreseen what calamity would ensue? Moon Fairy saw in the doctor's house his son, Candidate Djang Hoo-piao, and fell in love with him. I wanted to inform myself about the Djang family before taking a decision, but Moon Fairy begged me insistently to have the betrothal announced soon, and my First Lady—the stupid woman!—supported her request, though she ought to have known better.

"When I had given my consent, a matchmaker was chosen, and the marriage contract drawn up. Then, however, my friend the business promoter Wan I-fan warned me that Dr. Djang was a libertine who some time previously had tried in vain to make Wan's daughter an instrument of his base lusts. I decided to annul the betrothal at once. But then Moon Fairy fell ill, and my First Lady maintained that the girl was lovesick and would certainly die if I didn't reconsider my decision. Moreover, Dr. Djang, loath to see his prey escape, refused to cancel the marriage contract."

Liu shot a venomous look at the professor, then went on.

"So, although with the greatest reluctance, I allowed the wedding to take place. The day before yesterday the red candles were lighted in the Djang mansion and the marriage solemnized before the soul tablets of the ancestors. The wedding feast was attended by more than thirty prominent citizens, including the guests who were present at the banquet on the flower boat.

"Now early this morning the professor came rushing to my house in great agitation, reporting that yesterday Moon Fairy had been found dead on the bridal couch. I asked at once why he hadn't immediately informed me. He replied that since his son, the bridegroom, had disappeared without trace, he had wanted to try to locate him first. I asked what had caused her death, but he just mumbled some unintelligible words. I wanted to go back with him to view my daughter's body. The man calmly told

61

me that she had been already encoffined and deposited in the Buddhist Temple!"

Judge Dee sat up. He wanted to interrupt Liu but on second thought decided to hear him to the end.

"A horrible suspicion arose in me," Liu went on. "I hurriedly went to consult my neighbor, Guildmaster Wang. He at once agreed with me that my daughter had been the victim of an unspeakable crime. I informed Dr. Djang that I would proceed to the tribunal to file an accusation. Master Wang went to fetch Wan I-fan to act as witness. Now I, Liu Fei-po, am kneeling in front of Your Honor's bench beseeching you to see to it that the wicked criminal gets his just punishment so that the soul of my poor daughter may rest in peace!"

Having thus spoken Liu knocked his forehead on the stone floor three times in succession.

Judge Dee slowly stroked his long beard. After a moment's thought he asked:

"Do you mean to say that Candidate Djang murdered his bride and then absconded?"

"I beg Your Honor's pardon!" Liu answered hurriedly. "I am quite upset, I don't express myself clearly. That weak-kneed youngster, Candidate Djang, is innocent. It's his father, that degenerate lecher, who is the culprit! He coveted Moon Fairy and, excited by the wine, he laid hands on her the very night she was to be his son's bride. My poor daughter killed herself, and Candidate Djang, horrified at the scandalous behavior of his own father, fled in despair. The next morning, when the wicked professor had slept off his debauch, he found my daughter's dead body. Afraid of the consequences of his dastardly deed, he had the corpse encoffined immediately, to conceal the fact that she had committed suicide. I therefore accuse Dr. Djang Wen-djang of having ravished and caused the death of my daughter, Moon Fairy."

Judge Dee told the senior scribe to read out Liu's accusation as he had noted it down. Liu agreed that it was correct and affixed his thumbmark to the document. Then the judge spoke.

"The accused Djang Wen-djang shall now give his version of what happened."

"This person," the professor began in a slightly pedantic voice, "begs Your Honor's forgiveness for his improper behavior. I wish to state that I fully realize that I have acted foolishly. The quiet life among my books has made

62

me sadly incapable of dealing efficiently with so horrible a crisis as suddenly befell my poor house. But I emphatically deny ever having as much as thought of my son's bride in an unseemly way, let alone having assaulted her. The following is a complete account of what really happened, true in every detail."

The doctor paused a moment to collect his thoughts, then went on:

"Yesterday morning when I was having breakfast in my garden pavilion, the maidservant Peony came and reported that she had knocked on the door of the bridal room and called out that she was bringing the morning rice, but there had been no answer. I said that the couple should not be disturbed, and ordered her to try again after an hour or so.

"Later in the morning, when I was watering the flowers, Peony came again and told me there was still no answer from the room. I began to feel somewhat alarmed. I went myself to the separate courtyard assigned to the young couple and vigorously knocked on the door. When there was no response I repeatedly shouted my son's name, but without result.

"Then I knew that something untoward must have happened. I hurriedly went to fetch my neighbor and friend, the tea merchant Koong, and asked his advice. He said it was my duty to have the door opened by force. I called my house steward. He took an ax and smashed the lock."

Dr. Djang paused. He swallowed, then went on in a toneless voice:

"The naked body of Moon Fairy was lying on the couch, covered with blood. My son was nowhere to be seen. I hastily stepped forward and covered her with a quilt. Then I felt her pulse. It had stopped beating and her hand was cold as ice. She was dead.

"Koong at once went to fetch the learned physican Dr. Hwa, who lives nearby, and he conducted the post-mortem. He reported that the cause of death had been severe hemorrhage resulting from defloration. I then knew that my son, distracted with grief, had fled the scene of his tragic misfortune. I was convinced that he had gone to some lonely place to kill himself, and wanted to go out at once to try to find him and prevent him from executing that desperate deed. When Dr. Hwa remarked that in this hot weather it was better to have the dead body encoffined immediately, I gave orders to call an undertaker for washing the body and placing it in a temporary coffin. Koong suggested to have it deposited in the Buddhist Temple, pending the decision regarding the place of interment. I asked all present to keep the matter secret until I would have found my son, dead or alive. Then I went to search for him, accompanied by Koong and my steward.

"The entire day we roamed through the city and the suburbs, inquiring everywhere, but when dusk was falling we had failed to obtain the slightest clue. When we came back home we found a fisherman waiting for us in front of the gate. He gave me a silk girdle that had caught his hook when he was fishing in the lake. There was no need for me to inspect the name embroidered on the lining. I at once recognized it as that of my poor son. This second shock was too much for me; I fell down in a faint. Koong and my steward put me to bed. Completely exhausted, I slept till this morning.

"As soon as I had risen I remembered my duty to the bride's father. I hastened to the Liu mansion and reported the fearful tragedy. Instead of joining me in lamentations over the cruel fate that had robbed us of our children, that heartless man heaped the wildest accusations on my head and threatened me with action in this tribunal. I pray Your Honor to see to it that justice is done to this person, who on one and the same day lost his only son and his young son's bride, and thus is faced with the terrible prospect that his family line will be broken off!"

Then the professor knocked his forehead on the floor several times.

Judge Dee gave a sign to the scribe. He read out his recorded version of Dr. Djang's statement and the latter affixed his thumbmark to it. Then the judge spoke.

"I shall now hear the witnesses of complainant and accused. Let the promoter Wan I-fan come forward!"

Judge Dee gave him a sharp look. He remembered that his name had also been mentioned in connection with the quarrel of the Kang brothers. Wan I-fan was a man of about forty with a smooth, beardless face, the pallor of which was set off by his short black mustache.

Wan stated that two years earlier Dr. Djang's Second Lady had died. Since his First and Third Lady had passed away previously, the professor was then all alone. He had approached Wan with the offer to take Wan's daughter as concubine. Wan had indignantly refused that proposal done without even a proper matchmaker. Thereupon Dr.

Djang, thwarted in the satisfaction of his lust, had spread malicious rumors averring that Wan was an impostor whose transactions couldn't bear the light of day. Having thus come to know the professor's wicked character, Wan had thought it his duty to warn Liu Fei-po to what kind of a family he was going to entrust his only daughter.

As soon as Wan I-fan had finished Dr. Djang shouted angrily:

"I beseech Your Honor not to believe that preposterous mixture of truth and falsehood! It is true that I have often commented unfavorably on Wan I-fan. I don't hesitate to state here formally that the man is a crook and a swindler. After the demise of my Second Lady, it was he who approached me offering his daughter as a concubine. He said that since his wife had died he was unable to look after his daughter properly. Evidently he wanted to extort money from me, and to prevent my criticizing his questionable business methods any further. It was I who at once refused that impudent proposal!"

Judge Dee crashed his fist on the table. He called out:

"I, the magistrate, am being trifled with! Evidently one of these two men is telling a brazen lie! Let it be understood that I shall thoroughly investigate this matter and woe to him who has tried to fool me!"

Angrily tugging at his beard, the judge ordered Guildmaster Wang to come forward.

Wang's statement supported Liu Fei-po as far as the facts were concerned. But he was very diffident in expressing an opinion on Liu's theory of the crime committed by Dr. Djang. He said he had agreed to it merely to calm down the excited Liu Fei-po, and that he wished to reserve his opinion as to what had actually happened on the wedding night.

Then Judge Dee heard the two witnesses for the defense. First the tea merchant Koong, who confirmed Dr. Djang's description of the events, and added that the professor was a man of frugal habits and the most elevated character. When Dr. Hwa was kneeling on the stone flags Judge Dee ordered the headman to call the coroner of the tribunal. Then the judge sternly addressed Dr. Hwa, saying:

"You, as a professional physician, should have known that in all cases of sudden death the body may not be encoffined before the full circumstances have been reported to this tribunal and before the coroner has examined the corpse. You have offended against the law and you shall be punished accordingly. Now you shall, in the presence of the coroner, describe in what condition you found the body, and how you arrived at your conclusion as to the cause of death!"

Dr. Hwa quickly embarked on a detailed description of the symptoms found on the dead girl. When he had finished, Judge Dee looked questioningly at the coroner, who said:

"I respectfully report to Your Honor that although the death of a virgin under the circumstances described is of rare occurrence, our medical books do indeed cite a few instances from the past. There can be no doubt that death occasionally ensues though prolonged unconsciousness is more common. The symptoms described by Dr. Hwa accord in all details with those recorded in authoritative medical treatises."

Judge Dee nodded. After he had condemned Dr. Hwa to a heavy fine, he addressed the audience, saying:

"I had planned this morning to review the case of the courtesan's murder, but this new case makes an immediate inspection of the scene of the alleged crime imperative."

He rapped his gavel and closed the session.

Sixth Chapter

JUDGE DEE EXAMINES THE LIBRARY OF A STUDENT; AN AUTOPSY IS CONDUCTED IN A DESERTED TEMPLE

IN THE CORRIDOR JUDGE DEE TOLD MA JOONG:

"Let the constables make my palanquin ready to proceed to Dr. Djang's house, and tell four of them to go to the Buddhist Temple, to prepare everything there for the autopsy. I'll go there as soon as I am finished with the professor."

Then he entered his private office.

Sergeant Hoong went to the tea table to make a cup of tea for the judge. Chiao Tai remained standing, waiting till Judge Dee would sit down. But the judge started pacing the floor with his hands on his back, a deep frown creasing his forehead. He stood still only when Hoong offered him a cup of tea. He took a few sips, then spoke.

"I can't imagine what made Liu Fei-po proffer that fantastic accusation! I admit that the hurried encoffining of the body seemed suspicious, but any man in his senses would first have insisted on an autopsy, instead of filing such a serious accusation! And last night Liu impressed me as a very calm and self-possessed man."

"Just now in the court hall he looked to me as if he was out of his mind, Your Honor," the sergeant remarked. "I saw that his hands were shaking, and there was foam on his lips!"

"Liu's accusation is utterly absurd!" Chiao Tai exclaimed. "If Liu was really convinced that the professor was a man of low character, why then did he consent to the marriage? He hardly seems the kind of man to let himself be tyrannized by his wife and daughter! And he could easily have had the marriage contract canceled unilaterally!"

Judge Dee nodded pensively.

"There must be more behind that marriage than meets the eye!" he said. "And I must say that Dr. Djang, despite his touching lament about the disaster that hit his house, seemed to take it rather calmly!"

Ma Joong entered and reported that the palanquin was ready. Judge Dee went out into the courtyard, followed by his three lieutenants.

Dr. Djang lived in an impressive mansion, built against the mountain slope, to the west of the tribunal.

The steward opened the heavy double door, and Judge Dee's palanquin was carried inside.

The professor assisted the judge respectfully in descending, then led him and Sergeant Hoong to the reception hall. Ma Joong and Chiao Tai stayed behind in the first courtyard with the headman and two constables.

While the judge was sitting opposite the professor at the tea table, he gave his host a good look. Dr. Djang was a tall, well-built man, with a sharp, intelligent face. He seemed about fifty years old, rather young to have been granted a pension already. He silently poured out a cup of tea for the judge, then sat down again and waited till his distinguished guest would begin the conversation. Hoong remained standing behind Judge Dee's chair.

The judge looked at the well-stocked bookshelves and inquired which literary subject had the professor's special interest. Dr. Djang gave, in well-chosen words, a concise explanation of his research into the critical study of some ancient texts. His answers to Judge Dee's questions on some details proved that he had completely mastered the subject. He made a few quite original remarks on the authenticity of a disputed passage, freely quoting by heart from lesser-known old commentaries. Although one might question the professor's moral integrity, there couldn't be the slightest doubt that he was a great scholar.

"Why," the judge asked, "did you when still comparatively young give up your chair in the School of the Temple of Confucius? Many persons retain that honorable position till they are seventy or even older."

Dr. Djang gave the judge a suspicious look. He replied stiffly: "I preferred to devote all my time to my own researches. The last three years I have confined my teaching to two private courses in classical literature here in my own house, for a few advanced students."

Judge Dee rose and said he wanted to see the scene of the tragedy.

The professor nodded silently. He led his two guests through an open corridor to a second courtyard, and stood still before a graceful arched door opening. He said slowly:

68

"Beyond is the courtyard which I had assigned to my son. I have given strict orders that no one shall enter there since the coffin has been removed."

Inside was a small landscaped garden. In the center stood a rustic stone table, flanked by two clusters of bamboos whose rustling green leaves made one forget the oppressive heat.

Upon entering the narrow portal, Dr. Djang first pushed open the door on the left and showed them a small library. There was just room for a writing desk in front of the window, and an old armchair. The book rack bore piles of books and manuscript rolls. The professor said softly:

"My son was extremely fond of his small library. He had chosen the pen name of Student of the Bamboo Grove, though the clusters of bamboos outside there could hardly be called a grove!"

Judge Dee went inside and examined the books on the rack. Dr. Djang and Sergeant Hoong remained standing outside. Turning round to them, the judge said casually to the professor:

"I see from his choice of books that your son had wide interests. It's a pity that those extended also to the damsels of the Willow Quarter!"

"Who in the world," Dr. Djang exclaimed angrily, "could have given Your Honor this ridiculous misinformation! My son was of a most serious disposition; he never went out at night. Who made that preposterous suggestion?"

"I thought I had heard a remark to that effect somewhere," Judge Dee answered vaguely. "I probably misunderstood the speaker. Since your son was such an industrious scholar I suppose that he wrote a very good hand?"

The professor pointed at a pile of papers on the desk and said curtly:

"That is the manuscript of my son's commentary on the Analects of Confucius, on which he was working of late."

Judge Dee leafed the manuscript through. "A very expressive handwriting," he commented as he stepped out into the portal.

The doctor took them to the sitting room opposite. He seemed still to nurse a grievance over Judge Dee's remark about his son's dissipated life. His face had a surly expression when he said:

"If Your Honor walks down the corridor you'll find the door of the bedroom. With Your Honor's leave I shall wait here."

Judge Dee nodded. Followed by Sergeant Hoong he passed through the dimly lit corridor. At the end they saw a door hanging loose on its hinges. The judge pushed it open and surveyed from the threshold the darkish room. It was fairly small, and lit only by the sunlight filtering in through the translucent paper pasted over the latticework of the only window.

Sergeant Hoong whispered excitedly:

"So Candidate Djang was Almond Blossom's lover!"

"And the fellow drowned himself!" Judge Dee replied testily. "We have found the Student of the Bamboo Grove and lost him at the same time! There is one curious point, though. His handwriting is quite different from that of the love letters." He stooped and continued: "Look, a film of dust covers the floor. Apparently the professor spoke the truth when he said that nobody entered this room after Moon Fairy's body had been removed."

The judge looked for a moment at the broad couch against the back wall. The reed mat that covered it showed some dark-red spots. On the right there was a dressing table, on the left a pile of clothes boxes. By the side of the couch stood a small tea table, with two tabourets. The air in the room was very close.

Judge Dee walked over to the window to open it. But it was locked by a wooden crossbar, covered with dust. He pushed it back with some difficulty. Through the iron bars he saw a corner of a vegetable garden surrounded by a high brick wall. There was a small door, apparently used by the cook when he came to gather vegetables.

The judge shook his head perplexedly. He said:

"The door was locked on the inside, Hoong, the window has solid iron bars and anyway hasn't been opened for several days at least. How in the name of Heaven did Candidate Djang leave this room that fateful night?"

The sergeant gave his master a puzzled look.

"This is very queer!" he said. And then, after some hesitation: "Perhaps this room has a secret door, Your Honor!"

Judge Dee rose quickly. They pushed the couch away from the wall and studied the wall and the floor inch

70

by inch. Then they examined also the other walls and the entire floor, but without result.

Judge Dee resumed his seat. Dusting his knees he said:

"Go back to the sitting room, Hoong, and order the professor to write out for me a list of all the friends and acquaintances of himself and his son. I shall stay here for a while and have a look around."

After the sergeant had left, Judge Dee folded his arms. So now there was a new riddle to be solved. In the case of the dead dancer there were at least some definite leads. The motive was clear: the murderer wanted to prevent her from warning the judge about a secret plot. There were four suspects. A systematic investigation of their relations with the courtesan would show who the culprit was, and then the plot he was planning would soon be known. The investigation was well under way, and now this queer affair had cropped up, a case where there were two main persons, and both of them dead! And here there seemed to be no lead at all! The professor was a curious man, but he did not seem the type of a philanderer. On the other hand, appearances are often deceptive, and Wan I-fan would hardly have dared to lie in court about the affair of his daughter. But neither would the professor have dared to lie when he said that his son didn't frequent the Willow Quarter. Dr. Djang was clever enough to know that such things could easily be checked. Perhaps the doctor himself had had an affair with the dancer, and used his son's pen name in his love letters! He wasn't so young any more, but he had a strong personality, and anyway it was always difficult to know a woman's preference. In any case they would compare the doctor's writing with that of the love letters; the list Hoong would have him draw up would provide them with a specimen. But the professor couldn't have murdered the dancer, because he hadn't been on board! Perhaps after all the dancer's love affair had nothing to do with her murder.

Judge Dee shifted on his chair. Suddenly he had the uneasy feeling that he was being watched. He turned to the open window.

A pale, haggard face was looking at him with wide eyes.

The judge jumped up and ran to the window, but he stumbled over the second tabouret. He scrambled up but reached the window only in time to see the door in the garden wall close.

71

He rushed to the first courtyard and ordered Ma Joong and Chiao Tai to search at once the street outside for a man of medium height, his head shaved like that of a monk. Then he told the headman to assemble all the inmates of the household in the reception hall, and thereafter search the house to see that nobody was hiding there. He slowly walked over to the hall himself, his eyebrows knitted in a deep frown.

Sergeant Hoong and Dr. Djang came running out to see what all the commotion was about. Judge Dee ignored their questions. He curtly asked Dr. Djang:

"Why didn't you tell me there is a secret door in the bridal room?"

The professor stared at the judge in blank astonishment.

"A secret door?" he asked. "What would I, a retired scholar living in a reign of peace, need such a contraption for? I myself supervised the building of this house; I can assure Your Honor that there is no such thing in the entire building!"

"In that case," Judge Dee remarked dryly, "you had better find the explanation of how your son could have left his room. Its only window is barred, and the door was locked on the inside."

The doctor clapped his hand against his forehead. He said, annoyed:

"To think that I didn't even realize that!"

"I'll give you an opportunity to ponder over that puzzle!" the judge said curtly. "Until further notice you shall not leave this house. I shall now go to the Buddhist Temple and have an autopsy conducted on Moon Fairy's body. I deem this step necessary in the interests of justice, so you can spare yourself the trouble of protesting!"

Dr. Djang looked furious. But he restrained himself. He turned round and left the hall without another word.

The headman herded about a dozen men and women into the hall. "That's all there was, Your Honor!" he announced.

Judge Dee quickly looked them over. No one showed any resemblance to the apparition he had seen outside the window. He questioned the maid Peony about her trying to rouse the newlywed couple, but her answers tallied exactly with the statement made by the professor.

When the judge had dismissed them, Ma Joong and Chiao Tai came in. The former wiped the sweat from his brow and said:

"We have searched the entire neighborhood, Your Honor, but without result. We found no one about but a lemonade vendor who sat snoring by the side of his cart. Because of the midday heat the streets were deserted. Next to the garden door we found two bundles of firewood, evidently left there by a pedlar, but the man himself was nowhere to be seen."

Judge Dee told them briefly about the weird man who had been watching him from outside the window. Then he ordered the headman to go to the houses of Liu Fei-po and Guildmaster Wang, and to summon them to the Buddhist Temple for the autopsy. Ma Joong was to go there too, to see that the constables had put everything in order. To Chiao Tai he said: "You'll stay here with two constables and see to it that Dr. Djang doesn't leave the house! And keep your eyes skinned for that queer fellow who watched me!"

The judge went to his palanquin, angrily swinging his sleeves. He ascended together with Sergeant Hoong, and they were carried to the temple.

As he climbed the broad steps of the gatehouse Judge Dee noticed that they were overgrown with weeds and that the red lacquer was peeling off the high pillars of the monumental gate. He remembered having heard that a few years before the monks had left and that the temple was now in charge of an old caretaker.

He walked with Hoong through a dilapidated corridor to the side hall of the temple. There he found Ma Joong waiting for him, together with the coroner and the constables. Ma Joong introduced three other men as the undertaker and his two assistants. On the right stood a high altar, completely bare. In front of it was the coffin, resting on two trestles. On the other side of the hall the constables had placed a large table for the temporary tribunal, flanked by a smaller table for the scribe. Before he went to sit behind the table, Judge Dee called the undertaker and his two men. As they were kneeling down he asked the undertaker:

"Do you remember whether the window of the bridal room where you washed the corpse was open or closed?"

The man looked, dumfounded, at his assistants. The younger one replied at once:

"It was closed, Your Honor! I wanted to open it because it was rather hot in the room, but the crossbar had become stuck, and I could not push it back."

The judge nodded. Then he asked again:

"Did you notice while you were washing the body any signs of violence? Wounds, bruises or discolored spots?"

The undertaker shook his head.

"I was rather astonished by all that blood, Your Honor, and therefore examined the body with special care. But there was no wound, not even a scratch! I may add that the girl was sturdily built. She must have been rather strong for a young lady of her class."

"Did you place the body immediately in the coffin after you had washed it and put it in the shroud?" Judge Dee asked.

"We did, Your Honor. Mr. Koong had ordered us to bring a temporary coffin, because the parents would have to decide later on when and where she would be buried. The coffin was made of thin boards, and it took little time to nail the lid on."

In the meantime the coroner had spread out a thick reed mat on the floor in front of the coffin. He now placed there a copper basin with hot water.

Then Liu Fei-po and Guildmaster Wang came in. After they had greeted Judge Dee, he went to sit in the armchair behind the table. He rapped three times with his knuckles and said:

"This special session of the tribunal has been convened to settle some doubts that have arisen concerning the manner in which Mrs. Djang Hoo-piao, *nee* Liu, met her death. The coffin shall be opened and the coroner of this tribunal shall conduct an autopsy. Since this is not an exhumation but merely a sequel to the routine preliminary examination, the parents' consent is not required. I have, however, requested Liu Fei-po, the father of the deceased, to be present as a witness, and the Guildmaster Wang, in the same capacity. Dr. Djang Wen-djang is unable to attend since he has been placed under house arrest."

On a sign of the judge a constable lighted two bundles of incense sticks. One he laid on the edge of Judge Dee's table, the other he put in a vase which he placed on the floor next to the coffin. When the thick gray smoke filled the hall with its acrid smell, Judge Dee ordered the undertaker to open the coffin.

He inserted his chisel under the lid. His assistants started to pry loose the nails.

As the two men were lifting the lid, the undertaker

74

suddenly backed away with a gasp. His frightened assistants let the lid clatter to the floor.

The coroner quickly stepped up to the coffin and looked inside.

"A ghastly thing has happened!" he exclaimed.

Judge Dee rose at once and rushed over to his side. After one look he drew back involuntarily.

In the coffin lay the body of a fully dressed man. His head was a mass of clotted blood.

Seventh Chapter

A GRISLY DISCOVERY CREATES NEW COMPLICATIONS; THE JUDGE GOES TO VISIT TWO EMINENT PERSONS

THEY STOOD SILENTLY ROUND THE COFFIN, STARING with unbelieving eyes at the hideous corpse. The forehead had been cleft by a fearful blow. Covered with dried blood, the head presented a sickening sight.

"Where is my daughter?" Liu Fei-po suddenly screamed. "I want my daughter!" Guildmaster Wang put his arm round the shoulder of the stricken man and led him away. He was sobbing wildly.

Judge Dee turned round abruptly and went back to the bench. He rapped the table hard and said testily:

"Let everyone return to his appointed place! Ma Joong, go and search this temple! Undertaker, let your assistants take the body out of the coffin!"

Slowly the two men lifted the stiff corpse from the coffin and lowered it onto the reed mat. The coroner knelt by its side and carefully removed the bloodstained clothes. The jacket and trousers were of rough cotton, showing clumsy patches. He folded these articles and put them in a neat pile. Then he looked up expectantly at the judge.

Judge Dee took his vermilion writing brush and wrote at the head of an official form: "One male person of unknown identity." He gave the form to the scribe.

The coroner dipped a towel in the copper basin and removed the blood from the head, revealing the terrible, gaping wound. Thereafter he washed the entire body, examining it inch by inch. Finally he rose and reported:

"One body of a male person, musculature well developed, age approximately fifty years. Rough hands with broken nails, pronounced callosity on the right thumb. Thin, short beard and gray mustache, bald head. Cause of death: one wound in the middle of the forehead, one inch broad and two inches deep, presumably inflicted by a two-handed sword or a large ax."

When the scribe had entered these details on the form,

the coroner added his thumbmark on it and presented the paper to the judge. Then Judge Dee ordered him to search the clothes of the dead man. The coroner found in the sleeve of the jacket a wooden ruler, and a soiled scrap of paper. He laid these objects on the table.

The judge gave the ruler a casual look, then smoothed out the piece of paper. He raised his eyebrows. While putting the scrap of paper in his sleeve he said:

"All present shall now file past the corpse and try to identify it. We shall begin with Liu Fei-po and Master Wang."

Liu Fei-po looked cursorily at the disfigured face, then shook his head and quickly passed on. His face was of a deadly pallor. Guildmaster Wang wanted to follow his example but suddenly he uttered an astonished cry. Suppressing his aversion he stooped over the corpse, then exclaimed:

"I know this man! It's Mao Yuan, the carpenter! Last week he came to my house to repair a table!"

"Where did he live?" the judge asked quickly.

"That I don't know, Your Honor," Wang replied, "but I'll ask my house steward; it was he who called him."

Judge Dee silently caressed his side whiskers. Then he suddenly barked at the undertaker:

"Why didn't you, a professional undertaker who is supposed to know his job, immediately report to me that the coffin had been tampered with? Or isn't it the same one in which you placed the dead woman? Speak up and tell the truth!"

Stuttering with fear the undertaker answered:

"I . . . I swear it's the same coffin, Your Honor! I bought it myself two weeks ago and burnt my mark in the wood. But it could easily be opened, Your Honor! Since it was only a temporary coffin we didn't hammer the nails in very carefully and—"

Judge Dee cut him short with an impatient gesture.

"This corpse," he announced, "shall be properly clad in a shroud and replaced in the coffin. I shall consult the family of the deceased regarding the burial. Until then two constables shall stand guard in this hall, lest also this corpse disappear! Headman, bring the caretaker of this temple before me! What is that dog's-head doing anyway? He should have presented himself here!"

"The caretaker is a very old man, Your Honor," the headman said quickly. "He lives on a bowl of rice that some pious people bring twice daily to his cell next to the gatehouse. He is deaf, and nearly blind."

"Blind and deaf, forsooth!" the judge muttered angrily. He said curtly to Liu Fei-po:

"I shall without delay institute an investigation into the whereabouts of your daughter's body."

Then Ma Joong came back into the hall.

"I respectfully report," he said, "that I have searched this entire temple, including the garden behind it. There is no trace of a dead body having been concealed or buried there."

"Go now back with Master Wang," Judge Dee ordered him, "find out the address of the carpenter, and proceed there at once. I want to know what he has been doing these last days. And if he should have male relatives, I want them brought to the tribunal for questioning."

Having thus spoken, the judge rapped the table and declared the session closed.

Before leaving the hall he walked over to the coffin and scrutinized its inside. There were no bloodstains. Then he examined the floor all around it, but among the confused mass of footprints in the dust he could discover no smudges or other signs of blood having been wiped up there. Evidently the carpenter had been killed somewhere else, and his body brought to the hall and placed inside the coffin after the blood had already coagulated. He took leave of the company and left the hall, followed by Sergeant Hoong.

Judge Dee remained silent all the way back. But when he was in his private office and Hoong had helped him change into a comfortable house robe, his morose mood left him. As he sat down behind his desk he said with a smile:

"Well, Hoong, plenty of problems to solve! By the way, I am glad that I placed the professor under house arrest. Look what the carpenter carried in his sleeve!"

He pushed the scrap of paper over to Hoong, who exclaimed, astonished:

"The name and address of Dr. Djang are scribbled here, Your Honor!"

"Yes," Judge Dee said with satisfaction, "our learned doctor apparently overlooked that! Let me now see that list you had him draw up, Hoong."

The sergeant took a folded piece of paper from his sleeve. As he handed it to the judge he said dejectedly:

"As far as I can see, Your Honor, his handwriting is quite different from that of the love letters."

"You are right," the judge said. "There isn't the slightest resemblance." He threw the sheet on the table and continued: "When you have had your noon rice, Hoong, you might try to locate in the chancery a few samples of the handwriting of Liu, Han, Wang and Soo; all of them will have sent at one time or another letters to the tribunal." He took two of his large red official visiting cards from the drawer and gave them to the sergeant, adding: "Have these cards forwarded to Han Yung-han and Councilor Liang, with the message that I shall pay them a visit this afternoon."

When Judge Dee rose the sergeant asked:

"What on earth could have happened to the corpse of Mrs. Djang, Your Honor?"

"It is no use, Hoong," the judge replied, "to ponder over a puzzle as long as all pertaining pieces have not yet been assembled. I shall now put that entire problem out of my mind. I am going to eat my noon rice in my own house, and have a look how my wives and children are getting on. The other day my Third Lady told me that my two sons are already writing quite nice essays. But they're a couple of rascals, I tell you!"

Late in the afternoon, when Judge Dee came back to his private office, he found Sergeant Hoong and Ma Joong standing by his desk, bent over several sheets of paper. Hoong looked up and said:

"Here we have samples of the handwriting of our four suspects, Your Honor. But none of them resembles that of the dancer's letters."

Judge Dee sat down and carefully compared the various letters. After a while he said:

"No, there's nothing there! Liu Fei-po is the only one whose brush stroke reminds me a bit of that of the Student of the Bamboo Grove. I could imagine that Liu disguised his hand when he wrote those love letters. Our writing brush is a very sensitive instrument. It is very difficult indeed not to betray one's manner of handling it, even if one uses a different type of writing."

"Liu Fei-po could have known Candidate Djang's pen name through his daughter, Your Honor!" the sergeant said eagerly, "and used it for signing his letters for want of a better!"

"Yes," the judge said pensively. "I must get to know

more about Liu Fei-po. That is one of the subjects I plan to raise with Han and the Councilor; they will be able to tell me more about him. Well, Ma Joong, what did you learn about the carpenter?"

Ma Joong sadly shook his large head.

"There's not much to be found out there, Your Honor! Mao Yuan lives in a hovel way down near the lake, near the fish market. There's only his old woman; you have never seen such an ugly old harpy! She hadn't been worrying at all about her husband's absence, because when he was on a job he would often stay away several days. And I don't blame the fellow either, cursed as he is with a woman like that! Well, three days ago he left in the morning saying that he was going to the house of Dr. Djang to repair some furniture for the coming wedding feast. He told his wife he would find a place to sleep in the servants' quarters there, for the job would take several days. That was the last she saw of him!"

Ma Joong pulled a face and went on:

"When I told his pleasant mate the sad news, she only said that she had predicted long before that her old man would come to a bad end, because he always went to wine houses and gambling dens with his cousin Mao Loo. Then she asked for the blood money!"

"What an impious woman!" Judge Dee exclaimed angrily.

"I told her," Ma Joong said, "that she couldn't get that before the murderer had been caught and convicted. She started to call me names and accused me of having pocketed the money! I hurriedly left the harridan, and went to make inquiries in the neighborhood. The people there say that Mao Yuan was a good-natured, hard-working fellow and no one blames him for drinking a bit too much on occasion, for married to a woman like that a man needs some consolation. But they added that his cousin Mao Loo is a real bad lot. He is also a carpenter by profession, but he has no fixed place to live. He roams all over the district looking for odd jobs in wealthy houses, and pilfers there what he can. He spends all his money drinking and gambling. Of late no one has seen him in that neighborhood. There's a rumor that he was expelled from the Carpenters' Guild because he wounded another carpenter with a knife during a drunken brawl. Mao Yuan had no other male relatives."

80

Judge Dee slowly sipped his tea. Then he wiped off his mustache and said:

"You did well, Ma Joong! We know now at least the meaning of that scrap of paper we found in the sleeve of the murdered man. You'd better go now to the professor's residence and find out together with Chiao Tai, who is watching there, when Mao Yuan arrived in Dr. Djang's house, what work he did, and when exactly he left there. Also keep an eye on that neighborhood; perhaps you may yet find that weird fellow who watched me through the window." He rose and continued to the sergeant: "While I am away, Hoong, you can go to the street where Liu Fei-po lives and have a look around there. Try to collect in the shops in that neighborhood some gossip about him and his household. He is the complainant in the case of Liu versus Djang, but at the same time he is one of our main suspects in the case of the murdered dancer!"

He emptied his teacup and walked across the courtyard to the gatehouse where his palanquin stood waiting for him.

In the street outside it was still quite hot. Fortunately, the Han mansion was not far from the tribunal.

Han Yung-han stood inside the monumental gate waiting for the judge. After the exchange of the usual courtesies he led his guest into a dimly lit hall cooled by two round copper basins loaded with blocks of ice. Han made Judge Dee sit down in a capacious armchair next to the tea table. As he busied himself giving orders for tea and refreshments to the obsequious steward, the judge looked round. He estimated that the house was well over a hundred years old. The wood of the heavy pillars and of the carved roof-beams above was blackened by age, and the scroll paintings decorating the walls had acquired a mellow tinge of old ivory. The hall was pervaded by an atmosphere of quiet distinction.

After fragrant tea had been served in antique cups of eggshell porcelain, Han cleared his throat and said with stiff dignity:

"I offer Your Honor my humble apologies for my unseemly behavior last night."

"It was a most unusual situation," Judge Dee said with a smile. "Let's forget about it! Tell me, how many sons do you have?"

"I have only a daughter," Han replied coldly.

81

There was an awkward pause; it had not been a very fortunate opening. But the judge reflected that he could hardly be blamed. One would expect a man of Han's status, with many wives and concubines, to have some sons. He continued unabashed:

"I'd better tell you frankly that I am completely baffled by that murder on the flower boat, and that queer case of Liu Fei-po's daughter. I hope you'll kindly let me have your opinion on the character and background of the persons connected with these two cases."

Han bowed politely and replied:

"I am entirely at Your Honor's service. The quarrel of my friends Liu and Djang has shocked me deeply. Both are prominent citizens of our small town. I hope and trust that Your Honor will be able to effect an amiable settlement; that would—"

"Before thinking of any attempt at conciliation," Judge Dee interrupted him, "I'll first have to decide whether the bride died a natural death and, if not, punish the murderer. But let's begin with the case of the dead dancer."

Han raised his hands. He exclaimed, annoyed:

"But those two cases are as far apart as Heaven and Earth, Your Honor! The courtesan was a beautiful woman, a talented woman, but after all only a professional dancer! Those girls often get involved in all kinds of unsavory affairs. Heaven knows how many of them die a violent death!" Leaning over to the judge he continued confidentially: "I can assure Your Honor that nobody who counts here will raise any objection if that case is treated by the tribunal a bit, ah . . . superficially. And I hardly think that the higher authorities will evince much interest in the death of a light woman. But the case of Liu versus Djang—Heavens! that affects the reputation of our city, Your Honor! All of us here would deeply appreciate it if Your Honor could persuade them to agree to a compromise, perhaps by suggesting—"

"Our views on the administration of justice," Judge Dee interrupted him coldly, "are evidently too far apart to admit fruitful discussion. I confine myself to a few questions. First, what was your personal relation to the dancer Almond Blossom?"

Han grew red in the face. His voice trembled in suppressed anger as he asked:

"Do you expect an answer to that question?"

"Certainly!" the judge said affably, "else I wouldn't have asked it!"

"Then I refuse!" Han burst out.

"Here and now that is your good right," the judge remarked calmly. "I shall pose the same question to you in the tribunal, and you will have to answer it, so as not to be guilty of contempt of court—on penalty of fifty lashes. It's only to spare your feelings that I ask you that question now."

Han looked at the judge with blazing eyes. He mastered himself with difficulty and replied in a flat voice:

"The courtesan Almond Blossom was good-looking, she was an expert dancer, and her conversation was entertaining. Therefore I thought she was qualified to be hired to amuse my guests. Apart from that, the woman didn't exist for me; whether she is alive or dead leaves me completely indifferent."

"Didn't you tell me just now that you have a daughter?" Judge Dee asked sharply.

Han apparently considered this question as an attempt at changing the subject. He ordered the steward who stood waiting at a discreet distant to bring candied fruit and sweetmeats. Then he said amicably:

"Yes, Your Honor; her name is Willow Down. Though one shouldn't praise one's own child, I dare say she is a remarkable girl. She displays a great talent for painting and calligraphy. She even has—" He had no sooner spoken than he caught himself up self-consciously: "But my household affairs will hardly interest Your Honor."

"I now come to my second question," Judge Dee said. "What is your estimate of the character of the guildmasters Wang and Soo?"

"Many years ago," Han replied in a formal voice, "Wang and Soo were unanimously elected by the members of their guild to act on their behalf and look after their interests. They were elected because of their elevated character and irreproachable conduct. I have nothing to add to that."

"Now a question about the case Liu versus Djang," the judge resumed. "Why did the professor resign so early?"

Han shifted uncomfortably on his chair.

"Must that old affair be raked up again?" he asked testily. "It has been established beyond all possible doubt that the girl student who lodged the complaint was deranged in mind. It is most commendable that Dr. Djang still insisted on tendering his resignation, because he opined that a professor of the Temple School should never get talked about, even if he were proved completely innocent."

"I'll consult our files about that case," Judge Dee said.

"Oh, Your Honor won't find anything about it in the dossiers," Han said quickly. "Fortunately, the case has never been before the tribunal. We, the notables of Hanyuan, have heard the persons concerned and settled the case, together with the Rector of the School. We deem it our duty, Your Honor, to spare the authorities unnecessary work."

"So I noticed!" the judge remarked dryly. He rose and thanked Han for his kind reception. When Han was conducting him to his palanquin the judge reflected that this interview didn't seem to have laid the foundation for a lasting friendship.

Eighth Chapter

JUDGE DEE CONVERSES WITH A BIRD AND FISHES; HE SUMS UP HIS THEORIES FOR HIS ASSISTANTS

WHEN JUDGE DEE HAD ASCENDED HIS PALANQUIN THE bearers told him that the Councilor's house was just around the corner. He hoped that this interview would prove more profitable than that he had just had with Han Yung-han. Councilor Liang, an outsider in Han-yuan like himself, would not be obsessed by Han's scruples about supplying information on the citizens of Han-yuan.

The Councilor's house had an imposing gate. The two heavy pillars that flanked the double doors were carved with an intricate pattern of clouds and fabulous birds.

In the front courtyard, overshadowed by old trees, a young man with a long, sad face came to welcome the high guest. He introduced himself as Liang Fen, the Councilor's nephew, who acted as his secretary. He began elaborate excuses for the Councilor not coming out to bid the magistrate welcome in person. Judge Dee cut him short, saying:

"I know that His Excellency is in poor health. I would never have dared to importune him were it not that I have to discuss with him urgent official business."

The secretary bowed deeply and led the judge into a broad, semiobscure corridor. There were no servants in evidence.

When they were about to cross a small garden, Liang Fen suddenly halted in his steps. Nervously rubbing his hands together, he said:

"I realize this is quite irregular, Your Honor. I deeply regret that I have to put forward this request in such an abrupt manner. . . . Would Your Honor deign to grant me the opportunity for a brief private conversation, after the interview with my master? I am in great difficulties. I really don't know—"

He didn't manage to conclude his sentence. The judge gave him a searching look, then nodded his assent. The young man seemed greatly relieved. He led the judge across the garden to a large porch, and opened a heavy door. "His Excellency shall presently make his appearance!" he announced. Then he stepped back, and closed the door noiselessly behind him.

Judge Dee blinked his eyes. The spacious room was pervaded by a dim, diffuse light; at first he could discern only a white square in the back wall. It proved to be a low, broad window, pasted over with a grayish paper.

He advanced gingerly over the thick carpet, afraid of barking his shins against a piece of furniture. But when his eyes had got adjusted to the darkness, he saw that his fear had been unfounded. The room was sparsely furnished: next to a high desk in front of the window with a large armchair behind it, the only furniture consisted of four high-backed chairs against a side wall, underneath a set of well-stocked bookshelves. The nearly empty room breathed a curious, desolate atmosphere, as if no one really lived there.

Noticing a large goldfish bowl of colored porcelain that stood on a stand of carved blackwood next to the desk, the judge stepped up to it.

"Sit down!" a strident voice screeched suddenly.

Judge Dee stumbled backward.

There were shrill sounds of laughter that came from the window. Perplexed, he looked in that direction. Then he smiled. He now saw a small cage of silver wire, suspended by the side of the window. Inside a myna bird was hopping up and down excitedly, fluttering its wings.

The judge went over to it. He tapped on the silver cage and said reprovingly:

"You gave me quite a fright, you naughty bird!"

"Naughty bird!" the myna squeaked. He cocked his small smooth head, and peered shrewdly at the judge with one glittering eye. "Sit down!" he screeched again.

"Yes, yes!" said the judge. "But I'll first have a look at those goldfish if I may!"

When he bent over the bowl, half a dozen small black-and-gold fish with long trailing tails and fins came to the surface, and looked solemnly up at him with their large protruding eyes.

"I am sorry I have no food for you!" Judge Dee said. He saw in the middle of the bowl a small statue of the Flower Fairy, raised above the water on a pedestal in the shape of a piece of rock. The statue was delicately molded in colored porcelain; the smiling face of the goddess had daintily rouged cheeks and her straw hat seemed real. Judge Dee stretched out his hand to touch it, but the goldfish started an indignant uproar and splashed around near the surface in great excitement. The judge knew how highly strung these costly, carefully bred small creatures were and was afraid that thrashing about as they were they would damage their long fins. Therefore he quickly went over to the bookshelves.

Then the door opened and Liang Fen came in with an old, bent man leaning on his arm. The judge made a deep bow and stood waiting respectfully while the secretary led his master, step by step, to the armchair. While leaning with his left hand on the young man's arm, the Councilor supported himself with his right on a long crooked staff of red-lacquered wood. He was clad in a wide robe of stiff brown brocade; on his large head he wore a high cap of black gauze with an inwoven gold-thread pattern. On his forehead he had a black eyeshade in the shape of a moon sickle, so that the judge could not see his eyes. He was impressed by the heavy, gray mustache and long whiskers, and the full white beard that covered the old man's breast in three thick strands. As the old Councilor let himself down slowly into the armchair behind the desk, the myna bird started to flutter in its silver cage. "Five thousand, cash!" it screeched suddenly. The old man made a move with his head. The secretary quickly hung his handkerchief over the cage.

The Councilor put his elbows on the table and let his large head hang forward. The stiff brocade stood out on both sides of his shoulders like two wings; as the judge saw his hunched shape outlined against the window it resembled that of a huge bird of prey come to roost. But his voice was weak and indistinct as he mumbled:

"Take a seat, Dee! I presume you are the son of my colleague, the late State Councilor Dee, eh?"

"Indeed, Excellency!" the judge answered respectfully. He sat down on the edge of one of the chairs against the wall. Liang Fen remained standing by his master's side.

"I am ninety, Dee!" the Councilor resumed. "Bad eyes, rheumatism . . . But what can one expect, at my age?"

His chin sank down deeper on his breast.

"This person," Judge Dee began, "offers his humble excuses for daring to disturb Your Excellency. I shall state my business as succinctly as possible. I find myself confronted with two baffling criminal cases. Your Excellency is doubtless aware of the fact that the citizens of Han-yuan are not very communicative. They—"

He saw that Liang Fen frantically shook his head at him. The young man came over to him quickly and whispered:

"The Councilor has fallen asleep! He is often taken that way of late; he will now sleep for hours on end. We'd better go to my study; I'll warn the servants."

Judge Dee cast a pitying glance at the old man, who was now lying bent over the table, with his head on his arms. He heard his irregular breathing. Then he followed Liang Fen, who brought him to a small study at the back of the house. The door stood open; it gave on a small but well-kept flower garden surrounded by a high fence.

The secretary made Judge Dee sit down in the large armchair by the desk, piled with ledgers and books. "I'll now call the old couple that looks after His Excellency," he said hurriedly. "They'll bring him to his bedroom."

Left alone in the quiet study, Judge Dee slowly stroked his beard. He reflected dejectedly that his luck was not in that day.

Liang Fen came back and busied himself about the tea table. When he had poured a scalding-hot cup of tea for the judge, he sat down on a tabouret and said unhappily:

"I deeply regret that His Excellency had one of his spells just when Your Honor came to see him! Can I perhaps be of any service?"

"Well, no," Judge Dee replied. "Since when has the Councilor had these fits?"

"It began about half a year ago, Your Honor," Liang Fen said with a sigh. "It is now eight months since his eldest son in the capital sent me here to act as his father's private secretary. For me it was a godsend to obtain this post, for to tell you the truth I belong to an impoverished branch of the family. Here I found food and shelter, and sufficient spare time to prepare myself for my second literary examination. The first two months everything went well; the Councilor had me come every morning to his library for an hour or so and dictated letters to me, or told me all kinds of interesting anecdotes from his long career when he felt in the mood. He is very nearsighted, so he had nearly all the furniture removed from that room, to avoid bumping himself.

He also used to complain of rheumatism; but his mind was wonderfully clear. He himself directed the administration of his extensive landed property, and he did it very well.

"About six months ago, however, he must have had a stroke during the night. He suddenly spoke with difficulty, and often seemed completely dazed. He summoned me only once a week or so, and then would doze off in the middle of our conversation. Also, he will often stay in his bedroom for days on end, feeding only on tea and pine seeds, and drinking infusions of herbs which he prepares himself. The old couple think that he is trying to find the Elixir of Immortality!"

Judge Dee shook his head. He said with a sigh:

"It's not always a blessing to reach such an advanced age!"

"It's a calamity, Your Honor!" the young man exclaimed. "It's therefore that I felt I had to ask Your Honor's advice! Despite his illness, the Councilor insists on conducting all his own financial affairs. He writes letters which he doesn't show me, and he had long discussions with Wan I-fan, a business promoter whom Mr. Liu Fei-po introduced to him some time ago. I am not allowed to take part in those. But I have to keep the books, and I noticed that of late the Councilor has been engaging in fantastic business transactions. He is selling large lots of good arable land for a ridiculously low price! He is selling out his possessions, Your Honor, at a tremendous loss! The family will hold me responsible, but what can I do? They can't expect me to give unasked-for advice to His Excellency!"

The judge nodded comprehendingly. This was indeed a delicate problem. After a while he said:

"It won't be an easy or agreeable task, Mr. Liang, but you will have to apprise the Councilor's son of the situation. Why don't you propose to him that he come here for a few weeks; then he'll see for himself that his father is in his dotage."

Liang Fen didn't seem to relish the idea. The judge felt sorry for him; he fully realized how awkward it was for a poor relation of such an illustrious person to communicate to the family the unwelcome news about the head of their clan. He said:

"If you could show me some actual examples of the Councilor's mismanagement, I shall be glad to draw up a note for you that I, the magistrate, have personally convinced myself that the Councilor is not any longer capable of conducting his affairs."

The young man's face lit up. He said gratefully:

"That would be a tremendous help, Your Honor! I have here a summary of the Councilor's most recent transactions, which I drew up for my own orientation. And here is the ledger with His Excellency's instructions, written by himself, in the margin. The writing is very small, because of his nearsightedness, but the meaning is clear enough! Your Honor'll see that the offer for that piece of land was far below its actual value. It is true that the buyer paid cash in gold bars, but—"

Judge Dee seemed deeply engrossed in the summary Liang had given him. But he didn't take in the content; he looked only at the handwriting. It resembled closely that of the love letters which the Student of the Bamboo Grove sent to the dead dancer.

He looked up and spoke.

"I'll take your summary with me for a closer study." As he rolled it up and put it in his sleeve he said: "The suicide of Candidate Djang Hoo-piao must have been a big blow to you."

"To me!" Liang Fen asked, astonished. "I have heard people talk about it, of course, but I have never met that unfortunate youth. I hardly know anybody in this town, Your Honor; I seldom go out, practically only to the Temple of Confucius, for consulting the books in the library there. I use all my spare time for my studies."

"Yet you do find time for visiting the Willow Quarter, don't you?" Judge Dee asked coldly.

"Who has been spreading that slanderous talk!" Liang Fen exclaimed indignantly. "I never go out at night, Your Honor; the old couple here will confirm that! I haven't the slightest interest in those light women, I . . . Besides, where in the world would I get the money for such escapades?"

The judge made no response. He rose and went to the garden door. He asked:

"Used the Councilor to walk out there when he was still in good health?"

Liang Fen shot the judge a quick look. Then he replied:

"No, Your Honor; this is only a back garden. That small gate over there leads to the alley behind the house.

The main garden is over on the other side of the compound. I trust that Your Honor doesn't give any credence to those evil rumors about me? I really can't imagine who—"

"It doesn't matter," Judge Dee interrupted him. "I shall study your summary at leisure, and in due time let you know."

The young man thanked him profusely, then led him to the first courtyard and helped him to ascend his palanquin.

When Judge Dee came back to the tribunal, he found Sergeant Hoong and Chiao Tai waiting for him in his private office. Hoong said excitedly:

"Chiao Tai has made an important discovery in the house of Dr. Djang, Your Honor!"

"That's welcome news!" the judge remarks as he sat down behind his desk. "Speak up. What did you find, Chiao Tai?"

"It isn't much, really," Chiao Tai said deprecatingly. "With the main business we didn't get any forrader! I made a second search for that queer fellow who spied on Your Honor in the bridal room, and Ma Joong helped me after he had come back from the Buddhist Temple, but we didn't find the slightest clue to him or to his whereabouts. Neither did we find out anything special about that carpenter, Mao Yuan. The steward had summoned him two days before the wedding. The first day he made a wooden platform for the orchestra, and slept in the gatehouse. The second day he repaired some furniture and the roof of the bridal room, which was leaking. He again slept with the doorman, and the following morning repaired the large dining table. Then he lent a hand in the kitchen, and when the feast had started he helped the servants to drink the wine that was left over. He went to bed dead drunk! The next morning the dead body of the bride was discovered, and Mao stayed on out of curiosity till the professor came back from his fruitless search for his son. Then the steward saw Mao standing talking outside in the street with the fisherman who had found Candidate Djang's belt. Mao left with his toolbox and his ax. All those days Dr. Djang didn't speak with Mao; it was the housemaster who gave him his instructions and who paid him off."

Chiao Tai pulled at his short mustache, then went on: "This afternoon, when the professor was taking his siesta, I had a look at his collection of books. I found a fine old illustrated work on archery which greatly interested me. When I put it back, I saw an old book that had been lying behind it. It was a chess manual. I leafed it through, and found on the last page the problem that the dead dancer carried in her sleeve."

"Excellent!" Judge Dee exclaimed. "Did you bring the book with you?"

"No, Your Honor. I thought that the professor might become suspicious if he discovered that it was missing. I left brother Ma to watch the house and went to the bookshop opposite the Temple of Confucius. When I mentioned the title of the book, the shopkeeper said he still had one copy, and began at once about that last problem! He said that the book was published seventy years ago by the great grandfather of Han Yung-han, an old eccentric whom the people here used to call Hermit Han. He was famous as a chess expert, and his manual is still widely studied. Two generations of chess lovers have pondered over that last problem, but no one has ever succeeded in discovering its meaning. The book gives no explanation of it; therefore it is now generally assumed that the printer added that last page by mistake. Hermit Han died suddenly while the printing was still in progress; he didn't see the proofs. I bought the book. Your Honor can see for yourself."

He handed the judge a dog-eared, yellow volume.

"What an interesting story!" Judge Dee exclaimed. He eagerly opened the book and quickly read through the preface.

"Han's ancestor was a fine scholar," he remarked. "This Preface is written in a very original, but excellent, style." He leafed the book through till the end, then took from his drawer the sheet with the chess problem and laid it next to the printed book. "Yes," he pursued, "Almond Blossom tore that sheet from a copy of this book. But why? How could a chess problem that was printed seventy years ago have anything to do with a plot that is being hatched now in this city? It's a strange affair!" Shaking his head, he put the book and the loose sheet in the drawer. Then he asked the sergeant: "Have you found out more about Liu Fei-po, Hoong?"

"Nothing that has a direct bearing on our cases, Your Honor," Hoong replied. "Of course, the sudden death of his daughter and the disappearance of her body have set tongues wagging in that neighborhood. They say that Liu must have had a premonition that the marriage would be an unlucky one, and therefore tried to have it annulled. I had a cup of wine with one of Liu's palanquin bearers in the wine shop on the corner near the Liu mansion. The fellow told me that Liu is fairly popular with his personnel; he is a bit strict, but since he is away traveling so often they have on the whole an easy life of it. He told me one strange thing, though. He maintains that Liu sometimes practices a kind of vanishing trick!"

"Vanishing trick?" the judge asked, amazed. "What did he mean by that?"

"Well," Hoong said, "it seems it has happened several times that after Liu had retired to his library, when the steward went there to ask him something he found the room empty. He then looked for his master all over the house, but he was nowhere to be seen, and nobody had seen him go out. Then, at dinnertime, the steward would suddenly meet him walking in the corridor, or in the garden. The first time it happened the steward told Liu that he had been looking everywhere for him in vain, but then Liu had flown into a rage and cursed him for a doddering fool, blind as a bat. He said he had been sitting in his garden pavilion all the time. Later, when the same thing repeated itself, the steward didn't dare to remark on it any more."

"I fear," Judge Dee said, "that the palanquin bearer had had a drop too much! Well, as regards the two calls I made this afternoon, Han Yung-han let it slip out that Dr. Djang retired before his time because one of his girl students accused him of an offense against morality. Han maintains that the professor was innocent, but according to him all prominent citizens of Han-yuan are high-minded persons! Thus Liu's accusation about Dr. Djang assaulting his daughter may, after all, not be as improbable as it seemed to us at first sight. Second, Councilor Liang has a nephew living with him whose handwriting seems to me to resemble closely that of our elusive Student of the Bamboo Grove! Give me one of those letters!"

Judge Dee took the summary Liang Fen had given him from his sleeve, and studied it together with the letter Hoong placed before him. Then he hit his fist on the table and muttered peevishly:

"No, it's the same thing we are running up against every time in this vexing case! It just doesn't fit! Look:

93

it's the same style of calligraphy, written with the same ink and the same kind of brush! But the strokes are not the same, not quite!" Shaking his head he went on: "It would all tally nicely, though. The old Councilor is in his dotage, and except for an aged couple there are no other servants in that large mansion. That fellow Liang Fen has his quarters on a small back yard, with a door to an alley behind the house. Thus he has an ideal situation for a secret rendezvous with a woman from outside. Perhaps it was there that the dead courtesan used to spend her afternoons! He could have made her acquaintance in a shop somewhere. He maintains he didn't know Candidate Djang, but he knows very well we can't check that, because he is dead! Does the name Liang occur on that list the professor drew up for you, Hoong?"

The sergeant shook his head.

"Even if Liang Fen had an affair with Almond Blossom, Your Honor," Chiao Tai remarked, "he couldn't have killed her because he wasn't on the boat! And the same goes for Dr. Djang."

Judge Dee folded his arms across his chest. He remained deep in thought, his chin on his breast. At last he spoke.

"I admit frankly that I can't make head or tail of it! You two can go now and have your meal. Thereafter Chiao Tai goes back to the house of Dr. Djang to take over there from Ma Joong. On your way out, Sergeant, you can tell the clerk to serve my evening rice here in my office. Tonight I shall reread all documents pertaining to our two cases, and see whether I can't find a lead." He angrily tugged at his mustache. Then he resumed: "For the time being our theories don't look very promising! Number one: the murder on the flower boat. A dancer is murdered in order to prevent her from betraying a criminal plot to me. Four persons had the opportunity: Han, Liu, Soo and Wang. The plot has something to do with an unsolved chess problem that is only seventy years old! The dancer also had a secret love affair—that perhaps has nothing to do with her murder. Her lover was Dr. Djang, who was familiar with the pen name found on the love letters, or Liu Fei-po, for the same reason plus the resemblance of his handwriting, or Liang Fen, because of the resemblance of the handwriting plus the fact that he had an excellent opportunity for having secret meetings with her in his quarters.

94

"Number two: a professor of profound learning but questionable morals assaults his daughter-in-law, who commits suicide. The groom also commits suicide. The professor tries to have the body buried without an autopsy, but a carpenter suspects the truth because he had a talk with a fisherman—make a note that we try to locate that fellow, Hoong!—and that carpenter is promptly murdered, apparently with his own ax! And the professor sees to it that the dead body of the bride disappears without a trace.

"That's all! But now don't you two start thinking that there's something afoot here! Goodness, no. This is a sleepy little town; nothing ever happens here—says Han Yung-han! Well, good night!"

Ninth Chapter

THE JUDGE ENJOYS THE MOON ON THE MARBLE TERRACE; HE HEARS A STRANGE STORY DURING A NIGHTLY VISIT

WHEN JUDGE DEE HAD FINISHED HIS DINNER HE TOLD the clerk to serve tea on the terrace.

The judge slowly ascended the broad stone staircase and seated himself in a comfortable armchair. A cool evening breeze had swept away the clouds. The full moon cast its eerie radiance over the wide expanse of the lake.

He sipped the hot tea; the clerk disappeared noiselessly on his felt shoes. The judge was all alone on the broad terrace. With a contented sigh he loosened his robe, leaned back in the chair and looked up at the moon.

He tried to review the events of the past two days. He found to his dismay, however, that he could not concentrate his thoughts. Disconnected images kept flitting across his mind's eye. The face of the dead courtesan staring up at him from under the water, the horribly disfigured head of the murdered carpenter, the haggard face outside the window of the bridal room—all those kept turning round and round in quick succession.

Judge Dee got up impatiently. He went to stand by the marble balustrade. The town below was alive with human activity. He could hear faintly the din from the market place in front of the Temple of Confucius. This was his town, with thousands of people entrusted to his care. Yet foul murderers stalked about there planning who knew what new crimes. And he, the magistrate, was unable to stop them.

Greatly vexed, the judge started pacing the terrace, his hands on his back.

Suddenly he stopped; he thought for a while, then turned round and hurriedly left the terrace.

In his deserted private office he opened a box containing discarded articles of clothing. He selected an old, tattered robe of faded blue cotton. Having donned that disreputable garment, he added an old patched jacket on top of it which he fastened with a rope round his waist.

He took off his gauze cap, loosened his topknot, and bound up his hair with a dirty rag. After he had put two strings of cash in his sleeve, he went outside and tiptoed across the dark courtyard. He left the tribunal compound by the side door.

In the narrow alley outside he scooped up a handful of dust and rubbed that in his beard and whiskers. Then he crossed the street and walked down the steps leading into the city.

When he got to the market place he soon found himself in the midst of a seething crowd. He elbowed his way to a street stall and bought an oil cake baked in rancid fat. He forced himself to take a bite from it, smearing the fat in his mustache and over his cheeks.

Walking idly hither and thither, he tried to strike up an acquaintance with some of the vagabonds hanging around there, but all seemed bent on their own business. He tried to begin a conversation with a meatball vendor. But before he had opened his mouth the man hastily pressed a copper coin in his hand and hurried on, shouting lustily: "Finest meatballs, only five coppers apiece!"

Judge Dee reflected that a cheap eating house might afford better opportunity for getting into contact with the underworld. He entered a narrow side street where he had seen a red lantern advertising hot noodles. He drew aside the dirty door curtain.

The smell of burning fat and cheap liquor met him. A dozen or so coolies were seated at the wooden tables, noisily gobbling their noodles. Judge Dee sat down on a bench behind a corner table. A slovenly waiter walked up to him, and the judge ordered a bowl of noodles. He had studied the ways of the underworld so that he could freely use their jargon, yet the waiter gave him a suspicious look.

"Where might you be from, stranger?" he asked in a surly voice.

The judge realized with dismay that he had overlooked the fact that in such a small, self-contained community any stranger was apt to be noticed. He answered hurriedly:

"I just arrived here this afternoon from Chiang-pei. What is it to you anyway! You get me my noodles and I'll get you your coppers. Get a move on!"

The man shrugged and shouted the order to the kitchen at the back.

Suddenly the door curtain was roughly drawn aside

and two men came in. The first was a tall, burly fellow with baggy trousers, his torso covered by a sleeveless jacket that left his long, muscular arms bare. He had a nearly triangular face with a stiff short beard and a bristling mustache. The other was a lean fellow dressed in a patched robe. His left eye was covered by a black plaster. He nudged his companion and pointed at the judge.

They quickly stepped over to his table and sat down on either side of him.

"Who asked you to sit down here, you dog's-heads?" the judge growled.

"Shut up, you dirty interloper!" the tall man hissed. The judge felt the point of a knife prodding his side. The one-eyed man pressed close to him; he exuded an offensive odor of garlic and stale sweat. He said with a sneer:

"I myself saw you pocketing a copper in the market place. Do you think we beggars will allow a dirty interloper to lap from our rice bowl?"

In a flash the judge understood the full extent of his folly. By exercising the profession of a beggar without having joined their guild he had gravely offended against age-old, unwritten rules.

The point of the knife became more insistent. The tall man rasped: "Come along outside! Behind there is a quiet yard. Our knives will decide whether you have a right to be here or not!"

Judge Dee thought quickly. He was a good boxer and an expert swordsman, but he was completely ignorant of the knife fighting practiced in the underworld. To reveal his identity was, of course, out of the question; he would rather die than become the laughing-stock of the entire province! The best plan was to goad the ruffians into a fight here and now. The coolies would probably join the fray and that would give him a better chance. With a powerful push he shoved the one-eyed man onto the floor. At the same time he knocked the knife away with a backward blow of his right elbow. He felt a sharp pain in his side. But now he could jump up, crashing his fist into the knife wielder's face. He kicked the bench away and ran round the table. He picked up a tabouret and, after wrenching off one leg for a club, raised it as a shield. Cursing loudly, the two ruffians scrambled up and went for the judge, now openly displaying their long knives. The coolies turned round. Far from joining the scuffle, they settled down contentedly to watch gratis a good fight.

The tall man lunged forward with his knife. The judge parried the blow with the tabouret, then hit out with his improvised club for the other's head. As the man ducked quickly, a truculent voice called out loudly from the door:

"Who is making trouble here?"

A cadaverously lean man with a slight stoop came toward them. The two ruffians hastily put away their knives and bowed. Resting his hands on a knobstick the old man stood there surveying them with crafty eyes from under gray tufted eyebrows. Although clad in an old brown robe and wearing a greasy skullcap, he had an unmistakable air of authority. Looking at the husky man he said sourly:

"What are you at now, Mao Loo? You know that I don't like killings inside the city."

"The rule is that an interloper be killed!" the other muttered.

"That's for me to decide!" the old man said gruffly. "As head of the Beggars' Guild I have my responsibilities. I don't condemn a fellow before I have heard him. Hey, you, what do you have to say for yourself?"

"I just wanted to have a bite before I went to see you," Judge Dee answered sullenly. "I came to this accursed town only a few hours ago, but if a man can't eat his noodles in peace here I'd better return where I came from!"

"It's true, boss!" The waiter now joined the conversation. "He said he had come from Chiang-pei when I talked to him just now."

The graybeard looked speculatively at the judge. He asked:

"Have you any money?"

The judge took a string of cash from his sleeve. The other snatched it from his hand with amazing quickness, then said placidly:

"The entrance fee is half a string, but I'll accept the whole string, as mark of your good will. Every night you'll come to the Inn of the Red Carp and hand me ten per cent of your earnings." He threw a dirty slip of wood inscribed with a number and some cabalistic signs on the table and added: "This is your membership tally. Good luck!"

The tall ruffian gave him a nasty look.

"If you ask me—" he began.

"I don't scare!" the head of the beggars snapped at him. "Don't forget that it was me who took you on when the Guild of the Carpenters' had kicked you out! What are you doing here anyway! I was told that you had gone to Three Oaks Island!"

Mao Loo muttered something about having to see a friend first. The one-eyed man said with a leer:

"A friend in skirts! He had come to fetch his wench but she pretended to be ill! That's why he is in that nasty temper!"

Mao Loo cursed.

"Come along, you fool!" he growled. The two men bowed to their boss and left.

Judge Dee wanted to engage the graybeard in some further conversation, but that worthy had lost interest in him. He turned round and was respectfully conducted to the door by the waiter.

The judge resumed his former seat. The waiter placed a bowl of noodles and a beaker in front of him and said, not unkindly:

"An unfortunate misunderstanding, brother! Here; the manager gives you a cup of wine, for free! Come in often!"

Judge Dee quietly ate his noodles and found them surprisingly appetizing. He thought to himself that it had been a good lesson. If ever again he would go out in disguise, he would choose the part of an itinerant doctor or soothsayer. For those stay as a rule only a few days in one place, and they are not organized in guilds. When he had finished his noodles he noticed that the wound in his side was bleeding. He paid his coppers and left.

He went to a pharmacy in the market place. While the assistant was washing his wound he remarked:

"You were in luck, my man! It's only a flesh wound, this time. I trust you hit the other fellow better!"

He covered it with an oil plaster; the judge paid five coppers, and went uptown again. As he slowly climbed the steps leading up to the street of the tribunal, the shopkeepers were already putting up their wooden shutters. He heaved a sigh of relief when he came to the level road running in front of the tribunal. After having ascertained that none of the guards was about, he quickly crossed the street and slipped into the narrow alley where the side entrance was. Suddenly he stood still, then pressed himself against the wall. Farther ahead he saw a figure, clad in black, in front of the side door. The man was stooping, apparently studying the lock.

Judge Dee strained his eyes to see what he was doing. Suddenly the man righted himself and looked round to the entrance of the alley. The judge couldn't see his face; he had wound a black scarf around his head. He saw the judge and quickly turned to flee. But Judge Dee was on him in three jumps and grabbed his arm.

"Leave me alone!" the black figure cried. "I'll shout if you don't!"

Greatly amazed, the judge let go. It was a woman.

"Don't be afraid!" he said quickly. "I am from the tribunal. Who are you?"

The woman hesitated. Then she said with a trembling voice:

"You look like a footpad!"

"I went out in disguise on a special mission!" the judge said, irritated. "Now speak up, what are you doing here?"

The woman lowered the scarf. It was a young girl with an intelligent, very attractive face. She said:

"I have to see the magistrate on urgent business."

"Why, then, didn't you present yourself at the main gate?" Judge Dee asked.

"Nobody of the personnel must know that I have come to see the magistrate," the girl said quickly. "I hoped to attract the attention of a maidservant, and let her take me to the private residence of the judge." Giving him a searching look she asked: "How do I know that you are from the tribunal?"

The judge took a key from his sleeve and unlocked the door. He said curtly:

"I am the magistrate. Follow me!"

The girl gasped. Stepping up to him, she said in an urgent whisper:

"I am Willow Down, the daughter of Han Yung-han, Your Honor! My father sent me; he has been attacked and wounded. He begs you to come quickly! He told me that only Your Honor must know about this; it's of the utmost importance!"

"Who attacked your father?" Judge Dee asked, astonished.

"It was the murderer of Almond Blossom, the courtesan! Please come now to our house, Your Honor; it isn't far!"

The judge went inside. He broke two red roses from the

shrub that grew against the garden wall. Then he stepped back into the alley, locked the door and handed the two flowers to the girl. "Stick these in your hair," he ordered. "Then lead the way to your house!"

The girl did as he had said, and walked toward the entrance of the alley, the judge following a few paces behind her. If they should meet the night watch or some late passer-by, they would think she was a prostitute going home with a client.

A short walk brought them to the sumptuous gate of the Han mansion. She quickly led him round the house to the kitchen door. She opened it with a small key she took from her bosom, and went inside, with Judge Dee close behind her. They crossed a small garden to a side building. Willow Down pushed a door open, and motioned the judge to go inside.

The back wall of the small but luxuriously appointed room was taken up almost entirely by a large, high couch of carved sandalwood. On the couch Han was lying back among a number of large silk pillows; the light of the silver candle on the tea table by the window shone on his pale, haggard face. When he saw the judge in his unusual attire, he uttered a frightened cry and wanted to get up. Judge Dee said quickly:

"Don't be afraid. It is I, the magistrate! Where are you wounded?"

"He was felled by a blow on his temple, Your Honor!" Willow Down said. As the judge sat down on the tabouret by the couch, she went to the tea table and took a towel from the hot-water basin. She wiped her father's face with it, then pointed at his right temple. Judge Dee leaned forward and saw that there was indeed a nasty-looking, dark-blue bruise. Willow Down carefully held the hot towel against it. Now that she had shed her black mantle, the judge saw that she was a very elegant and attractive girl indeed. The anxious look she gave her father proved that she was very fond of him.

Han stared at the judge with wide, frightened eyes. He was quite a different man from that of the afternoon. All his haughty airs were gone. There were pouches under his bleary eyes, and lines of strain around his mouth. He whispered hoarsely:

"I am most grateful that Your Honor came! I was kidnaped tonight, Your Honor!" He cast an anxious look at

102

the door and the window, then added in a low voice:
"By the White Lotus!"

Judge Dee straightened up on the tabouret.

"The White Lotus!" he exclaimed incredulously. "Stuff
and nonsense! That sect was exterminated scores of years
ago!"

Han slowly shook his head. Willow Down went to the
table to prepare tea.

The judge gave his host a hard and wary look. The
White Lotus had been a nationwide conspiracy to overthrow the Imperial House. The movement had been led
by some discontented high officials who claimed that
Heaven had granted them supernatural powers, and had
given them to understand by certain portents that the
Mandate of the Imperial House was about to be with-
drawn, and that they should found a new dynasty. Great
numbers of over-ambitious and wicked officials, leaders
of robber bands, army deserters and ex-convicts had
joined the secret society. It had ramifications all over the
Empire. But their treacherous plans had leaked out, and
the strong measures of the authorities had nipped the plot
in the bud. The leaders had been executed, together with
their entire families, and all members mercilessly pros-
ecuted and killed. Although all this had happened during
the preceding reign, the attempted rebellion had shaken
the Empire to its core, and even now few people dared to
mention that dangerous, dreaded name. But the judge had
never heard about attempts to revive the antidynastic
movement. He shrugged his shoulders and asked:

"Well, what happened?"

Willow Down offered the judge a cup of tea, then gave
one to her father. Han drank greedily, then began:

"After the evening meal I often take a brief stroll in
front of the Buddhist Temple, to enjoy the evening breeze.
I never take an attendant with me. Tonight there were few
people about there, as usual. Passing in front of the temple gate, I only met a closed palanquin, borne by six
bearers. Then suddenly a thick cloth was thrown over
my head from behind. Before I knew what was happening
my arms had been bound on my back; I was lifted up and
thrown inside the palanquin. Then my legs were tied together with a piece of rope, and the palanquin was borne
away at a quick pace.

"The thick cloth prevented me from hearing anything,
and I nearly suffocated. I started kicking with my bound

feet against the side of the palanquin; then someone loosened the cloth a little, so that I could breathe again. I don't know how long the trip lasted; it took at least one hour, I would say. Then the palanquin was put down. Two men roughly pulled me out of it, and carried me up a flight of stairs. I heard a door open. They put me down, cut the rope round my ankles, and made me walk inside. I was pressed down into an armchair, and they took the cloth from my head."

Han took a deep breath. Then he pursued:

"I found myself sitting at a square blackwood table in a small room. On the other side sat a man in a green robe. His head and shoulders were completely covered by a white hood, with only two slits for his eyes. Still half-dazed and stuttering, I began to protest. But the man angrily hit his fist on the table and—"

"What did his hand look like?" Judge Dee interrupted.

Han hesitated. He thought a moment, then replied:

"I really don't know, Your Honor! He was wearing thick hunting gloves. There was absolutely nothing by which I would be able to identify him; his green robe was hanging loosely around him, so that his body was just a formless shape, and the hood muffled his voice. Where was I now? Oh, yes. He cut my protest short, saying: 'This is a warning, Han Yung-han! The other night a dancer told you something she shouldn't have told. You know what happened to her. It was very wise of you that you didn't tell the magistrate, Han, very wise! The White Lotus is powerful, as proved by our execution of your paramour Almond Blossom!'"

Han felt the bruise on his temple with his fingertips. Willow Down hurried over to him, but he shook his head and continued in a plaintive voice:

"I hadn't the faintest idea what the man was talking about, Your Honor! The dancer my paramour, forsooth! And you know yourself that during the banquet she had hardly spoken to me at all! Well, I said angrily that he was talking nonsense. He laughed; I can tell you it sounded horrible from behind the mask. He said, 'Don't lie, Han! It's no use! Shall I tell you exactly what she said to you? Listen! She said: "I must see you later. A dangerous conspiracy is plotted in this town!"' When I looked at him, dumbfounded by that nonsense, he went on with a nasty sneer: 'You have nothing to say to that, eh, Han? The White Lotus knows everything! And we are also all-powerful, as you found out tonight. Obey my command, Han, and forget what she said, all of it, and for good!' He gave a sign to someone who must have been standing behind my chair and went on: 'Help that lecher to forget, and not too gently, mind you!' I received a fearful blow on my head, and I lost consciousness."

Han heaved a deep sigh, then concluded:

"When I came to, I was lying in front of the back door of my house here. Fortunately, there was no one about. I scrambled up, and succeeded in reaching my small study here. I had my daughter called, and told her to go to Your Honor at once. But nobody must know that I reported this, Your Honor! My life is at stake! And I am convinced that the White Lotus has its spies everywhere—even inside the tribunal!"

He leaned back against the pillows, and closed his eyes.

Judge Dee pensively caressed his side whiskers. Then he asked:

"What did that room look like?"

Han opened his eyes. He frowned and seemed to think deeply. After a while he replied:

"I could see only the section that was in front of me, I have the impression that it was a small, hexagonal room. I would have thought it was a garden pavilion, but the air was much too close for that. The only other piece of furniture besides the square table was a black-lacquered cabinet against the wall, behind the chair of the hooded man. I also seem to remember that the walls were covered with faded green hangings."

"Have you any idea," Judge Dee asked again, "in what direction your kidnapers took you?"

"Only some vague impression," Han answered. "At first I was so confused by the attack on me that I didn't pay much attention, but I am sure that generally we kept to an easterly direction. I think we descended a slope; thereafter, the last three-quarters of our way we went over level ground."

Judge Dee rose. The wound in his side was throbbing; he was eager to go home.

"I appreciate it that you reported this matter so promptly to me," he said. "I am inclined to believe that somebody played a prank on you. Do you have some enemy who could have indulged in this ill-timed and wholly irresponsible practical joke?"

"I have no enemies!" Han exclaimed indignantly. "And

105

a prank? Let me assure you that the fellow was in dead earnest!"

"I was thinking of a practical joke," Judge Dee said calmly, "because I have come to the conclusion that after all it probably was one of the oarsmen who murdered the courtesan. I noticed among them one rascal who seemed very ill at ease when I heard him. I think I'd better question him in the tribunal with legal severities."

Han's face lit up.

"Didn't I say so at once, Your Honor?" he exclaimed triumphantly. "At the very first moment when we heard about the murder, my friends and I knew that the criminal would be found among those oarsmen! Yes, now I come to think of it I feel inclined to agree that my kidnaping was only a trick. I'll try to think who could have done me that ill turn!"

"I also shall institute a few inquiries," the judge said. "Very discreetly, of course. I shall keep you informed."

Han seemed pleased. He said with a smile to his daughter:

"The doorman will be asleep already; lead His Excellency to the main gate, my girl! It isn't seemly for our magistrate to leave our house as a thief by the back door!"

He folded his pudgy hands and reclined on the pillows with a deep sigh.

Tenth Chapter

A CHARMING GUIDE SHOWS SOME RELICS OF THE PAST; A CONFIDENTIAL CONVERSATION UNDER BUDDHA'S EYES

WILLOW DOWN BECKONED JUDGE DEE. HE FOLLOWED her outside into a pitch-dark corridor.

"I don't dare to take a candle," she whispered. "My father's women sleep nearby. But I'll guide you!"

He felt her small hand groping for his. As she pulled him along, her silk dress swished against his jacket and he noticed that she used a delicate perfume of orchids. He thought it a quite unusual situation.

When they came out on a large, paved courtyard, Willow Down let go of his hand. Here there was sufficient moonlight to see by. The judge noticed on the right a door that stood ajar. A ray of light came through it; the heavy scent of Indian incense hung in the air. He stood still and whispered:

"Can we pass there without somebody noticing us?"

"Oh, yes!" the girl replied. "That is our Buddhist chapel, built by my great-grandfather. He was a devout Buddhist, and left strict instructions that day and night a lamp should be kept burning near the altar, and that the door should never be closed. There's nobody there. Won't you have a look inside?"

Judge Dee readily agreed, although he felt very tired. He knew he must not miss this opportunity for learning more about the author of the mysterious chess problem.

More than half of the space inside the small chapel was taken up by a high square altar of brick built against the back wall. In the front of the altar was a plaque of green jade, more than four feet square, with an engraved inscription. On the altar stood a magnificent gilded statue of the Buddha, sitting cross-legged on a lotus throne. In the semidarkness high up under the ceiling the judge could faintly discern the serene, smiling face. The walls of the chapel were painted with scenes from the Buddha's life; on the floor in front of the altar lay a round prayer An-cushion. The oil lamp stood on a stand of worked iron.

"This chapel," Willow Down said with evident pride, "was built under the personal supervision of my ancestor. He was such a wise and good man, Your Honor! He has become a kind of a legend in our family. He never would take part in the literary examinations; he preferred to live in retirement here, and to devote himself to his manifold interests. The people here therefore called him Hermit Han!"

Judge Dee saw her enthusiasm with pleasure. So few young women now had an understanding for family traditions. He said:

"I seem to remember that Hermit Han was also a great chess player. Are your father or you also fond of the game?"

"No, Your Honor," the girl answered. "We like to play card games and dominoes. Chess takes up too much time, you know, and only two persons can play at it. Does Your Honor see that inscription? Hermit Han was so clever with his hands—a real expert in engraving—and he himself carved that inscription!"

The judge stepped closer to the altar. He read the text aloud:

> Thus spoke the Enlightened One: If ye wish to follow Me, ye must promulgate the Supreme Truth to all beings to make them understand My Message that all pain and sorrow that depress them are essentially non-existent. For these words express the Supreme Truth. Thus ye shall, by saving all others, also yourselves enter this Gate of Nirvana, and find peace ever-lasting.

He nodded and said:

"Hermit Han executed this work beautifully, and the text he chose expresses a lofty thought. I myself am a staunch follower of our great Master, Confucius, but I readily admit that also the Buddhist creed has many admirable points."

Willow Down looked reverently at the jade plaque. She said:

"Of course it was impossible to find one piece of jade that size. Therefore Hermit Han carved every word separately in a small square piece of jade, and later those were joined together like a kind of mosaic. He really was an extraordinary man, Your Honor! He possessed enormous riches, but after his sudden death the treasury where he had stored his gold bars proved to be empty. It is assumed that during his lifetime he secretly gave away all that gold to various charitable organizations. Our family didn't need it anyway, for he had much valuable landed property, which is still owned by us. The proceeds thereof are more than sufficient for our needs."

Judge Dee looked at her with interest. She was really a most attractive young woman; her finely chiseled, sensitive face had a natural distinction. He said:

"Since you are so keen on historical subjects, I suppose you knew Moon Fairy, the daughter of Mr. Liu Fei-po? Her father told me that she also was of a studious turn of mind."

"Yes," Willow Down said softly, "I knew her very well indeed. She often came to visit me in our women's quarters here. She felt lonely because of the frequent travels of her father. She was such a strong, enterprising girl, Your Honor! She was good in hunting and riding; she ought to have been a boy. And her father always encouraged her; he was so fond of his daughter. I really can't understand what brought about her death, and she still so young!"

"I am doing my best to discover that," Judge Dee replied. "And you can help me by telling me more about her. You say that she was so fond of sports; but didn't she also take a course with Dr. Djang?"

The girl smiled a little.

"Well," she answered, "I suppose there's no harm in telling you; everybody in the women's quarters knows it! Moon Fairy's interest in literature dated from the day she met Candidate Djang! He made rather an impression on her, you see, and therefore she persuaded her father to let her join that course, so that she could see Candidate Djang more often. Those two were really very fond of each other. And now both are—"

She shook her head disconsolately. The judge waited awhile, then resumed:

"What did Moon Fairy really look like? You'll have heard that her dead body has disappeared."

"Oh, she was handsome!" Willow Down exclaimed. "And not so thin as I; she was a robust girl. She resembled that poor dancer Almond Blossom, you know."

"Did you know that courtesan?" Judge Dee asked, astonished.

"No," Willow Down replied, "I never spoke to her. But father often had her called here to the house to entertain his guests in the large hall, and I peeped through the window whenever I could because she danced so well. Almond Blossom had the same oval face, with those curved eyebrows, as Moon Fairy, and the same beautiful figure. They could have been sisters! Only the eyes of the dancer were quite different. They frightened me a little, Your Honor! I used to stand in the dark corridor outside; I am sure that she couldn't see me. And yet she often looked me straight in my eyes when she danced past the windows; she had an uncanny, piercing stare. The poor girl, what a life she had! Always to be obliged to show yourself to all those men . . . And now she has come to her end in such a grisly manner. Does Your Honor think that the lake had . . . anything to do with it?"

"I don't think so," the judge answered. "I suppose that her death has been a great blow for Guildmaster Soo; he seemed to be quite fond of her."

"Soo only worshiped her from a distance, Your Honor!" the girl said with a smile. "He has been coming to our house as long as I can remember. He is terribly shy, and always horribly embarrassed by his colossal strength. Once he inadvertently crushed one of father's fine antique tea-cups in his fist! He still hasn't married. He stands in deadly fear of women! Guildmaster Wang—now that is quite a different man! They say he is very fond of female company. But I'd better stop. Your Honor will think me a fearful gossip! I must not detain Your Honor any longer."

"On the contrary!" Judge Dee said quickly. "This conversation is most instructive. I always like to learn as much as possible about the background of all persons connected with a criminal case. We have not talked yet about Liu Fei-po. Do you think he could tell me more about the dead courtesan?"

"I hardly think so, Your Honor. He must, of course, have known her because she regularly danced at banquets. But Mr. Liu is such a serious, silent man; he hasn't the slightest interest in frivolous amusements. Before Mr. Liu started building his summer villa here in Han-yuan, he stayed in our house for a week or so. I noticed that when there was a party, he just sat there with a rather bored air. Except for his business, he is interested only in old books and manuscripts; they say that he has a magnificent collection of those in his house in the capital.

And, of course, his daughter! He would brighten up as soon as my father inquired after her. It was a link between those two, you see, because father also has only me. Moon Fairy's death has been a shattering blow to poor Mr. Liu; father says he has become a changed man. . . ."

She went to the lampstand and refilled the oil from an earthenware jar standing below it. Judge Dee looked pensively at her delicate profile and the graceful movements of her slender hands. Evidently she was very close to her father—but Han would have taken good care to conceal his evil mind from her. After Han's story, the judge suspected him of murder and a sly attempt at intimidation. He suppressed a regretful sigh, then asked:

"In order to complete our list, have you ever met the old Councilor Liang or his nephew?"

Suddenly Willow Down blushed.

"No," she replied quickly. "Father has paid the Councilor a courtesy visit, but he never came to our house. Of course, he didn't need to, seeing that he is such a high-ranking official. . . ."

"I was told," Judge Dee remarked, "that his nephew is a dissolute young fellow."

"That's a wicked slander!" Willow Down exclaimed angrily. "Liang Fen is a very serious young man; he works regularly in the library of the Temple!"

Judge Dee gave her a searching look.

"How do you know that?" he asked quickly.

"Oh," the girl said, "I sometimes go with my mother for a walk in the Temple garden, and I saw Mr. Liang there."

Judge Dee nodded.

"Well, Miss Han," he said, "I am very grateful for all this most useful information."

He turned to the door, but Willow Down quickly stepped up to him and said softly:

"I do hope that Your Honor will find those awful people who maltreated father. I can't believe it was a prank. Father is a bit stiff and formal, Your Honor, but he really is such a good man. He never thinks ill of anybody! I am so worried about him; he must have some enemy without himself even suspecting it. They are out to harm him, Your Honor!"

"You can rest assured that the problem has my full attention," Judge Dee said.

Willow Down gave him a grateful look. She said:

"I want to give Your Honor something as a small souvenir of this visit to Hermit Han's chapel. But you must not tell father about it, because it should really be given to members of our family only!"

She went quickly to the altar, and took a roll of paper from a recess beside it. She peeled off one sheet, and presented it to the judge with a deep bow. It was a carefully-traced copy of the inscription on the altar.

Judge Dee folded the sheet up and put it in his sleeve. He said gravely:

"I feel greatly honored by this gift!"

He saw with pleasure that she still wore the two roses, which became her very well. The girl led him through a long, winding corridor to the gatehouse. She unlocked the heavy door; the judge bowed silently and stepped out into the deserted street.

Eleventh Chapter

MA JOONG HAS SOME DISAPPOINTING EXPERIENCES; JUDGE DEE LEAVES TOWN TO INSPECT HIS DISTRICT

THE NEXT MORNING, JUST AFTER DAWN, WHEN TWO servants went to Judge Dee's private office to sweep the floor, they found him fast asleep on the couch. They quickly withdrew, and warned the clerk who came to prepare the morning tea.

An hour later Judge Dee woke up. Sitting on the edge of the couch, he lifted a corner of the plaster and inspected his side. He saw that the wound was healing well. Rising stiffly, he made a perfunctory toilet, then sat down behind the desk and clapped his hands. When the clerk appeared he told him to serve breakfast, and call his three lieutenants.

The sergeant, Ma Joong and Chiao Tai sat down on tabourets. While the judge was eating his rice, Hoong reported that he had just come back from a visit to the tea merchant. Koong had told him that he and Dr. Djang had been so distressed about the finding of Candidate Djang's belt that they hadn't thought of asking the fisherman who discovered it for his name. It wouldn't be easy to locate the man.

Then Ma Joong reported that nothing worth mentioning had happened during the night in the Djang mansion. That morning he and Chiao Tai had left there, leaving two constables in charge.

Judge Dee laid down his chopsticks. Sipping his tea, he told them about his adventure in the noddle restaurant. When he had finished, Ma Joong exclaimed, disappointment on his face:

"Why didn't Your Honor take me along on that trip?"

"No, Ma Joong," the judge said, "I by myself attracted too much attention! And you'll meet Mao Loo anyway, for I want you to get him here, so that I can verify whether he met his cousin the night he was murdered, and whether he knows something about Moon Fairy's death. Go now to that Inn of the Red Carp, Ma Joong, and ask the head of the beggars where you can find Mao Loo. Arrest him and bring him here. At the same time you can give the graybeard these two silver pieces; the fellow did me a good turn. Say that he gets that money from the tribunal as a bonus, because it came to my knowledge that he maintains a strict discipline among the beggars."

Ma Joong turned to go, but Judge Dee raised his hand.

"Just a moment!" he said. "I haven't yet finished my story! It was rather a long night, yesterday!"

Thereupon he told them his conversation with Han Yung-han. He didn't mention the White Lotus Society; that dreaded name should not be used lightly. He merely said that Han's kidnaper had claimed to be the leader of a powerful robber band. When he had concluded, Chiao Tai burst out:

"I have never heard such an improbable story! I trust Your Honor didn't believe one word of what the rascal said?"

Judge Dee said calmly:

"Han Yung-han is a cold-blooded and wily criminal. Of course, he overheard what the dancer said to me that night on the flower boat; he only feigned to be asleep. Thus he knew that she was about to tell me about the nefarious scheme he is working on. When I visited him yesterday afternoon, he tried to talk me into hushing up the murder of the courtesan. When he saw that I didn't let myself be persuaded, he resolved to try intimidating me. Last night he did so, and very cleverly too! He told intentionally a most improbable story, not in order to hoodwink me, mind you, but only because he wanted to disguise his threat in such a manner that I could never accuse him of attempted intimidation. You can imagine what the higher authorities would think of me if I accused Han, quoting that fantastic story! They would argue that if Han really had wanted to deceive me, he would certainly have concocted a better tale! And it was cleverly staged, his telling me the story in the presence of his daughter, his showing her and me the bruise—which was self-inflicted, of course. You see what a dangerous customer the fellow is!"

"Let's put the fat crook on the rack!" Ma Joong exclaimed angrily.

"Unfortunately we haven't a shred of direct proof!" Judge Dee retorted. "You can't question a man under torture without convincing proof of his guilt. And there'll be much difficult work ahead before we have collected that proof! Well, I gave Han to understand that I got his hint and told him that I suspected one of the oarsmen. I hope that now Han thinks he has succeeded in cowing me he'll become careless and make a wrong move."

Sergeant Hoong, who had been listening intently, now asked:

"Is Your Honor quite sure that no one was standing behind your table when Almond Blossom spoke to you? Perhaps a waiter, or one of the courtesans?"

Judge Dee looked soberly at him. Then he replied slowly:

"No, Hoong, I can't say I am certain about that. At least not as regards the waiters. I only know it couldn't have been one of the courtesans, because all five of them were in view, right in front of me. But as to the waiters ... One is apt to take their presence for granted. . . ."

He pensively pulled at his mustache.

"In that case, Your Honor," Sergeant Hoong resumed, "I think we must reckon with the possibility that Han's story is true. A waiter may have overheard what the dancer said, but wrongly thought she was addressing Han. Almond Blossom was standing in between you two, and from behind the man couldn't see that Han was dozing off. That waiter must have been an accomplice of the man who is engaged in the criminal scheme the dancer referred to; he warned his principal, and that man murdered her. Thereafter the murderer had to make sure that Han wouldn't report the warning to Your Honor, and therefore he kidnaped and threatened him."

"You are quite right, Hoong!" Judge Dee said. But then he added quickly: "No, wait a moment! That waiter can't have made a mistake; I remember distinctly that Almond Blossom addressed me as 'Your Honor!'"

"Perhaps the fellow didn't catch all she said," Hoong remarked. "He must have left in a hurry directly after he had overheard her first remark; he didn't hear what she said about playing chess. For Han's kidnaper didn't quote those words."

Judge Dee made no response. He suddenly felt greatly alarmed. If Han's story was true, then it was also true that the White Lotus was being revived! Not even the most reckless criminal would ever dare to use that fearful name in vain. And then the courtesan had discovered a treacherous plot against the Imperial House! Heavens, this was

115

more than a murder case, it was a nationwide conspiracy that affected the security of the State! With a great effort he got hold of himself and said composedly:

"The only one who can settle the problem of whether or not some one was standing behind me is Anemone. After you have arrested Mao Loo, Ma Joong, you may go to the Willow Quarter, and have a talk with Anemone, as a reward! Let her give you an exact account of how she noticed that Han was dozing, how she went to fetch a beaker of wine for him, everything. And in between, you then ask casually who was standing behind us at that time. Do your best!"

"Absolutely, Your Honor!" Ma Joong said happily. "I'd better go right now, before Mao Loo has left his lair!"

In the door opening he nearly collided with the senior scribe, who came in with an armful of dossiers. When the scribe had put those on the desk, Sergeant Hoong and Chiao Tai pulled their chairs closer and started sorting the papers out. Then they assisted the judge in going over them. There were a number of administrative matters that had come in; the morning was well advanced when Judge Dee closed the last dossier.

He leaned back in his chair and waited till Hoong had poured him a cup of tea. Then he spoke.

"I can't put that kidnaping story out of my mind. Quite apart from what Ma Joong may learn from that girl Anemone, we also have another means of checking Han's tale. Go to the chancery, Hoong, and fetch me a good map of the district!"

The sergeant came back with a thick roll under his arm. Chiao Tai helped him to unroll it on the desk. It was a detailed pictorial map of the district Han-yuan, executed in full colors. Judge Dee studied it attentively; then he pointed with his forefinger and said:

"Look; here is the Buddhist Temple where Han allegedly was kidnaped. He said they then went off in an easterly direction. That seems to fit: you first get a level stretch through the uptown villa quarter, then you go down the mountain slope into the plain. If Han spoke the truth, this is the only way they could have taken. For if they had gone downtown he would certainly have noticed their going down those steep steps, and if they had gone north or west they would have got deeper and deeper into the mountains. But he says that after descending a slope, they went the last three-quarters of the way on level ground.

116

That could well apply to this highroad here that crosses the rice plain in the eastern half of our district, right through to the military post at the bridge over the river that forms the boundary between Han-yuan and the neighboring district of Chiang-pei. If this had been a normal, walled city, our problem would have been solved soon. A simple inquiry with the guards of the east gate would have settled it! Anyway, we can come near enough as it is. Han was taken up and down between the city and that mysterious house in one evening. The interview can't have lasted long, so we won't be far wrong if we assume that the trip took about one hour. How far do you think a palanquin could advance in one hour from the city along that road, Chiao Tai?"

Chiao Tai bent over the map. He said:

"It's cooler at night; the bearers could have kept up a good pace. I guess about to here, Your Honor."

With his finger he made a circle round a village in the plain.

"That's good enough!" Judge Dee said. "If Han didn't lie, we must find thereabouts a country house, probably built on a slight elevation because Han mentioned that a number of steps led up to the gate."

The door opened and Ma Joong came in. He greeted the judge with a downcast air. Sitting down heavily on one of the tabourets, he growled:

"Today everything went wrong, I tell you!"

"You certainly look it!" Judge Dee remarked. "What happened?"

"Well," Ma Joong began, "first I go to the fish market. I have to ask the way a hundred times till in a maze of stinking alleys I locate the Inn of the Red Carp. An inn, hey? It's no more than a hole in the wall! The old duffer sits dozing in a corner, I hand him the two silver pieces, with explanation as per instruction. Is he glad? No, the old geezer thinks I am playing him a dirty trick. I have to show him my pass, and then he still nearly breaks his rotting teeth biting on the silver to see whether it isn't false! Well, at last he accepts the money. Then he tells me that Mao Loo is staying with his wench in a brothel nearby. I leave the graybeard still convinced that he's been had!

"So I go to the brothel. Heavens, what a dirty hole, reserved exclusively and permanently for coolies and chair bearers! The only thing I learn from the harridan who owns the joint is that early this morning Mao Loo, his wench and his one-eyed friend left for Chiang-pei. So that was that.

"Then I go on to the Willow Quarter, simple fellow as I am, assuming that a visit there'll cheer me up! Oh, no. That girl Anemone has the father and mother of all hangovers, and the temper she was in! Well, I get out of her that maybe somebody was standing behind Your Honor. But whether it was a waiter or the Prime Minister of the Empire, the dull bit of skirt can't say! Well, that's all!"

"I'd have thought," Judge Dee observed, "that you'd perhaps also have another talk about the dead dancer with that girl friend of yours."

Ma Joong shot him a reproachful look.

"That girl," he muttered morosely, "had a hangover even worse than Anemone's!"

"Well," Judge Dee said with a twinkle of amusement in his eyes, "It can't be sunshine every day, Ma Joong! Now look here, we'll make a tour of inspection through the eastern part of the district, and see whether we can locate the house Han was talking about. If not, we'll know that Han lied, and we'll have had an opportunity for seeing that region; it's the granary of the district and I haven't yet had time to inspect it. We'll go on to the eastern boundary, and pass the night in the village there. Then we'll at least get an impression of the countryside, and clear the cobwebs from our brains! Go and select three good horses, Ma Joong, and cancel today's sessions of the tribunal. I can't announce to the citizens any progress in our two cases anyway!"

Ma Joong left the room with Chiao Tai, looking slightly more cheerful. The judge said to Sergeant Hoong:

"That long ride through the hot plain will be too tiring for you, Hoong; you'd better stay here and look after the chancery. You might collect in our archives all documents relating to the guildmasters Wang and Soo. After the noon meal I want you to go to the quarter where Wan I-fan lives. He's connected with the case Liu versus Djang, and also with that of the spendthrift Councilor. I find it strange that such a wealthy and well-known person as Liu Fei-po protects such an obscure business promoter. Check especially his story about that daughter of his, Hoong!"

Judge Dee stroked his beard, then resumed:

"I am worried about Councilor Liang, Hoong! Since the nephew informed me about the Councilor's state, his family will from now on hold me responsible also, and expect me to take adequate measures to prevent the old gentleman from squandering his entire fortune. But I can't do anything about that until I have ascertained whether it isn't the nephew who is stealing his employer's money, and whether he is implicated in the dancer's murder."

"Shall I go and visit that young man this afternoon, Your Honor?" the sergeant asked. "I might go over all the accounts with him, and try to find out what part Wan I-fan plays in this affair."

"That's an excellent proposal!" Judge Dee said. He took up his writing brush and wrote a brief letter of introduction for the sergeant, addressed to Liang Fen. Then he selected a sheet of official stationery and jotted down a few lines. As he impressed the large red seal of the tribunal on it he said:

"This is a request to my colleague, the magistrate of Ping-yang in Shansi Province, to send me by returning courier all data about the Fan family, and more especially about Miss Fan Ho-i, here called Almond Blossom. It is very strange that she insisted on being sold in this distant city of Han-yuan. Perhaps the roots of her murder lie in her native place! Have this letter dispatched by special messenger."

He rose and concluded:

"Put my light hunting dress out, Hoong, and my riding boots. I'd better be off. I feel I can do with a change of air!"

Twelfth Chapter

**MA JOONG AND CHIAO TAI DISPERSE AN UNRULY
CROWD; A SWINDLER EXPLAINS THE SECRET WAYS
OF KIDNAPERS**

MA JOONG AND CHIAO TAI STOOD WAITING IN THE COURT-
yard with three horses.

After Judge Dee had inspected the horses, the three
men swung themselves into the saddle, the guards pushed
open the heavy gate, and the cavalcade left the tribunal.

Riding toward the east, they left the city and soon
found themselves on a kind of headland. Below, a fertile
plain spread out as far as they could see.

The descent was quickly made. When they were down
in the plain, Judge Dee looked with interest at the sea of
waving, green paddy on both sides of the road.

"It looks promising!" he remarked with satisfaction.
"We'll have a good harvest this autumn! But I don't see
any country house!"

They halted in a small village, and ate a simple noon
meal in the local inn. When the village headman came to
pay his respects Judge Dee inquired about the country
house. But the old man shook his head. He said:

"In this entire neighborhood there's no house built of
brick. The landlords live in the mountains; it's cooler
there."

"Didn't I say that Han is a crook?" Ma Joong muttered.

"We may have better luck farther on," the judge said.

After half an hour they reached the next village. Passing through a narrow road lined by hovels, Judge Dee
heard loud shouting in front. Arriving in the market place,
he saw a crowd of peasants assembled under the old tree
in the center, brandishing sticks and clubs and shouting
and swearing at the top of their voices. High on his horse,
the judge could see that they were beating and kicking
a man lying at the foot of the tree. He was covered with
blood.

"Stop that at once!" Judge Dee shouted. But no one
paid him the slightest attention. He turned round in his

saddle and angrily ordered his two assistants: "Break up that crowd of yokels!"

Ma Joong jumped down from his horse and rushed into the crowd followed by Chiao Tai. Ma Joong grabbed the first man he could lay hands on by his neck and the seat of his trousers, lifted him over his head and threw him in the middle of the crowd. Then he jumped after him and made his way by placing blows and elbow thrusts on left and right, Chiao Tai protecting his rear. In a few moments they had fought their way to the tree and separated the attackers from their groaning victim. Ma Joong shouted:

"Lay off, you clodhoppers! Don't you know that His Excellency the Magistrate has arrived?" And he pointed to the rear.

All heads turned round. When they saw the commanding figure on horseback they quickly lowered their weapons. An elderly man came forward and knelt by Judge Dee's horse.

"This person," he said respectfully, "is the headman of this village."

"Report what is going on here!" the judge ordered. "If that man you are beating to death is a criminal, you should have brought him to the tribunal in Han-yuan. As village head you ought to know that it's a heinous offense to take the law into your own hands!"

"I beg Your Excellency's forgiveness," the headman said. "We were acting rashly, but the provocation was great. We of this village slave from morning till night to scrape together a few coppers for our daily bowl of rice, and then that swindler comes and robs us! The young fellow over there discovered that the crook used loaded dice. I beg Your Excellency's favorable consideration!"

"Let the fellow who discovered the cheating come forward!" Judge Dee ordered. To Ma Joong he added: "Bring that wounded man here!"

Soon a stalwart peasant and a weird, disheveled elderly person were kneeling on the road.

"Can you prove that this man cheated?" the judge asked.

"The proof is here, sir!" the peasant answered, taking from his sleeve two dice. Just as he was rising to hand them to the judge, the wounded man rose too and with amazing celerity snatched the dice from the peasant's hand. Waving them up and down in his hand, he shouted excitedly:

"May all the curses of Heaven and Earth descend upon this poor man if these dice are loaded!"

He handed them to the judge with a deep bow.

Judge Dee let the dice roll along the palm of his hand, then scrutinized them carefully. He gave the accused a sharp look. He was a scraggy man of about fifty. His hair, streaked with gray, hung over a long, deeply lined face disfigured by a bleeding wound on the forehead. He had a mole the size of a piece of copper cash on his left cheek, from which sprouted three hairs several inches long. Judge Dee said coldly to the peasant:

"These dice aren't loaded; neither have they been tampered with in any other way!" He threw them at the headman. He caught them and started to study them together with the others, muttering in astonishment.

The judge addressed the crowd in a stern voice:

"Let this be a lesson to you! If you are oppressed by robbers or treated unjustly by your landlords, you can always come to the tribunal and I'll carefully consider your plaints. But don't ever again have the nerve to take the law into your own hands, or you'll be severely punished. Go back to your work now, and don't squander your time and money on gambling!"

The headman knelt and knocked his forehead on the ground to express his gratitude for this leniency.

Judge Dee ordered Ma Joong to let the wounded man sit behind him on his horse; then the cavalcade moved on again.

In the next village they halted to let the man wash himself at the well and clean his clothes. Judge Dee had the headman called and asked him whether he knew about a country house in that neighborhood, built on a slight elevation. The man replied that there was none that he knew of. He asked what it looked like, and who the owner was; there might be such a house farther along the road. Judge Dee said that it didn't matter.

The wounded man bowed deeply before the judge and wanted to take his leave. But Judge Dee, noting his limp and the deadly pallor of his face, said curtly:

"You go with us to the boundary post my man; you need a doctor. I don't hold with professional gamblers, but I can't leave you here as you are."

Late in the afternoon they arrived at the boundary village. Judge Dee ordered Ma Joong to take the wounded man to the local physician. He himself rode on with

Chiao Tai to inspect the military guard post on the bridgehead.

The corporal in charge ordered his twelve soldiers to line up. The judge saw that their iron helmets and mail jackets were well polished; the men looked neat and efficient. While the judge was inspecting the armory, the corporal said there was a brisk traffic on the river even though it was but a branch of the Great River, which flowed through the neighboring district of Chiang-pei. He said all was quiet on their side of the river, but that there had been several armed robberies in Chiang-pei. The garrison there had recently been strengthened.

The corporal escorted them to a small hostel. An obsequious manager came out to meet them. While a groom led away the horses, the manager himself assisted the judge in taking off his heavy riding boots. When Judge Dee had been supplied with comfortable straw sandals, he was taken upstairs to a poorly furnished but scrupulously clean room. The manager opened the window, and the judge saw over the rooftops the broad expanse of the river, reflecting the red rays of the setting sun.

A servant brought lighted candles and a basin with hot towels. While the judge was refreshing himself, Ma Joong and Chiao Tai came in. Ma Joong poured a cup of tea for the judge, then said:

"That gambler is a queer fellow, Your Honor! He told me that in his youth he had been a clerk in a silk store, down south. The manager took a liking to his wife and trumped up a charge of theft against him. The constables gave him a beating but he succeeded in escaping. While he was away, the manager took his wife as concubine. When the hue and cry had subsided, he secretly came back and begged his wife to flee with him, but she laughed and said she liked it better where she was. He says that during the ensuing years he roamed all over the Empire. He talks like a doctor of literature and calls himself a commission agent, but I think he is nothing but a 'guest of rivers and lakes,' or in plain language, an itinerant swindler!"

"Those fellows always have a tale of woe ready!" Judge Dee remarked. "We'll never see him again!"

There was a knock on the door. Two coolies entered, carrying four large hampers. One contained three fine large fishes, stewed in ginger sauce, the other a large bowl with rice and salted eggs. A red visiting card proclaimed

123

this to be a present from the corporal. In the two other baskets they found three roasted chickens, three plates with stewed pork and vegetables and a jar with soup. This proved to be the welcome gift of the headman and the village elders. A waiter brought three jars of wine, by courtesy of the manager of the hostel.

When the dishes had been placed on the table, Judge Dee gave the coolies some silver wrapped up in a piece of red paper as return present; then he said to his two assistants:

"Since we are on the road together, I won't stand on ceremony! Sit down, we'll dine together."

Ma Joong and Chiao Tai protested vehemently, but the judge insisted and finally they sat down opposite him. The long ride had given them an excellent appetite; they ate with gusto. Judge Dee was in high spirits. Han's story had proved to be a lie; he now knew that Han was the criminal and sooner or later he would find a way to get him. He now could dismiss his worries about the White Lotus being revived; all that had been nothing but an invention.

When they were enjoying their after-dinner tea, a waiter brought in a large envelope addressed to Judge Dee. It contained an elegantly phrased and neatly written intimation that a certain Tao Gan begged to be allowed to call on His Excellency the Magistrate.

"That'll be one of the village elders," Judge Dee said. "Show the gentleman up!"

To their amazement the thin figure of the gambler appeared in the door opening. After his visit to the doctor he had evidently patronized the village shops. He had a bandage over his forehead, but he now presented a very neat appearance. He wore a simple blue robe with a black silk sash, and on his head he carried with perfect confidence a high cap of black gauze such as is favored by elderly gentlemen of leisure. Bowing deeply, he said in an educated voice:

"This insignificant person, named Tao Gan, respectfully greets Your Honor. Words don't suffice to express—"

"Enough, my man!" Judge Dee said coldly. "Don't thank me; thank Providence that saved you! Don't think I have any sympathy for you; the beating you got is probably not more than you deserved! I am convinced that somehow or other you cheated those peasants, but I won't have lawlessness in my district. That's the only reason why I protected you!"

"Even so," the gaunt man said, completely unperturbed by this harsh address, "I hoped to be allowed to offer Your Honor my humble assistance, as a slight mark of my profound gratitude. For I presume that Your Honor is engaged in the investigation of a kidnaping case."

With difficulty Judge Dee concealed his astonishment. "What are you talking about, my man?" he asked curtly.

"The exercise of my profession," Tao Gan replied with a deprecating smile, "necessarily encourages a sharpening of one's powers of deduction. I happened to overhear Your Honor asking about a country house. But I noticed that Your Honor was unconversant with its appearance and the name of its occupant."

He slowly wound the long hairs sprouting from his cheek round his forefinger, then continued placidly:

"Kidnapers will bandage the eyes of their victim and take him to a distant place where by dire threats they force him to send a letter to his family, asking them to send a large ransom. After the money has been received, they either kill their victim, or send him home again with his eyes bandaged as before. In the latter case such an unfortunate man may have a vague impression of the direction in which he was taken. But, of course, he doesn't know what the house looked like, or the name of its owner. Since I thus deduced that a victim of such a dastardly crime had reported to Your Honor's tribunal, I made bold to offer my advice."

Again the gaunt man bowed deeply.

Judge Dee said to himself that this was a remarkably astute fellow. He said:

"Let's for the sake of argument assume that your deduction is correct. What would then be your advice?"

"In the first place," Tao Gan answered, "I have been all over this district; in this plain there is no such house. On the other hand, I know several of such villas in the mountains north and west of Han-yuan."

"Now suppose that the victim remembered distinctly that the greater part of the journey went along a level road?" the judge asked.

A sly smile spread over Tao Gan's sardonic face.

"In that case, Your Honor," he answered, "the house is located inside the city."

"What a preposterous remark!" Judge Dee exclaimed angrily.

"Not quite, Your Honor," the other said calmly. "The only thing those rascals need is a house with a fairly large garden and a raised terrace. Having brought their victim in a palanquin inside the compound, they'll carry him slowly round about there for an hour or so. They are very skillful; they create the impression of passing a mountainous region by climbing up and down the terrace, muttering from time to time: 'Look out for that ravine!' or similar remarks. Those crooks have carefully studied that technique, Your Honor, and excute it in a most convincing manner."

The judge looked thoughtfully at the thin man, slowly caressing his side whiskers. After a while he said:

"An interesting theory! I'll keep it in mind for future reference. Before you go, listen to my advice. Change your life, my friend; you are clever enough to earn your living in a decent way!" He wanted to dismiss him, but asked suddenly: "By the way, how did you fool those peasants? I am just curious to know; I shan't take action against you."

The thin man smiled faintly. He called the waiter and ordered him:

"Go downstairs and bring His Excellency's right riding boot!"

When the waiter returned with the boot, Tao Gan, with nimble fingers, removed two dice from its folded rim, and handed them to the judge. He said:

"After I had snatched these loaded dice from the yokel who was going to give them to Your Honor, I presented to you for inspection a pair of normal dice, which I had kept concealed in the palm of my hand. While everybody was looking intently at Your Honor inspecting those dice, I took the liberty of depositing the false ones in Your Honor's boot, temporarily, I hoped."

Judge Dee couldn't help laughing.

"Without boasting," Tao Gan continued earnestly, "I can say that my knowledge of the tricks and ruses of the underworld is equaled by few in the Empire. I am thoroughly familiar with forging documents and seals, drawing up ambiguous contracts and false declarations, picking all kinds of ordinary and secret locks on doors, windows and strongboxes, while I am also an expert on hidden

126

passages, secret trap doors and such-like contrivances. Moreover, I know what people are saying at a distance by watching their lips, I—"

"Halt!" Judge Dee interrupted him quickly. "Do you mean to say that the last item of your imposing catalogue is really true?"

"Certainly, Your Honor! I may add only that it is easier to practice lip reading on women and children than on, for instance, old men with heavy beards and mustaches."

The judge made no comment. In this manner the words of the courtesan could have been intercepted by others in the room besides Han Yung-han. When he looked up, Tao Gan said in a low voice:

"I have already told your lieutenant the unfortunate occurrence which made me a bitter man. After that galling experience I completely lost faith in my fellow men. For nearly thirty years I have been roaming over the Empire, taking delight in swindling and cheating whom I could. But I swear that I have never inflicted grave bodily harm on anyone; neither did I ever cause irreparable loss. Today, Your Honor's kindness has given me a new outlook on life; I want to give up my career as a guest of rivers and lakes. My various abilities, while necessary for the exercise of my profession, can, I presume, also be employed in the detection of crime and the apprehension of miscreants. I therefore place before Your Honor my humble request that I be allowed to serve in Your Honor's tribunal. I have no family—I broke with them long ago when they sided with my wife. Further, I have saved some money. Thus the only reward I hope for is an opportunity to make myself useful and receive Your Honor's instruction."

Judge Dee looked hard at this curious person. He thought he could detect in that cynical face the signs of genuine emotion. Also, this man had already supplied him with two important pieces of information, and he possessed a store of special knowledge and experience none of his other assistants had. Under suitable supervision he might indeed prove a useful addition to his personal staff. At last he spoke.

"You'll realize, Tao Gan, that I can't give you a definite answer here and now. Since, however, I do believe that you are in earnest, I shall allow you to work as a volunteer

127

in my tribunal for a few weeks or so. Then I shall decide whether or not I can accept your proposal."

Tao Gan knelt and touched his forehead to the floor three times, to express his gratitude.

"These men," Judge Dee went on, "are my two lieutenants. You'll assist them to the best of your ability, and they on their part will instruct you in the affairs of the tribunal."

Tao Gan made his bow in front of each. Chiao Tai looked the gaunt man up and down with a noncommittal expression, but Ma Joong clapped him on his bony shoulder and exclaimed, highly pleased:

"Come along downstairs, brother! You can teach me a few of your gambling tricks!"

Chiao Tai snuffed all but one candle; then he wished the judge a good night, and followed the two others downstairs.

After he had gone, Judge Dee remained sitting at the table. For a long time he idly observed the swarm of gnats buzzing around the candle flame, deep in thought.

Now that Tao Gan had shown that Han's story could be true, even though they had not been able to locate the house he was abducted to, he had again to consider the possibility that the White Lotus Society was indeed weaving its evil web of treachery and corruption over the Empire. Han-yuan was a small, isolated town, but it occupied a strategic position, being very close to the hub of the realm, the Imperial capital. Thus it was a most suitable location for the headquarters of a conspiracy against the Throne. That was, then, the explanation of the oppressive atmosphere of hidden evil that he had felt by intuition soon after his arrival.

Since, as he now knew, any guest in the dining room on the flower boat could have read the dancer's words from her lips, any one of them could have been a member of the White Lotus and decided to murder her. Han Yunghan could be innocent, or he could be their leader! And so could Liu Fei-po! Liu's great wealth, his frequent travels, his resentment against the government—all these factors seemed to point to him as a likely suspect. Heavens, the entire company present at the banquet could have conspired together to murder the courtesan! He angrily shook his head; the awful threat of the White Lotus was having an effect already: it prevented him from thinking logically. He must reconsider once more all the facts, beginning from the beginning. . . .

The candle started to splutter. The judge got up with a sigh. He took off his upper robe and cap, and stretched himself out on the wooden couch.

Thirteenth Chapter

SERGEANT HOONG IS SUSPECTED OF IMPROPER INTENTIONS; A FALSE PRIEST IS CAUGHT TOGETHER WITH HIS ACOLYTE

THE FOLLOWING MORNING, AT DAWN, JUDGE DEE AND his three companions left the boundary village. A brisk ride took them back to the city before noon.

The judge went straight to his own quarters, took a hot bath and put on a summer dress of thin blue cotton. Then he went to his private office, and introduced Tao Gan to Sergeant Hoong. Then Ma Joong and Chiao Tai also came in. All seated themselves on tabourets in front of Judge Dee's desk. He noticed that Tao Gan behaved himself with the modesty expected of a newcomer, yet without undue humility. This strange man could evidently adapt himself to any situation.

Judge Dee told Hoong they had found no country house, but that Tao Gan's theory opened new possibilities. Then he ordered the sergeant to report.

Hoong took a sheet with notes from his sleeve and began:

"We have in the archives only a few routine documents concerning Guildmaster Wang: registrations of his children, tax declarations, etc. But our senior scribe knows him fairly well. He told me that Wang is very wealthy; he owns the two largest gold and jewelry shops in town. Although he is admittedly fond of wine and women, he is considered a sound businessman and is trusted by everyone. He seems to have had some financial setbacks of late; he had to postpone payments of some large amounts due to dealers who supply his gold stock, but since they know that before long he'll recoup his losses, they don't worry in the least.

"Soo also has a good reputation. People regretted, however, that he fell in love so deeply with the courtesan Almond Blossom, who would have none of him. Soo was very depressed about that. It is generally said that it's all for the best that she died; people hope that Soo, when

130

he has got over his grief, will marry a decent, steady woman."

The sergeant consulted his notes and continued:

"Then I strolled to the street where Wan I-fan lives. He is not very popular; people think he is an underhanded fellow who loves to drive a hard bargain. He is a kind of handyman of Liu Fei-po, and occasionally collects small debts for him. Of course, I didn't want to ask in the shops about Wan's daughter, so as not to compromise her. But when I saw on the street corner an old crone selling combs, rouge and face powder I struck up a conversation with her. Those women frequent the women's quarters and always know all that goes on there. I asked her whether she knew Wan's daughter."

The sergeant gave the judge a self-conscious look, then went on diffidently:

"The old woman said at once: 'You are still very enterprising for your age, aren't you, sir? Well, she asks two strings of coppers for the evenings and four for the whole night, but the gentlemen are always very satisfied.' I explained to her that I was a matchmaker, acting on behalf of a grocer in the west quarter, and that the people there had mentioned Miss Wan. 'Those of the west quarter never know what they are talking about!' the procuress said contemptuously. 'Everybody here knows that after her mother's death, Miss Wan started to live freely. Wan tried to sell her to a professor, but that fellow knew better! Now she earns her own money, and her father turns a blind eye to it. He is as stingy as they make them, and he's mighty glad he needn't provide for her!'"

"That means that the impudent rascal has lied in court!" Judge Dee exclaimed angrily. "He'll hear about this! Well, how did it fare at Councilor Liang's?"

"Liang Fen seems an intelligent youngster," Hoong replied. "I have been working with him more than two hours on the accounts. Everything points indeed to the conclusion that the Councilor is selling out his estates at considerable loss in order to obtain quickly a large amount of gold. But we couldn't trace what he is doing with all that money. I can well imagine that the secretary is worried."

Tao Gan, who had been listening intently, now observed:

"They say that figures don't lie, Your Honor, but nothing is farther from the truth. It all depends on the way they

131

are handled! Perhaps the nephew manipulated the books in order to conceal his own malversations!"

"That possibility had already occurred to us," the judge remarked. "It's an annoying situation!"

"While riding back to the city this morning," Tao Gan resumed, "Ma Joong told me about the case Liu versus Djang. Is it quite certain that besides the old caretaker no other monk is living in the Buddhist Temple?"

Judge Dee looked questioningly at Ma Joong, who answered at once:

"Absolutely! I searched the entire temple, including the garden."

"That's queer!" Tao Gan said. "When I was in town the other day I happened to pass there. I saw a monk standing behind a pillar at the gate, craning his neck to peer inside. Since I am of an inquisitive disposition I walked up to him to assist him in peering. Then he gave me a startled look and quickly went away."

"Did that monk have a pale, haggard face?" Judge Dee asked eagerly.

"No, Your Honor," Tao Gan replied, "it was a hefty fellow with a bloated look. In fact he didn't look like a real monk to me."

"Then it can't have been the fellow whom I saw outside the bridal room," said the judge. "I have now a job for you, Tao Gan. We know that when the carpenter Mao Yuan left Dr. Djang's house he had just been paid, and we also know that he liked drinking and gambling. It is possible that he was murdered for his money, for we didn't find one copper on the corpse. You know that I suspect Dr. Djang of being concerned in his murder, but we must explore all possibilities. Go now and make the rounds of the gambling dens of this city, and inquire about Mao Yuan. I assume that you know how to find those places! Ma Joong, go back once more to the Inn of the Red Carp, and ask the head of the beggars to what place in Chiang-pei Mao Loo went. In the noodle restaurant he mentioned it, but I have forgotten what the place is called. What matters must be dealt with during the noon session, Hoong?"

While the sergeant and Chiao Tai started laying out several dossiers on the desk, Ma Jong and Tao Gan left the office together.

In the courtyard Tao Gan said to Ma Joong:

"I am glad I can do that job about the carpenter right

now. News travels fast in the underworld; it'll be known soon that I am now working for the tribunal. By the way, where is that Inn of the Red Carp? I thought I knew this town fairly well already, but I never saw the place."

"You didn't miss anything!" Ma Joong replied. "It's a dirty joint, somewhere behind the fish market. Good luck!"

Tao Gan went downtown, and entered the west quarter. He went through a rabbit warren of narrow alleys, and halted in front of a small vegetable shop. Picking his way carefully among the vats of pickled cabbage, he grunted a greeting at the shopkeeper and made for the staircase at the back.

On the second floor it was pitch dark. Tao Gan felt along the cobweb-covered plaster wall till he found the door. He pushed it open and remained standing there surveying the dimly lighted, low-ceilinged room. Two men were sitting at a round table with a depression in the center for throwing dice. One was a fat man with a heavy jowled, expressionless face and a closely shaved head. He was the manager of the gambling den. The other was a thin fellow with a pronounced squint. Men with this defect are in great demand as supervisors of gambling games because persons who cheat never know whether they are being watched or not.

"It's brother Tao," the fat man said without much enthusiasm. "Don't stand hanging about there. Come inside! It's too early for a game, but there'll be people in soon."

"No," Tao Gan said. "I am rather in a hurry. I only look in to see whether the carpenter Mao Yuan is here. I want to collect some money he owes me."

The two men laughed heartily.

"In that case," the fat manager sniggered, "you'll have to go a long way, brother! All the way to the King of the Nether World! Don't you know that old Mao is dead?"

Tao Gan swore volubly. He sat down in a rickety bamboo chair.

"That would be my cursed luck!" he said angrily. "Just when I need the money! What happened to the bastard?"

"It's all over the town," the man with the squint remarked. "He was found in the Buddhist Temple with a hole in his head you could put your fist in!"

"Who did it?" asked Tao Gan. "I might approach that fellow and blackmail him into paying me the money, with a bit extra for good luck!"

The fat man nudged his neighbor. Both started laughing again.

"What's the joke now?" Tao Gan asked sourly.

"The joke is, my friend," the manager explained, "that Mao Loo is probably mixed up in that murder. Now you travel to Three Oaks Island, brother Tao, and blackmail the fellow!"

The man with the squint bellowed with laughter.

"You have him again, boss!" he exclaimed, guffawing.

"What nonsense!" Tao Gan exclaimed. "Mao Loo is the carpenter's own cousin!"

The fat man spat on the floor.

"Listen, brother Tao," he said, "listen carefully; then perhaps even you will understand! Three days ago Mao Yuan comes in here late in the afternoon. He has just finished a job and there's money in his sleeve. He finds a good crowd here; the fellow has luck, he wins a nice bit of money. Then who should come in but his cousin. Now Mao Yuan hasn't been too keen on that cousin of his lately, but what with the wine in his belly and the money in his sleeve he greets him like a long-lost brother. They drink four jars of the best together; then Mao Loo invites his cousin to have a meal with him somewhere outside. And that is the last we see of them. Mind you now, I don't say anything against Mao Loo. I just state the facts!"

Tao Gan nodded comprehendingly.

"That's bad luck!" he said ruefully. "Well, I'd better be on my way."

Just as he was rising the door opened and a powerfully built man clad in a ragged monk's robe came in. Tao Gan hurriedly sat down again.

"Ha, there's the monk!" the manager exclaimed.

The man thus addressed sat down with a grunt. The manager pushed a teacup toward him. The monk spat on the floor.

"Have you nothing better to serve than that filthy stuff?" he asked gruffly.

The fat man lifted his right hand, making a circle with the thumb and forefinger.

The monk shook his head.

"Nothing doing!" he said disgustedly. "Wait till I have beaten that mealy youth to pulp; then I'll show you some real money!"

The manager shrugged his shoulders. He said indifferently:

"Then it'll have to be tea, monk!"

"I think I have met you once," Tao Gan said, joining the conversation. "Didn't I see you in front of the Buddhist Temple?"

The newcomer shot him a suspicious look.

"Who's the scarecrow?" he asked the manager.

"Oh, that's Brother Tao," the manager replied. "A good fellow, but not too bright. What did you do in the temple? Do you really think of joining the clergy now, monk?"

The man with the squint laughed loudly. The monk barked at him: "Stop your stupid sniggering!" As the manager gave him a sour look he went on in a calmer voice: "Well, I am in a foul temper and I don't care who knows it. The day before yesterday I see that fellow Mao Loo behind . . . where was it now? Yes, it was somewhere near the fish market. You could see the coppers weighing in his sleeves! 'Where's the Treasure Tree, brother?' I ask, friendly like. 'There's plenty more where that came from!' says he. 'You just go and have a look at the Buddhist Temple!' Well, I went there."

The monk gulped the tea down. Making a face, he continued:

"And what do you think I find there? An old dodderer who has even less than me, and a coffin!"

The fat manager burst out laughing. The monk's eyes glittered with rage, but he didn't dare to curse him.

"Well, well," the manager said, "you better go then with Brother Tao here to Three Oaks Island! He also wants to talk with Mao Loo!"

"So he got you too, hey?" the monk asked a little more cheerfully.

Tao Gan grunted his assent.

"I am all for milking that young fellow you were talking about," he said dryly. "That should be a little easier than tackling Mao Loo!"

"That's what you think, brother!" the monk said disgustedly. "I meet that youngster in the deep of night, running as if the King of Hell was on his heels. I grab him by his neck and ask him where he's running to. He says: 'Leave me alone!' I see that he's a wealthy youngster, the weak-kneed type that eats with silver chopsticks. I know the fellow has done something he shouldn't. So I pat

135

him on the head, sling him over my shoulder and carry him all the way to my place."

The monk cleared his throat noisily and spat in the corner. He groped for the teapot, then thought better of it and went on:

"Imagine the fellow refusing to tell me a thing! And that after all the trouble I took for him! Now here I am with a fine blackmail case in the hollow of my hand, and the fellow won't talk! And not for lack of persuasion either!" he added with a cruel grin.

Tao Gan got up.

"Well," he said with a resigned sigh, "that's how it always is with us people, monk! Nothing but bad luck! If I were a strong fellow like you I could make thirty silver pieces tonight. Anyway, good luck!"

He went to the door.

"Hey!" the monk shouted, "why the hurry? Thirty silver pieces did you say?"

"None of your business!" Tao Gan snapped and opened the door.

The monk jumped up and dragged him back by his collar.

"Keep your hands off, monk!" the manager said sharply. And to Tao Gan: "Why be unreasonable, Brother Tao? If you can't do the job yourself, why don't you let the monk here in on it and pocket a commission?"

"Of course, I had thought of that!" Tao Gan said testily. "But you know I am new here and I didn't quite catch the name of the place where they gather. Since they said they needed a hefty fellow who could fight I didn't inquire further."

"The stupid son of a dog!" the monk exclaimed. "Thirty silver pieces! Think, bastard!"

Tao Gan knitted his eyebrows. Then he shrugged. "It's no use. I only remember something about a carp or so!"

"That's the Inn of the Red Carp!" the manager and the monk exclaimed at the same time.

"There you have it!" Tao Gan said. "But I don't know where it is."

The monk rose and took Tao Gan by his arm.

"Come along, brother!" he said. "I know that place!"

Tao Gan shook himself loose. He held up his hand, with the palm upward.

"Five per cent of my share!" the monk said gruffly.

Tao Gan made for the door.

"Fifteen or nothing!" he said over his shoulder.

"Seven for you and three for me!" the manager interrupted. "So that's settled now. You take the monk there, Brother Tao, and tell them that I personally guarantee that the monk knows his job! Get going!"

Tao Gan and the monk left the room together.

They went to the poor quarter east of the fish market. As the monk let Tao Gan into a smelly, narrow side street, he pointed to the door of a ramshackle wooden shed.

"You go in first!" he whispered hoarsely.

Tao Gan opened the door. He heaved a sigh of relief. Ma Joong was still there, sitting in a corner with the head of the beggars. They were the only occupants of the sparsely furnished room.

"How are you, brother!" Tao Gan said cordially to Ma Joong. "Here's exactly the man your boss was looking for!"

The monk bowed with an ingratiating grin.

Ma Joong rose and walked up to him. Looking him up and down, he asked:

"What would the boss be wanting this ugly dog's-head for?"

"He knows too much about the murder in the Buddhist Temple!" Tao Gan said quickly.

The monk stepped back, but not fast enough. Before he had raised his hands Ma Joong had landed a straight blow in his heart region that made him fall backward over a small table.

But the monk had been in such situations before. He didn't attempt to get up. Quick as lightning he drew a knife and threw it at Ma Joong's throat. Ma Joong ducked and the knife stuck in the doorpost with a dull thud. Ma Joong grabbed the small table and crashed it on the monk's half-raised head. It hit the floor. The monk lay motionless.

Ma Joong unwound the thin chain he carried round his waist. He turned the monk over on his face and secured his hands behind his back. Tao Gan said excitedly:

"He knows more about Mao Yuan and his cousin than he'll admit, and besides, he is a member of a kidnaping gang!"

Ma Joong grinned broadly.

"That's good work!" he said with approval. "But how

did you get the rascal here? I thought you didn't know this inn?"

"Oh," Tao Gan said airily, "I told him a story and he himself took me here."

Ma Joong gave him a sidelong glance.

"You look inoffensive enough," he said thoughtfully. "Yet I have a feeling that in your own way you are as nasty a piece as they make them!"

Ignoring that remark, Tao Gan went on:

"He has recently kidnaped a young man of good family. Probably the bastard belongs to the same gang that Han Yung-han reported about! Let's make him take us to their hideout; then we'll have something worthwhile to report!"

Ma Joong nodded. He dragged the unconscious man to his feet and threw him in a chair against the wall. Then he shouted to the graybeard to bring incense sticks. The old man hastily disappeared in the back of the room. He returned with two incense sticks that sent forth a pungent smell.

Ma Joong jerked the head of the monk up and held the burning sticks close under his nose. Soon the man started to cough and sneeze violently. He looked up at Ma Joong from bloodshot eyes.

"We'll have a look at your home, Frogface!" Ma Joong said. "Speak up; how do we get there?"

"You have something coming to you when the manager hears about this!" the monk said thickly. "He'll tear your liver out!"

"I can look after myself!" Ma Joong said cheerfully. "Come on; answer my question!"

He held the incense sticks close to the monk's cheek. He looked apprehensively at them, and quickly mumbled some directions. One had to leave the city by a footpath that began somewhere behind the Buddhist Temple.

"That'll do!" Ma Joong interrupted him. "The rest you'll show us yourself!"

He told the graybeard to bring an old blanket, and to call two coolies with a stretcher.

Ma Joong, together with Tao Gan, rolled the monk from head to foot in the blanket. The monk protested that it was very hot. But Tao Gan kicked him in his ribs and said: "Don't you know that you have a fever, bastard?"

The monk was loaded on the stretcher and they set off.

"Get a move on, dog's-head!" he snapped.

"Be careful!" Ma Joong growled at the coolies. "My friend is very ill!"

When they had arrived at the pine forest behind the Buddhist Temple, Ma Jong told the coolies to put the stretcher down and paid them off. As soon as they were out of sight, he freed the monk from his blanket. Tao Gan took an oil plaster from his sleeve and pasted that over the monk's mouth.

"When we are near there you stop and point the place out to us!" he ordered the monk, who scrambled up with difficulty. "Those rascals have special whistles and other warning signals," Tao Gan explained to Ma Joong. Ma Jong nodded. He sent the monk into precipitate action by an accurately placed kick.

The monk took them along a footpath that led up the mountain. Then he left it and picked his way through the dense forest. He halted and pointed with his head at a cliff that loomed through the trees some distance ahead. Tao Gan ripped the plaster off his mouth. He said nastily:

"We aren't nature lovers! We want the house!"

"I have got no house!" the monk said sullenly. "I live in a cave over there."

"A cave?" Ma Joong shouted angrily. "Do you think you can fool us? Bring us to the headquarters of your gang or I'll throttle you!" And he gripped the monk by his throat.

"I swear it!" the monk gasped. "The only gang I belong to is the gambling ring! I have been living alone in that cave ever since I came to this accursed place!"

Ma Joong let him go. He took out the knife the monk had thrown at him. Giving Tao Gan a meaningful look, he asked:

"Shall we do some pruning on him?"

Tao Gan shrugged his shoulders.

"Let's first have a look at that cave, anyway!" he said.

The monk led them to the cliff, trembling on his legs. He separated the undergrowth with his foot. They saw a dark cleft of about a man's height.

Tao Gan went down on his belly and crept inside, holding a wicked-looking thin knife between his teeth.

After a while he reappeared, this time walking upright.

"There's nobody there but a whimpering youngster!" he announced in a disappointed voice.

139

Ma Joong followed him inside, dragging the monk behind him.

After a dozen steps or so through a dark tunnel he saw a large cave lighted by a crevice in the ceiling. On the right stood a roughly made wooden bed and a battered leather box. On the other side a young man was lying on the floor, wearing only a loincloth. His hands and feet were tied with rope.

"Let me go! Please, let me go!" he groaned.

Tao Gan cut his ropes. The young man raised himself with difficulty to a sitting position. They saw that his back was beaten raw.

"Who has been beating you?" Ma Joong asked gruffly.

The youngster silently pointed at the monk. As Ma Joong slowly turned round to him the monk fell on his knees.

"No, Your Excellency, please!" he cried. "The bastard is lying!"

Ma Joong gave him a contemptuous look. He said coldly:

"I'll save you for the headman of the constables; he likes that kind of work!"

Tao Gan had helped the young man to sit down on the bed. He seemed about twenty years old. His head had been crudely shaved, and his face was distorted with pain. But it was easy to see that he was an educated man of good family.

"Who are you, and how did you get yourself in this state?" Tao Gan asked curiously.

"That man kidnaped me! Please take me away from him!"

"We'll do better than that!" Ma Joong said. "We'll take you to His Excellency the Magistrate!"

"No!" the youngster shouted. "Let me go!"

He made an attempt to rise.

"Well, well!" Ma Joong said slowly. "So that's how the land lies! You come along to the tribunal, my young friend!" He barked at the monk: "Hey there! Since you don't even belong to a kidnaping gang I don't care who sees us! You won't be cuddled and carried this time!"

He lifted the weakly protesting youngster from the bed and placed him with legs astride on the monk's neck. He threw an old blanket over the young man's shoulders. Then he took a blood-stained willow branch from the corner and hit the monk's calves.

Fourteenth Chapter

A YOUNG SCHOLAR TELLS A MOST AMAZING STORY;
JUDGE DEE QUESTIONS THE OWNER OF A BROTHEL

LATE IN THE MORNING, SHORTLY BEFORE THE NOON
meal, Judge Dee opened a session of the tribunal. The
court hall was crowded; the citizens of Han-yuan thought
that a session held at such an unusual hour could only
mean that important new facts had come to light regarding the two sensational cases that had occurred in
their midst.

To their disappointment, however, the judge began at
once with one of the matters he had been studying with
Sergeant Hoong and Chiao Tai that morning, namely a
quarrel between the fishermen and the management of the
fish market regarding the methods of fixing prices. Judge
Dee had representatives of both parties explain again
their standpoint, then proposed a compromise that, after
some discussion, was accepted.

He was just going to broach a taxation problem when
loud shouts were heard outside. Ma Joong and Tao Gan
entered, each dragging along a prisoner. They were followed by a dense crowd that had joined them on the
way. The spectators stormed them with excited questions;
the court hall was in confusion.

Judge Dee rapped his gavel three times.

"Silence and order!" he shouted in a thunderous voice.
"If I hear one more word I'll have the hall cleared!"

All fell silent. No one wanted to miss the questioning of
the incongruous pair that was now kneeling in front of the
dais.

The judge looked at the prisoners with an impassive
face. But inwardly he was far from calm, for he had immediately recognized the young man.

Ma Joong reported how he and Tao Gan had arrested
the two men. Judge Dee listened, slowly stroking his beard.
Then he addressed the youngster:

"State your name and profession!"

"This insignificant person," he replied in a low voice,

141

"respectfully reports that his name is Djang Hoo-piao, a Candidate of Literature."

A murmur of astonishment rose from the hall. The judge angrily looked up and rapped his gavel. "This is my last warning!" he shouted. To the youngster he continued: "It was reported to this tribunal that Candidate Djang drowned himself in the lake four days ago!"

"Your Honor," the young man said in a faltering voice, "it distresses me beyond words that I, in my foolishness, created that wrong impression. I fully realize that I have acted with extreme rashness and showed a most reprehensible lack of decision. I can only hope that Your Honor, having taken cognizance of the special circumstances, will kindly view my case leniently."

Here he paused. Deep silence reigned in the court hall. Then he went on:

"Be it never given another man to undergo such a shattering transition from supreme bliss to deepest despair as I went through on my wedding night! United for one brief moment with my beloved, I found that my very love had killed her."

He swallowed with difficulty, then went on:

"Distracted with grief and horror, I stared at her still body. Then panic seized me. How was I to face my father, who had always tended me, his only son, with the greatest love and care—I, who had deprived him of the hope of seeing his family continued? The only thing I could do was to end my wretched life.

"I hastily put on a light robe and made for the door. But then I reflected that the feast was still going on, and that the house was full of people. I would never be able to leave unnoticed. Suddenly I remembered that the old carpenter who had come the other day to mend the leaking roof of my room had left two boards of the ceiling loose. 'That'd be a useful place for storing valuables!' he had remarked to me. I stood on a tabouret, pulled myself up on a beam, and crept up in the loft. I replaced the boards and climbed out on the roof. Then I let myself down into the street.

"Since it was deep in the night there was no one about; I reached the bank of the lake unnoticed. I stood on a large boulder over the water and took off my silk girdle. I was going to strip, for I feared that my robe would keep me afloat and thus prolong my death struggle. Then, looking down in the black water I, miserable coward, became afraid. I remembered the macabre stories told about the foul creatures roaming in the water. I thought I could discern indistinct shapes moving about and malicious eyes staring up at me. Although it was very hot I stood there shivering; my teeth clattered in my mouth. I knew that I couldn't execute my plan.

"My girdle had dropped into the water, so I drew my robe close and ran away from the lake. I don't know where my feet took me. I came to myself only when I saw the gate of the Buddhist Temple looming ahead. Then that man there suddenly stepped out from the shadow and grabbed me by the shoulder. I thought he was a robber and tried to shake myself loose, but he hit me on the head and I lost consciousness. When I came to, I was lying in that horrible cave. The next morning that man immediately asked me my name, where I lived and what crime I had committed. I realized that he intended to blackmail me or my poor father, and refused. He just grinned and said that it was my good fortune that he had brought me to the cave, for the constables would never discover me there. He shaved my head despite my protests, saying that thus I would pass for his acolyte and that I wouldn't be recognised. He ordered me to gather firewood and cook rice gruel, then went away.

"I passed that entire day debating with myself what to do. Now I would decide to flee to some faraway place, then again I thought it would be better to go back home and face my father's wrath. At night the man came back drunk. Again he started questioning me. When I refused to give any information he bound me with rope and beat me mercilessly with a willow wand. Then he let me lie there on the floor, more dead than alive. I passed a terrible night. The next morning the monk took off the ropes, gave me a drink of water, and when I had somewhat recovered ordered me to gather firewood. I decided to flee from that cruel man. As soon as I had collected two bundles, I hurried away to the city. With my shaven head and tattered robe nobody recognized me on the road. I was well-nigh exhausted; my feet and back were sore. But the thought of seeing my father again gave me force, and I reached our street."

Candidate Djang paused to wipe the perspiration from his face. On a sign of the judge the headman gave him a cup of bitter tea. After he had drunk that he resumed:

"Who shall describe my horror when I saw constables

of the tribunal in front of our door! That could mean only that I came too late; my father, unable to bear the shame I had brought over his house, had himself put an end to his life. I had to make certain, and slipped inside through the garden door, leaving my bundles of firewood in the street outside. I looked through the window of my bedroom. Then I saw a fearful apparition! The King of the Nether World was staring at me with burning eyes! The ghosts of Hell were persecuting me, the patricide! I lost my head completely. I ran out again into the deserted street and fled to the forest. By dint of much searching through the woods I at last found the cave.

"The man was waiting for me. When he saw me he flew into a violent rage. He stripped me and again beat me cruelly, shouting all the time that I should confess my crime. Finally I fainted, unable to bear the torture any longer.

"What followed then was a terrible nightmare. I got fever and lost all notion of place and time. The man would wake me up only to give me a drink of water, then beat me again. He never took off the ropes. Apart from this physical agony there was always present in my feverish brain the dreadful thought that I had killed the two people I cared for most, my father and my bride. . . ."

His voice trailed off. He swayed on his feet, then sank unconscious to the floor, completely exhausted.

Judge Dee ordered Sergeant Hoong to have him carried to his private office. "Tell the coroner," he added, "to revive this unfortunate youth and dress his wounds. Then give him a sedative and supply him with a decent robe and cap. Report to me as soon as he has recovered. I want to ask him one question before we send him home."

The judge leaned forward and asked the monk coldly: "What have you to say for yourself?"

Now the monk had, during his checkered career, always managed somehow or other to steer clear of the authorities. He was, therefore, unfamiliar with the severe rules of the tribunal and the drastic methods used to enforce those rules. During the latter part of Candidate Djang's statement he had been muttering angrily, but he had been silenced by vicious kicks from the headman. Now he spoke up in an insolent voice.

"I, the monk, want to protest against—"

Judge Dee gave a sign to the headman. He hit the

monk in the face with the heavy handle of his whip, hissing:

"Speak respectfully to His Excellency!"

Livid with rage, the monk rose to attack the headman. But the constables were fully prepared for such an eventuality. They at once fell on him with their clubs.

"Report to me when the man has learned to speak civilly!" Judge Dee told the headman. Then he started to sort out the papers before him.

After some time the sloshing of water on the stone-flagged floor indicated that the constables were reviving the monk by throwing buckets of water over him. Presently the headman announced that he could be questioned.

Judge Dee looked over the bench. The monk's head was bleeding from a number of gashes and his left eye was closed. The other stared up at the judge with a dazed look.

"I have heard," the judge said, "that you told a few gamblers about your dealings with a man called Mao Loo. I now want the truth, and the complete truth. Speak up!"

The monk spat a mouthful of blood on the floor. Then he began with a thick tongue:

"The other day, after the first night watch, I decide to go to the city for a walk. Just as I am coming down the path behind the Buddhist Temple, I see a man digging a hole under a tree. The moon comes out and I see it's Mao Loo. He is in a mighty hurry, using his ax as hoe. I think Brother Mao is up to some dirty trick. But although I am ready for him any time with bare hands or with a knife, I don't like that ax. So I stay where I am.

"Well, he had made his hole; then he throws in his ax, and a wooden box. When he starts shoving the earth in it with his hands, I come out and say: 'Brother Mao, can I help you?' joking-like. He only says: 'You are out late monk!' I say: 'What are you burying there?' He says: 'Nothing but a few old tools. But over there in the temple there's something better!' He shakes his sleeve, and I hear the good money clinking. 'What about a share for a poor man?' I say. He looks me up and down and says: 'This is your lucky night, monk! The people there saw me running away with part of the loot and they came after me, but I gave them the slip in the wood. Now there's only one fellow left in the temple. You go there now quick and grab what you can before they return. I have all I can carry!' And off he goes."

145

The monk licked his swollen lips. On a sign from the judge the headman gave the monk a cup of bitter tea. He emptied it in one draught, spat, and continued:

"I first started digging just to make sure there's nothing there he forgot to tell me about. But the fellow hadn't lied, for once. I find only a box with old carpenter's tools. So I go to the temple. I ought to have known better! The only thing I find is an old baldpate snoring in a bare cell, and a coffin in an empty hall! I know that the son of a dog has told me a story just to get rid of me. That's all, Judge. If you want to know more, just catch that bastard Mao Loo and ask him!"

Judge Dee caressed his side whiskers. Then he asked curtly:

"Do you confess having kidnaped and maltreated that young man?"

"I couldn't let him get away from your constables, could I?" the monk asked sullenly. "And you can't expect a man to hand out food and lodging for nothing. He refused to work, so naturally I had to encourage him a bit."

"Don't prevaricate!" the judge barked. "Do you admit having abducted him to your cave by force and beaten him repeatedly with a willow wand?"

The monk shot a sidelong gance at the headman, who was fingering his whip. He shrugged his shoulders and muttered: "All right, I confess!"

The judge gave a sign to the clerk, who read out his record of the monk's statement. The part about Candidate Djang was phrased more positively than the monk had expressed himself, but he agreed that it was correct and affixed his thumbmark to the document. Then the judge said:

"I can have you punished severely on more than one count. I shall defer my verdict, however, till I have verified your statement as to your meeting with Mao Loo. You'll now be put in jail to meditate on what will happen to you if I find that you have lied!"

When the monk was being led away, Sergeant Hoong came in and reported that Candidate Djang had somewhat recovered. Two constables led him in front of the bench. He was now clad in a neat blue robe, and wore a black cap that concealed his shaven head. Despite his haggard appearance one could still see that he was a handsome young man.

He listened carefully to the scribe reading out the

record of his statement, then impressed his thumbmark on it. Judge Dee looked at him gravely. He spoke.

"As you have stated yourself, Candidate Djang, you have behaved very foolishly, and thereby seriously impeded the course of justice. However, I deem your harrowing experiences of the past few days sufficient punishment for that. Now I have good tidings for you. Your father is alive and he doesn't blame you. On the contrary, he was deeply shocked when he thought you were dead. He was accused in this tribunal of having been involved in your bride's death; that's why you saw the constables at your house. The apparition you saw in your room was I. In your confused state of mind I must have appeared somewhat forbidding to you.

"I regret to inform you that the corpse of your bride has unaccountably disappeared. This court is doing everything in its power to have it recovered so that it can be given a proper burial."

Candidate Djang covered his face with his hands and started to cry softly. Judge Dee waited a little, then pursued:

"Before I let you return home, I want to ask you one question. Were there, besides your father, other persons who knew that you used the pen name Student of the Bamboo Grove?"

Djang replied in a toneless voice:

"Only my bride, Your Honor. I only started to use that pen name after I had met her, and I therewith signed the poems I sent her."

Judge Dee sat back in his chair.

"That's all!" he said. "Your tormentor has been thrown into jail; in due time he'll receive adequate punishment. You can go now, Candidate Djang."

The judge ordered Ma Joong to bring the youngster home in a closed palanquin, to recall the constables on guard in his father's house and to tell him that the house arrest had been canceled.

Then he rapped his gavel and closed the session.

When Judge Dee was sitting again in his private office, he smiled bleakly and said to Tao Gan, who was sitting opposite him together with Sergeant Hoong and Chiao Tai:

"You did your job very well, Tao Gan! The case Liu versus Djang is now solved, save for the problem of the vanished corpse!"

"Mao Loo shall tell us all about that, Your Honor!" the sergeant said. "Evidently Mao Loo killed his cousin for his money. When we have arrested him, he'll tell us what he did with the corpse of Mrs. Djang!"

Judge Dee didn't seem to agree. He said slowly:

"Why would Mao Loo have removed the corpse? I could imagine that Mao Loo, after he had murdered his cousin somewhere near the temple, went to look inside for a place to hide the corpse, and then found the coffin in the side hall. To open it was easy; he had his cousin's toolbox. But why didn't he then simply put the carpenter's body inside on top of that of the woman? Why remove her body—which left him with exactly the same problem as before, namely how to dispose of a dead body?"

Tao Gan, who had been listening silently, playing with the three long hairs sprouting from his cheek, now suddenly said:

"Perhaps a third person, as yet unknown to us, had removed the bride's body before Mao Loo found the coffin. That must have been a person who for some reason or other wanted to prevent at all cost that the corpse would be examined. The dead woman can't very well have walked off by herself!"

Judge Dee shot him a sharp look. He folded his arms in his sleeves and, huddled in his armchair, remained deep in thought for some time.

Suddenly he straightened himself. He hit his fist on the table and exclaimed:

"That's exactly what she did, Tao Gan! For that woman wasn't dead!"

His lieutenants looked at him in utter astonishment.

"How could that be, Your Honor?" Sergeant Hoong asked. "A professional physician pronounced her dead; an experienced undertaker washed her body. Then she was lying in a closed coffin for more than half a day!"

"No!" the judge said excitedly. "Listen to me! Don't you remember the coroner's saying that in such cases the girl would often faint, but that death was rare! Well, suppose she fainted and that the nervous shock caused her to fall into a condition of suspended animation! Our medical books record cases of persons who were in that state. There is complete cessation of breathing, no pulse of the wrist, the eyes lose their luster and sometimes the face will even show cadaveric characteristics. This state has been known to last for several hours.

148

"Now we know that she was encoffined in a great hurry, then carried at once to the Buddhist Temple. Fortunately, the coffin was only a temporary one of thin boards; I myself noticed the crevices. Else she would have died from suffocation. Then, when the coffin had been placed in the temple, and everybody gone, she must have regained consciousness. She'll have shouted and beaten against the walls of her wooden prison, but she was in a side hall of a deserted temple, and the caretaker was deaf!

"The following is just a theory. Mao Loo kills his cousin and steals his money. He searches the temple for a place to hide the body, and hears the sounds from the coffin!"

"That must have given him a bad fright!" Tao Gan remarked. "Wouldn't he have run away as fast as he could?"

"We must assume he didn't," Judge Dee said. "He took his cousin's tools, and opened the coffin. The woman must have told him what had happened and—" His voice trailed off. He frowned, then resumed with annoyance: "No, there we are up against a snag! Wouldn't Mao Loo, upon hearing her story, have realized at once that Dr. Djang would give him a generous reward for having saved his daughter? Why didn't he bring her back immediately?"

"I think she saw the carpenter's corpse, Your Honor," Tao Gan said. "That made her a witness to Mao Loo's crime, and he was afraid she would denounce him."

Judge Dee nodded eagerly.

"That must be it!" he said. "Mao must have decided to take her with him to some distant place, and keep her there till he would have heard that the coffin had been buried. Then he could let her make her own choice: either be sold as a prostitute, or be taken back home, on condition that she promised to tell Dr. Djang some trumped-up story about Mao Loo's saving her. In that manner Mao Loo would in either case earn a couple of gold bars!"

"But where was Mrs. Djang when Mao Loo buried the toolbox!" Hoong asked. "You may be sure that the monk searched the temple thoroughly, and he didn't discover her."

"We'll learn all that when we have caught Mao Loo," the judge said. "But we know already where Mao Loo concealed that unfortunate woman these last days, namely in the brothel behind the fish market! 'Mao Loo's wench,' as the one-eyed man referred to her, is nobody else but Mrs. Djang!"

A clerk came in carrying a tray with Judge Dee's noon

meal. While he was placing the bowls on the table, the judge resumed:

"We can easily verify our theory about Mrs. Djang. You three can have your noon meal now too; then Chiao Tai goes to the brothel and brings the owner here. He'll give us a description of the woman Mao Loo brought there."

He took up his chopsticks, and his three lieutenants left.

Judge Dee ate without really tasting his food. He was trying to digest the new facts that had come to light. There could hardly be any doubt that the case Liu versus Djang was now solved; only some details remained to be filled in. The real problem was to find the link between this case and the murder of the courtesan. One could now safely assume that the professor was innocent, but the whole affair threw a curious light on Liu Fei-po.

When the clerk had cleared the table and poured out a cup of tea, the judge took the documents relating to the murder on the flower boat from the drawer, and started rereading them, slowly caressing his side whiskers.

Thus his four lieutenants found him when they entered the private office. Ma Joong said:

"Well, I now have seen the professor show some real emotion! Wasn't he glad to see his son!"

"The others will have told you already," Judge Dee said to him, "that we have strong reasons to assume that Candidate Djang's bride is alive too. Did you bring the brothel owner here, Chiao Tai?"

"He did!" Ma Joong replied for him. "I saw that beauty waiting in the corridor outside!"

"Bring her in!" Judge Dee ordered.

Chiao Tai came back with a tall, rawboned woman with a coarse, flat face. She bowed deeply, then at once began in a whining voice:

"He didn't even give me time for changing my robe, Your Excellency! How can I appear before Your Excellency in this terrible attire! I said to him—"

"Be quiet and listen to your magistrate!" the judge cut her short. "You know I can close your establishment any time I choose, so you'd better be careful and tell the complete truth. Who was the woman brought to your place by Mao Loo?"

The woman fell on her knees.

"I knew the rascal would land me into trouble!" she wailed. "But what can a weak woman do, Your Excellency! He would have cut my throat, Excellency! Forgive me, Excellency!"

Crying loudly, she knocked her forehead on the floor.

"Stop all that noise!" Judge Dee commanded angrily. "Speak up; who was that woman!"

"How could I know the wench!" the woman cried out. "Mao Loo brings her to my house in the middle of the night; I swear I had never seen her before! She wears a queer, single robe, and looks rather frightened. Brother Mao says: 'The chicken doesn't know what's good for her. Can you imagine her refusing a fine husband like me? But I'll teach her a lesson!' I see the poor girl is really ill, so I tell Mao Loo to leave her alone for the night. That's how I am, Excellency. I always believe in treating them kindly. I put her in a nice room; I give her some good rice gruel and a pot of tea. I remember exactly what I said to her, Excellency. 'Go to sleep, my chicken,' I say, 'and don't worry! Tomorrow you'll see that everything is all right!' "

The woman heaved a deep sigh.

"Oh, you don't know those girls, Excellency! One would have thought that the next morning she'd at least say thank you to me. But no! She woke up the whole house, kicking against the door and shouting at the top of her voice. And when I went up to her she cursed me and Brother Mao and said all kinds of foolish things about her being kidnaped and belonging to a good family—the kind of story they'll always tell. Well, there's one way to make them see reason, and that is to give them a taste of a piece of rope. That shut her up, and when Brother Mao came she went quietly away with him. I swear that's all, Excellency!"

Judge Dee looked at her with contempt. He thought a moment of arresting her for having maltreated a girl, then reflected that she had only acted according to her lights. Those low-class brothels were a necessary evil; the authorities could control them so as to prevent excesses, but they could never eliminate entirely cruelty to the unfortunate inmates. He said sternly:

"You know very well that you are not allowed to give lodging to stray girls. For the time being, however, I'll let you go. But I'll check your story, and if you didn't tell the truth you are done for!"

The woman again began knocking her head on the floor,

protesting her gratitude. On a sign of the judge, Tao Gan led her away.

Judge Dee said gravely:

"Yes, our theory is correct. Candidate Djang's wife is alive, but perhaps it would have been better for her to die than to fall into Mao Loo's hands! We must arrest Mao Loo as quickly as possible and deliver her from that ruffian. They are in a place called Three Oaks Island, in the district Chiang-pei. Does anybody know where that is?"

Tao Gan said:

"I have never been there, Your Honor, but I have heard plenty about it! It's a cluster of islands, or rather a swamp, in the middle of the Great River. The swamp is covered by close-growing bush, half-submerged the greater part of the year. The higher places consist of a dense forest of old trees. Only the outlaws who have gathered there know the creeks and waterways that lead to and through the swamp. They levy a toll on all passing ships and often make raids on the villages along the riverbank. They say that robber band counts more than four hundred men."

"Why hasn't the government cleaned up that robber's nest?" the judge asked, astonished.

Pursing his lips, Tao Gan replied:

"That's not an easy undertaking, Your Honor! It would necessitate a naval operation that would cost many lives. The swamp would have to be approached in small craft, for war junks could not be used in those shallow waters. And the soldiers in those boats would be an easy target for the arrows of the outlaws. I have heard that the army has stationed a chain of military posts along the riverbank, and soldiers patrol the entire region. The idea is to blockade the swamp and thus force the outlaws to surrender. But they have been there for so many years now that they have many secret contacts among the population which are very difficult to trace. Up to now there are no signs that the robbers are short of food or anything else they need."

"That sounds bad indeed!" Judge Dee said. Looking at Ma Joong and Chiao Tai, he asked: "Do you think you could get Mao Loo and the woman out of there?"

"Brother Chiao and me will manage somehow, Your Honor!" Ma Joong answered cheerfully. "It's exactly the kind of job for us! We'd better go out there right now, to take stock of the situation!"

"Good!" said Judge Dee. "I'll write a letter introducing

you to my colleague the magistrate of Chiang-pei, and asking him to give you all assistance."

He took up his writing brush and quickly jotted down a few lines on a sheet of official paper. He impressed the large square seal of the tribunal on it, then gave it to Ma Joong saying:

"Good luck!"

Fifteenth Chapter

THE SERGEANT AND TAO GAN VISIT AN IMPORTANT PERSON; A BUSINESS PROMOTER CONCLUDES HIS VERY LAST DEAL

AFTER MA JOONG AND CHIAO TAI HAD LEFT, JUDGE DEE continued to Sergeant Hoong and Tao Gan:

"While our two braves are in Chiang-pei we shan't be idle either. When I was eating my noon rice I was thinking all the time about Liu Fei-po and Han Yung-han, our two main suspects of the murder of the courtesan. Let me tell you that I am not going to sit here quietly, waiting for the next move of those two gentlemen! I have decided to arrest Liu Fei-po today."

"We couldn't possibly do that, Your Honor!" Hoong exclaimed, aghast. "We have only some vague suspicions; how could we—"

"I certainly can arrest Liu, and I shall," the judge interrupted him. "Liu has proffered in this court a serious accusation against Dr. Djang, and that accusation has now proved to be false. I admit that nobody would blame me if I let the matter rest, especially because Liu was evidently beside himself with grief when he made the accusation, and because the professor hasn't brought forward a plaint against him for slander. Yet the law says that he who falsely accuses another of a capital crime shall be punished as if he himself had committed that crime. The law allows a broad margin of discretion in the application of this article, but in this case I choose to interpret it according to the letter."

Sergeant Hoong looked worried, but Judge Dee took his brush and wrote out an order for the arrest of Liu Fei-po. Then he selected a second form, and said while he was filling it out:

"At the same time I'll have Wan I-fan arrested, for giving false testimony in court regarding his daughter and Dr. Djang. Both of you go now with four constables to Liu's house and arrest him. On your way out, Hoong, tell the headman to take two men and arrest Wan I-fan. Let the two prisoners be conveyed here in closed palanquins, and have them locked up in cells that are far apart; they mustn't know that they share the hospitality of our jail! I shall hear both of them during the evening session. I think that then we'll learn a thing or two!"

The sergeant still looked doubtful, but Tao Gan remarked with a grin:

"It's the same as with gambling: if you rattle the dice well, you'll often throw a nice combination!"

When Hoong and Tao Gan had left, Judge Dee pulled out a drawer and took from it the sheet with the chess problem. He was by no means as sure of himself as he had made his two assistants believe. But he felt he had to start the attack, to take the initiative. And the two arrests were the only way he could think of to achieve that aim. He turned round in his chair and took a chessboard from the cupboard behind him. He placed the black and white men in the position indicated in the problem. He was convinced that it was this chess problem that contained the key to the plot discovered by the dead dancer. It had been made more than seventy years before, and the best chess experts had tried in vain to solve it. Almond Blossom, herself not a chess player, must have chosen it not as a chess problem, but because it could be given a double meaning which had nothing to do with chess. Was it perhaps a kind of rebus? Knitting his eyebrows, he began to rearrange the men, trying to read their hidden message.

In the meantime Sergeant Hoong had given the headman instructions regarding the arrest of Wan I-fan and went himself with Tao Gan to the house of Liu Fei-po. The four constables followed them at a discreet distance, with a closed palanquin.

Hoong knocked on the high, red-lacquered gate. When the barred peephole was opened he showed his pass and said:

"His Excellency the Magistrate has ordered us to have an interview with Mr. Liu."

The doorman opened the gate, and led the two men to the small waiting room in the gatehouse. Soon an elderly man appeared who introduced himself as Liu Fei-po's steward.

"I trust," he said, "that I'll be able to be of service. My master is just taking his siesta in the garden; he can't be disturbed."

"We have strict orders to speak to Mr. Liu in person,"

the sergeant said. "You'd better go and wake him up!"

"Impossible!" the steward exclaimed, horrified. "It would cost me my job!"

"Just take us to him," Tao Gan said dryly. "Then we'll wake him up ourselves! Get going, my friends; don't hinder us in the execution of our official duties!"

The steward turned round, his gray goatee quivering with rage. He crossed a spacious courtyard paved with colored tiles, Hoong and Tao Gan following on his heels. They walked through four winding corridors to a large walled-in garden. Porcelain pots with rare flowers lined a broad marble terrace; beyond there was an elaborate landscaped garden with a lotus lake in the center. Rounding the lake, the steward brought them to an artificial rockery in the back of the garden, consisting of large pieces of rock of interesting shape and color, luted together with cement. Next to it was an arbor, a bamboo framework overgrown with thick ivy. Pointing at the arbor the steward said testily:

"You'll find my master inside there. I'll wait here."

Sergeant Hoong parted the green leaves. In the cool interior he saw only a rattan reclining chair and a small tea table. There was nobody.

The two men quickly rejoined the steward. Hoong rasped at him:

"Don't try to fool us! Liu isn't there!"

The steward gave him a frightened look. He thought for a while, then said:

"He'll have gone to his library."

"Then we'll follow his example!" Tao Gan said. "Lead the way!"

The steward again took them through a long corridor. He halted in front of a black ebony door, decorated with metalwork showing an intricate flower pattern. He knocked several times but there was no answer. Then he pushed, but the door was locked.

"Stand clear!" Tao Gan growled impatiently. He took a small package with iron instruments from his capacious sleeve, and started to work on the lock. Soon there was a click, and he pushed the door open. They saw a spacious, luxuriously furnished library. The heavy chairs and tables and the high bookcases were all made of ebony, elaborately carved. But no one was there.

Tao Gan went straight to the writing desk. All its draw-

156

ers had been pulled out; the thick blue carpet was strewn with folders and letters.

"There's been a burglar here!" the steward cried out.

"Burglar nothing!" Tao Gan snapped. "Those drawers weren't forced; they have been opened with a key. Where is his safe?"

The steward pointed with a trembling hand at an antique scroll picture hanging in between two bookcases. Tao Gan went up there and pulled the painting aside. The square iron door in the wall behind it wasn't locked. But the safe was completely empty.

"This lock hasn't been forced either," Tao Gan remarked to the sergeant. "We'll search the house, but I fear that the bird is flown!"

After Hoong had called in the four constables, they went over the entire mansion, including even the women's quarters. But Liu Fei-po was nowhere, and no one had seen him after the noon meal.

The two men went back to the tribunal in a morose mood. In the courtyard they met the headman, who told them that Wan I-fan had been arrested without difficulty. He was now locked up in the jail.

They found Judge Dee in his private office, still absorbed in his study of the chess problem.

"Wan I-fan has been placed under lock and key, Your Honor," Sergeant Hoong reported, "but Liu Fei-po has disappeared without a trace!"

"Disappeared?" the judge asked, astonished.

"And taken along all his money and important papers!" Tao Gan added. "He must have slipped out through the garden gate, without telling anybody."

Judge Dee hit his fist on the table.

"I have been too late!" he exclaimed ruefully. He jumped up and started striding round the room. After a while he stood still and said angrily:

"It's all the fault of that silly bungler, Candidate Djang! If I had known sooner that the professor was innocent—" He pulled angrily at his beard. Then he said suddenly: "Tao Gan, go and bring Councilor Liang's secretary here, at once! There's still time to question him before the session begins!"

After Tao Gan had hurried outside, he continued to Sergeant Hoong:

"Liu's flight is a bad setback, Hoong! A murder is important, but there are things which are more important still!"

Hoong wanted to ask for some further explanation of that remark, but seeing Judge Dee's tight-lipped face he thought better of it. The judge resumed his pacing; then he stood himself in front of the window, his hands on his back.

In a surprisingly short time Tao Gan came back with Liang Fen. The young man seemed even more nervous than when the judge had seen him last. Judge Dee leaned against his desk; he didn't ask Liang Fen to sit down. Folding his arms across his chest and looking with great deliberation at the young man, he spoke.

"This time I'll speak in plain terms, Mr. Liang! I tell you that I suspect you of being concerned in a despicable crime. It's because I want to spare the old Councilor's feelings that I question you here instead of presently during the session of the court."

Liang's face turned ashen. He wanted to speak but the judge raised his hand.

"In the first place," he continued, "your touching story about the Councilor's reckless spending can also be explained as an attempt to cover up the fact that you are taking advantage of his condition for appropriating his money. Second, I have found in the room of the dead dancer, Almond Blossom, love letters written in your hand. The most recent letters proved that you wanted to break off the relationship, presumably because you had fallen in love with Willow Down, the daughter of Han Yung-han."

"How did you find that out?" Liang Fen burst out. "We had—" But again Judge Dee cut him short, saying:

"You can't have murdered the dancer because you were not on board the flower boat. But you did have a liaison with her, and had secret meetings with her in your room. You could easily let her in by the back door of your small garden. No, I haven't finished! I can assure you that I haven't the slightest interest in your private life; as far as I am concerned you may entertain all the damsels of the Willow Quarter. But you shall tell me all about your affair with the dead dancer. One foolish young man has already obstructed my investigation, and I will not have another repeating that stunt! Speak up, and tell the truth!"

"It isn't true, I swear it, Your Honor!" the young man wailed, wringing his hands in despair. "I don't know that

158

courtesan, and I have never appropriated one copper of my master's money! I admit, however, and do so gladly, that I am in love with Willow Down, and I have reason to assume that my feelings are reciprocated. I have never spoken to her but I see her often in the temple garden, and— But since Your Honor knows this, my deepest secret, you must also know that all the rest is not true!"

Judge Dee handed him one of the dead dancer's letters and asked:

"Did you write this or not?"

Liang Fen carefully examined it. Giving it back to the judge, he said calmly:

"The handwriting resembles mine; it even reproduces some personal peculiarities. Yet I didn't write it. The person who forged it must have had many examples of my handwriting at his disposal. That is all I can say!"

The judge gave him a baleful look. He said curtly:

"Wan I-fan has been arrested; I shall presently question him. You shall attend the session. You can go to the court hall now."

When the young man had taken his leave, Sergeant Hoong remarked:

"I think that Liang spoke the truth, Your Honor."

Judge Dee made no response. He motioned the sergeant to help him don his official robe.

Three beats on the gong announced the evening session. Judge Dee left his private office, followed by Hoong and Tao Gan. When he had seated himself behind the bench, he saw that there were only a dozen or so spectators. The citizens of Han-yuan had apparently for the time being given up hope of hearing sensational news. But he noticed Han Yung-han and Liang Fen standing in the front row, and behind them Guildmaster Soo.

As soon as he had called the roll, Judge Dee filled in a form for the warden of the jail. He gave it to the headman and ordered him to lead Wan I-fan before the bench.

Wan I-fan seemed completely unperturbed by his arrest. He gave the judge an impudent glance, then knelt down and answered in a steady voice the formal questions about his name and profession. Then Judge Dee spoke:

"I have obtained proof that you have lied to this court. It was you who tried to persuade Dr. Djang to buy your daughter. Do you want to hear the details, or do you confess?"

"This person," Wan I-fan replied respectfully, "acknowledges that he has misled Your Honor. He let himself be led astray by his eagerness to help his friend and patron, Mr. Liu Fei-po, in the latter's case against the professor. Since, according to the law, I can be freed on bail for this offense, pending the payment of a fine, I beg Your Honor to fix the amount due. No doubt Mr. Liu Fei-po will be found willing to put up bail, and pay the required sum."

"Second," Judge Dee said, "this court has also proof that you, taking advantage of the Councilor's lapsing into his second childhood, persuaded him to engage in reckless financial transactions, to your own personal gain."

This second accusation didn't seem to make any impression on Wan either. He said placidly:

"I deny emphatically ever having financially injured Councilor Liang. Mr. Liu Fei-po had introduced me to His Excellency; it is on Mr. Liu's advice that I recommended the Councilor to sell some of his estates which in the expert opinion of Mr. Liu were due to diminish considerably in value in the near future. I beg Your Honor to have Mr. Liu deliver testimony."

"I shan't be able to do that," Judge Dee said curtly. "Mr. Liu Fei-po has left without any previous warning, taking away with him his liquid funds and important papers."

Wan I-fan jumped up. His face had a deadly pallor as he shouted:

"Where did he go to? To the capital?"

The headman wanted to press Wan down on his knees again, but the judge quickly shook his head. He said:

"Mr. Liu has disappeared and his household is ignorant of his whereabouts."

Wan I-fan was rapidly losing his self-control. Sweat pearled on his forehead. He muttered, half to himself: "Liu had fled. . . ." Then he looked up at the judge and said slowly: "In that case I shall have to reconsider some of my previous statements." He hesitated, then went on: "I beg Your Honor to grant me time for reflection."

"Your request is granted," Judge Dee replied at once. He had seen the look of frantic entreaty in Wan's eyes.

When Wan had been led back to jail, Judge Dee raised his gavel to close the session. But just at that moment Guildmaster Soo came forward, together with two members of his guild. One proved to be a jadeworker, the other a retail dealer in jade. The latter had sold to the artisan a block of jade, but upon splitting it up into smaller pieces the jadeworker had found it had a defect, and he refused to pay. Since he had discovered that the block was faulty only after he had cut it up, he couldn't return it to the dealer either. Soo had tried to make them accept a compromise, but the men had rejected all his proposals.

Judge Dee listened patiently to the long-winded explanations of both parties. Letting his eyes rove over the court hall, he noticed that Han Yung-han had left. When Soo had again summed up the position, Judge Dee spoke to the dealer and the jadeworker:

"This court finds that both of you are at fault. The dealer, as an expert, ought to have noticed that the block was faulty when he purchased it, and the jadeworker, as an experienced professional, ought to have discovered the defect without cutting up the block. The dealer bought the block for ten silver pieces, and sold it to the jadeworker for fifteen. This court rules that the dealer shall pay the jadeworker ten silver pieces. The cut pieces shall be divided equally among them. Thus each pays a fine of five silver pieces for his lack in professional skill."

He rapped his gavel and closed the session.

Back in his private office Judge Dee said contentedly to the sergeant and Tao Gan:

"Wan I-fan wants to tell me something he didn't dare to reveal in the public session. It is against the rules to question a prisoner in private, but in this case I feel justified to make an exception. I shall have him brought here now. You'll have noticed that he said that Liu Fei-po fled. Now we shall hear more about—"

Suddenly the door flew open and the headman came running inside, followed by the warden of the jail. The former panted:

"Wan I-fan has killed himself, Your Honor!"

Judge Dee crashed his fist on the table. He barked at the jail warden:

"Didn't you search the prisoner, you dog's-head?"

The warden fell on his knees.

"I swear that he didn't have the pastry on him when I locked him in, Your Honor! Somebody must have smuggled that poisoned cake into his cell!"

"So you have admitted a visitor to the jail!" the judge shouted.

"Nobody from outside has come into the jail, Your Honor!" the warden wailed. "It's a complete riddle to me!"

Judge Dee jumped up and went to the door. Followed by Hoong and Tao Gan, he crossed the courtyard, passed through the corridor behind the chancery, and entered the jail. The warden led the way with a lighted lantern.

Wan I-fan was lying on the floor in front of the wooden bench that served as bed. The light of the lantern shone on his distorted face; his lips were covered with foam and blood. The warden pointed silently at a small round piece of pastry on the floor, next to Wan's right hand. One piece was missing; Wan had evidently taken only one bite from it. Judge Dee stooped. It was a round cake filled with sugared beans, as sold by every baker in town. But there was impressed on its top, instead of the usual baker's shop sign, a small picture of a lotus flower.

The judge wrapped the cake up in his handkerchief and put it in his sleeve. He turned round and walked back silently to his office.

Sergeant Hoong and Tao Gan looked worriedly at Judge Dee's tight face as he sat down behind his desk. The judge knew that the sign of the lotus had not been meant for Wan, for it was dark in his cell when a messenger brought him the deadly gift. The sign of the lotus was intended for him, the magistrate! It was a warning from the White Lotus. He said in a tired voice:

"Wan was murdered in order to seal his lips. The poisoned cake was given to him by a member of the personnel. There's treason here in my own tribunal!"

Sixteenth Chapter

TWO VAGABONDS HARASS THE DISTRICT CHIANG-PEI; A DASTARDLY ATTACK ON A PEACEFUL RIVER BOAT

MA JOONG AND CHIAO TAI HAD STUDIED IN THE CHANcery a map of the province, and had made a provisional plan for their expedition.

They selected two good horses, and left town in an easterly direction. After they had descended into the plain they followed the highway for half an hour or so. Then Ma Joong halted his horse and said:

"Don't you think that if we cut across the paddy fields on the right here, we should come soon to the boundary river? Say fifteen miles downstream from our military post at the bridge?"

"That should be about correct," Chiao Tai agreed.

The two men drove their horses along the narrow path that led through the fields. It was very hot and sultry here, and they were glad when they saw a small farm. They drank deeply from the pail of well water the peasant gave them. It was arranged that for a handful of coppers he would look after their horses. As soon as the man was walking the horses to the stable the two friends rumpled their hair and bound it up with rags. Then they exchanged their riding boots for the straw sandals they had brought along in their saddlebags. As he rolled up his sleeves Chiao Tai called out:

"Ho, brother! This is like the old days when we were still in the green woods together!"

Ma Joong clapped him on his shoulder, then each pulled a thick bamboo pole out of the fence, and they walked down the path to the river.

An old fisherman was drying his nets there. He ferried them across for two coppers. While he was paying him Ma Joong asked:

"There aren't any soldiers around here, are there?"

The graybeard gave them a scared look. He shook his head and scurried back to his boat.

The two men walked through the tall reed till they came on a winding country road. Chiao Tai said:

"That checks. According to the map this road leads to the village."

They shouldered their bamboo poles and walked on, lustily singing together a ribald song. After half an hour they saw the village.

Ma Joong went ahead and entered the inn on the small market place. He sat down heavily on a wooden bench and shouted for wine. Then Chiao Tai came in. As he sat down opposite his friend he said:

"I had a look around, brother. All is safe!"

Four old peasants seated at the other table gave the newcomers a frightened look. One put up his hand with index and little finger crooked—the sign for highwaymen. His companions nodded sagely.

The innkeeper came running in with two jugs of wine. Grabbing him by his sleeve, Chiao Tai rasped:

"What do you mean by that, you dog's-head? Take those miserable jugs away and bring the whole jar!"

The innkeeper shuffled out. He came back with his son, carrying between them a wine jar three feet high, and two bamboo ladles with long handles.

"That's better!" Ma Joong called out. "No fussing with cups and jugs!" They dipped the ladles into the jar and drank the wine in greedy draughts, for the walk had made them thirsty. The innkeeper brought a platter with salted vegetables. Chiao Tai scooped up a handful. He found it was mixed with a generous amount of garlic and red pepper. Smacking his lips, he said happily:

"Brother, that's better than those kickshaws you get in the city!"

Ma Joong nodded with his mouth full. When the jar was half-empty they ate a large bowl of noodles and rinsed their mouths with the country tea, which had a pleasant bitter taste. They stood up and reached in their belts for money. The innkeeper hurriedly refused, assuring them that it had been a great honor that they visited his house. But Ma Joong insisted, and added a generous tip.

The two friends walked outside. They lay down under the large fir tree and soon were snoring loudly.

Ma Joong was roused by a kick against his leg. He sat up and looked, then poked Chiao Tai in his ribs. Five men armed with clubs were standing over them, surrounded by a group of gaping villagers. They scrambled up.

164

"We are constables of the tribunal of Chiang-pei!" a squat man barked. "Who are you and where do you come from?"

"Are you blind!" Ma Joong asked haughtily. "Can't you see that I am the governor of this province, traveling in disguise?"

The crowd guffawed. The headman raised his club threateningly. Ma Joong quickly grabbed him by the lapels of his jacket, lifted him two feet from the ground and shook him until his teeth rattled. The constables wanted to help their chief, but Chiao Tai pushed his bamboo pole between the legs of the tallest man and made him topple over. Whirling the bamboo round, he let it swish just over the heads of the others, narrowly missing them. The constables ran away, jeered at by the crowd. Chiao Tai ran after them in pursuit, cursing loudly.

The headman was no coward; he fought hard to loosen Ma Joong's grip and placed a few nasty kicks against his legs. Ma Joong put him down with a thud and quickly took up the bamboo pole. He therewith parried the club blow that the headman aimed at his head, and hit the headman a sharp blow on his arm. The man let the club go, wanting to come to grips with Ma Joong, but the latter kept him off with a few blows with the bamboo that narrowly missed his head. The headman saw that he couldn't keep up this unequal fight. He turned round quickly and ran away.

After a while Chiao Tai came back.

"The bastards escaped!" he panted.

"You gave them a good lesson!" an old peasant remarked contentedly.

The innkeeper had been following the proceedings from a safe distance. Now he came up to Chiao Tai and said in an urgent whisper:

"You two had better get away quick! The magistrate has soldiers here; they'll come soon to arrest you!"

Chiao Tai scratched his head.

"I didn't know that!" he said ruefully.

"Don't worry!" the innkeeper whispered. "My son'll take you across the fields to the Great River. There's a boat there. In an hour or two you'll be at Three Oaks Island. The people there'll help you; just say that old Shao sent you!"

They thanked him hurriedly. Soon they were stealing through the paddy, following the youngster. After a long

165

walk through the muddy fields the young fellow halted. Pointing at a row of trees ahead, he said:

"You'll find a boat hidden in the creek there. Don't worry, the current will take you there all right; only watch out for the whirlpools!"

Ma Joong and Chiao Tai easily located the boat among the shrubs. They stepped inside and Ma Joong poled it out from under the low-hanging branches. Suddenly they saw the river.

Ma Joong put the pole down and took the paddle. They drifted down the mud-brown stream; the bank soon seemed far away.

"Isn't this a very small boat for such a big river?" Chiao Tai inquired anxiously, gripping the gunwales.

"Don't worry, brother!" Ma Joong said with a laugh. "Remember that I am a native of Kiangsu. I was reared on a boat!"

He paddled vigorously to avoid a whirlpool. They were in the middle of the river now; the reed banks appeared like a thin line in the distance. Then they disappeared entirely; there was nothing but the broad expanse of brown water around them.

"Seeing all that water makes me sleepy!" Chiao Tai said testily. He lay down on his back. For more than an hour nothing was said. Chiao Tai slept, and Ma Joong had to concentrate his attention on steering the boat. Suddenly he called out:

"Look, there's some green!"

Chiao Tai sat up. He saw a number of small green patches ahead, barely a foot above the water level and overgrown with weeds. After half an hour they found themselves among larger islands, covered with shrubbery. Dusk was falling and all around them they heard the eerie calls of water birds. Chiao Tai listened intently. Suddenly he said:

"Those are no ordinary birdcalls! They are secret signals as used by the army when reconnoitering!"

Ma Joong muttered something. He had difficulty in steering the boat through a winding creek. Suddenly the paddle was pulled from his hands. The boat rocked violently. A wet head appeared from the water near the poop, and two others emerged behind it.

"Sit still or we overturn the boat!" a voice growled. "Who are you?"

The speaker laid his hands on the gunwale. Dripping with muddy water, he looked like a weird river goblin.

"Old Shao from the village up the river told us to come here," Ma Joong said. "We got into a bit of trouble with the constables there."

"Tell your story to the captain!" the man said. He gave the paddle back, adding: "Row straight ahead to that light you see there!"

Six armed men stood waiting for them on a roughly made landing stage. In the light of the lantern carried by their leader Chiao Tai saw that they wore army uniforms, but without any insignia. They took the two men through a dense forest.

Soon they saw lights glimmering among the trees. They came out on a large clearing. About a hundred men were assembled round campfires, cooking rice gruel in iron pots. All were armed to the teeth. They were taken to the other end of the clearing to a group of four men sitting on footstools under three very old oak trees.

"These are the two fellows about whom our sentries reported, Captain!" the leader of their escort reported respectfully.

The man addressed as captain was a broad-shouldered fellow with a close-fitting mail jacket and baggy trousers of black leather. His hair was bound up with a red scarf. Looking the two men up and down with small, cruel eyes, he barked:

"Speak up, rascals! Your name? Where from? Why? The whole story!"

He spoke with the clipped voice of a military officer. Chiao Tai thought that he was probably a deserter.

"My name is Yoong Bao, Captain," Ma Joong said with an ingratiating smile. "Me and my mate are just two brothers of the green woods." He related how they had got into a fight with the constables, and how the innkeeper had sent them to Three Oaks Island. He added that they would deem it a great honor if the captain would take them into his service.

"First we'll check your tale!" the captain said. And to their guard he added: "Take them to the enclosure where the others are!"

Each got a wooden bowl with rice gruel; then they were led through the forest to another, much smaller clearing. The light of a torch shone on a hut built from logs. In front a man was squatting in the grass eating his rice. At

167

the edge of the enclosure a girl in the blue jacket and trousers of a peasant woman was kneeling under a tree, also busy with her chopsticks.

"You'll not leave this place!" their guard warned and walked off. Ma Joong and Chiao Tai sat down cross-legged opposite the squatting man, who gave them a morose look.

"My name is Yoong Bao," Ma Joong addressed him cordially. "What is yours?"

"Mao Loo," the other replied in a surly voice. He threw his empty rice bowl to the girl and growled: "Wash it up!"

She rose without a word and picked up the bowl. She waited till Ma Joong and Chiao Tai were ready, then also took their empty bowls. Ma Joong eyed her with approval. She was looking sad and she walked with some difficulty, but it was easy to see that she was a very handsome girl. Mao Loo had followed his look with an angry frown. He said gruffly:

"Nothing for you! That's my wife!"

"Pretty wench!" Ma Joong remarked indifferently. "Listen, why do they keep us apart here? One would think we were criminals!"

Mao Loo spat on the ground. He looked quickly at the shadows around them. Then he said in a low voice:

"They are far from friendly, brother! I came here the other day with a friend of mine, a good fellow. We said we wanted to join them. The captain asked all kinds of questions. My friend got annoyed and said a few straightforward things. D'you know what happened?"

Ma Joong and Chiao Tai shook their heads. Mao Loo passed his forefinger across his throat.

"Just like that!" he said bitterly. "They put me here, like in prison! Last night two fellows come sneaking along to drag my wife away; I have to fight with them, till the guards come and collar them. I must say that they are disciplined, but apart from that it's a nasty crowd, and I am sorry I came!"

"What are they up to?" Chiao Tai asked. "I thought they were decent robbers who'd welcome people like us!"

"You go and ask them!" Mao Loo sneered.

The girl reappeared and put the rice bowls under a tree. Mao Loo growled at her:

"Can't you talk to me?"

"Amuse yourself!" the girl replied calmly, and entered

168

the hut. Mao Loo went red with rage, but he made no attempt to follow her. He cursed and said:

"I saved that slut's life! And what do I get? Nothing but a sour face! She got a good beating with a bit of rope, but a fat lot it helped!"

"A woman needs miles of rope across her behind before you get her sensible," Ma Joong remarked philosophically. Mao Loo rose and walked over to the foot of a large tree. He kicked a heap of leaves together and lay down. Ma Joong and Chiao Tai found a place among the dry leaves on the other side of the enclosure. Soon they were sound asleep.

Chiao Tai was awakened by someone blowing on his face. Ma Joong whispered close to his ear:

"I have been out reconnoitering, brother. Two large junks are moored in the main creek, all ready to sail tomorrow morning. There are no watchmen. We could tap our friend Mao Loo on his head, and put him and the girl on one of those junks. But you and I couldn't possibly get that heavy junk out of the creek onto the river. Quite apart from the fact that one has to know the fairway."

"Let's hide in the hold!" Chiao Tai whispered. "Tomorrow, after the bastards have got the junk out on the river, we come out and take them by surprise."

"Splendid!" Ma Joong said contentedly. "Either we get them, or they get us. That's the kind of simple proposition I like. Well, as a rule they don't start before dawn; we still have time for a good nap."

Soon they were snoring.

An hour before dawn Ma Joong got up. He shook Mao Loo by his shoulder. When he sat up, Ma Joong hit him unconscious with a hard blow on his temple. He bound Mao Loo's hands and feet tightly with the thin rope he carried round his waist, and gagged him with a strip of cloth he tore from his jacket. Then he woke up Chiao Tai, and together they went into the hut.

Chiao Tai took out his tinderbox and made light while Ma Joong woke up the girl.

"Me and my mate are from the tribunal in Han-yuan, Mrs. Djang," he said. "We have orders to take you back to the city."

Moon Fairy looked them up and down suspiciously in the faint light. She said curtly:

"You can tell me many things! If you as much as touch me I'll shout!"

169

Ma Joong sighed and took out Judge Dee's letter, which he had concealed in the fold of the rag round his hair. She read it through, nodded, and asked quickly:

"How do we get away from here?"

After Ma Joong had explained their plan, she remarked:

"The guards bring the morning rice shortly after dawn. They'll raise the alarm when they find us gone."

"I have been busy one hour during the night laying a false trail through the forest, in the opposite direction," Ma Joong replied. "You can trust us to know our job, dearie!"

"Keep a civil tongue in your mouth!" the girl snapped.

"A spirited wench!" Ma Joong said with a grin to Chiao Tai. They went outside. Ma Joong loaded Mao Loo on his shoulders. He was an expert in woodcraft; he led Chiao Tai and the girl unerringly through the dark forest to the creek. The black hulls of two large junks loomed up before them.

When they had gone aboard the one in front, Ma Joong went straight to the trap door aft and let Mao Loo slide down the steep ladder. Then he jumped down after him, and Chiao Tai and Moon Fairy followed. They were in a small kitchen. Forward the hold was filled to the ceiling with piles of large wooden boxes, with thick straw ropes wound round them.

"Climb up there, Chiao Tai," Ma Joong said, "and try to shove the upper boxes of the second row aside a bit. That'll be a good place to hide. I'll be back presently."

He grabbed the toolbox that was lying in a corner and climbed up the ladder. While the girl inspected the kitchen, Chiao Tai hoisted himself up on top of the pile of boxes, and crawled into the narrow space between them and the ceiling. As he set to work moving the upper boxes he muttered:

"They are uncommonly heavy; the fellows must have stuffed them with stones!"

When he had made sufficient room for the four of them, he heard Ma Joong come back.

"I have drilled a couple of holes in the other junk," he said contentedly. "By the time they noticed that their hold is flooded, they won't find those holes so easily!" He helped Chiao Tai to hoist Mao Loo on top of the boxes. He had regained his senses and was wildly rolling his eyes. "Don't suffocate, please!" Chiao Tai said. "Remember that our magistrate wants to question you before you die!"

When they had deposited Mao Loo between two boxes, Ma Joong crawled over to the first row and stretched out his hands.

"Come up here!" he said to Moon Fairy. "I'll help you."

But the girl didn't respond; she was thinking, biting her lips. Suddenly she asked:

"How many men does the crew of such a junk consist of?"

"Six or seven," Ma Joong replied impatiently. "Get a move on!"

"I'll stay where I am!" the girl announced. Wrinkling her nose, she added: "I am not dreaming of crawling on those dirty boxes!"

Ma Joong cursed roundly.

"If you don't—" he began.

Suddenly heavy footsteps resounded up on deck; orders were shouted. Moon Fairy pushed open the hatch in the stern and looked outside. She stepped up to the pile of boxes and whispered:

"About forty armed men are boarding the junk behind us!"

"Come up here at once, I tell you!" Ma Joong hissed.

She laughed mockingly. She took off her jacket. With bare torso she started to wash the pans.

"Magnificent figure!" Ma Joong whispered to Chiao Tai. "But what in the name of Heaven does that bit of skirt think she's doing?"

Heavy ropes thudded down on the deck; the junk started to move. The sailors who poled it along began to sing a monotonous song.

Suddenly the ladder creaked. A hefty fellow remained standing halfway down, and stared openmouthed at the half-naked woman. She gave him a saucy look, then asked casually:

"Are you coming to help me?"

"I . . . , I must inspect the cargo," the man brought out. His eyes were glued to the girl's round bosom.

"Well," Moon Fairy said with a sniff, "if you prefer the company of those dirty boxes, just suit yourself! I can manage very well alone!"

"Not on your life!" the man exclaimed. He quickly went down and up to the girl. "Aren't you a looker!" he said with a broad grin.

171

"I don't think you are so bad either," Moon Fairy said. She let him fondle her a moment, then pushed him away and said: "Pleasure comes after work! Get me a bucket of water!"

"Where are you, Liu?" a hoarse voice called down through the trap door.

"Busy inspecting the cargo!" the man shouted back. "I'll come up by and by! You look whether the sail is ready!"

"For how many fellows must I cook rice?" the girl asked. "Do we have soldiers on board?"

"No, those are on the junk behind us," the man called Liu replied as he handed her the bucket. "You just cook something nice for me, dearie; I am the mate and the boss here, you see! The helmsman and the four sailors can eat what's left over!"

A clatter of arms sounded on deck.

"Didn't you say we have no soldiers on board?" Moon Fairy asked.

"Those are the guards of our last outpost," Liu replied. "They come to search the ship before she goes out on the river."

"I like soldiers!" the girl said. "Get them down here!"

The man quickly climbed up the ladder again. He pushed his head through the trap door and called out:

"I have just searched the entire hold, men! It's hot as Hell down here!" There was some altercation; then he came down with a satisfied leer. "I got rid of those!" he said. "I have been a soldier too, dear; I'll do my best!" He put his arm round her waist and started fumbling with the cord of her trousers.

"Not here!" Moon Fairy said. "I am a decent woman. You go and look on top of those boxes there; maybe there's a little cozy corner up there for us!"

Liu hurriedly went to the pile of boxes, and hoisted himself up. Ma Joong grabbed him by his throat, pulled him on top and tightened his grip till the man was unconscious. Then he jumped down into the kitchen. Moon Fairy quickly closed the hatch and put on her jacket again.

"That was a pretty piece of work, my wench!" Ma Joong whispered excitedly. Then he ducked behind the ladder. Two heavy boots came down through the trap door. "What in Hell are you at, Liu!" an angry voice asked.

Ma Joong jerked the man's legs backward. He tumbled down; his head hit the floor with a dull crash. He didn't move. Chiao Tai stuck out his hands from above, and together they got the unconscious man up on the boxes.

"Truss him up and come down here, brother Chiao!" Ma Joong whispered. "I'll climb on deck through the hatch. Be ready to receive the other bastards that I'll send down to you here!"

He climbed through the hatch, pulled himself up along the outside of the hull by the anchor rope, and stepped noiselessly on deck. When he had made certain that no one had seen him, he sauntered up to the helmsman, who was holding the heavy rudder beam with both hands, and remarked:

"It became too hot for me down in the hold!" He saw they were in the middle of the river now. The second junk was behind them. He stretched himself out on his back on the deck.

The helmsman gave him a startled look, then whistled. Three sturdy sailors came running aft.

"Who the devil are you?" the first asked.

Ma Joong folded his hands under his head. He yawned prodigiously and said:

"I am the guard, supposed to watch the cargo. I just finished checking the boxes with old Liu."

"The mate never tells us a thing!" the sailor muttered with disgust. "Thinks the world of himself, he does! I'll just go and ask how much sail he wants put on." He went toward the trap door. Ma Joong scrambled up and followed him together with the two others.

When the man stood over the trap door, Ma Joong suddenly gave him a kick that sent him tumbling down the ladder. He turned round quick as lightning and gave the sailor that came for him a blow under his jaw that made him stagger backward against the railing. Ma Joong followed up with a thrust of his heart region that sent him over the railing into the river. The third sailor lunged out at Ma Joong with a long knife. Ma Joong ducked; the knife passed over his back as he butted his head into his attacker's midriff. The man fell gasping over Ma Joong's back. Ma Joong righted himself and heaved the knife wielder over the railing.

"All good fish fodder!" he called out to the helmsman. "Just keep to your steering job, my friend, else you'll join them!" He peered at the second junk, which had now fallen far behind. It had developed a heavy list to starboard; a crowd of people was running in confusion

173

over the tilting deck. "Those men will never keep their shirts dry!" he remarked cheerfully. Then he went to adjust the large reed sail.

Chiao Tai stuck his head through the trap door.

"You sent me only one," he said. "Where are the others?"

Ma Joong pointed down to the water; he was intent on getting the sail right. Chiao Tai came on deck and said: "Mrs. Djang is making our noon rice."

There was a strong breeze; the junk made good speed. Chiao Tai searched the two distant banks. He asked the helmsman:

"When'll we arrive at a military post?"

"In a couple of hours," the man replied with a sullen face.

"Where were you bound for, bastard?" Chiao Tai asked again.

"For Liu-chiang, four hours downstream. There friends of ours are going to do a bit of fighting."

"You are lucky, fellow!" Chiao Tai remarked. "You won't have to join the fray!"

As they were sitting in the shadow of the sail eating their noon rice, Ma Joong related to Mrs. Djang the adventures of her husband. When he had finished her eyes were full of tears. "The poor, poor boy!" she said softly.

Ma Joong exchanged a quick glance with Chiao Tai. He whispered:

"Do you get what such a spanking wench sees in that mealy-mouthed weakling?"

But Chiao Tai didn't hear him; he was looking intently ahead. He exclaimed:

"Do you see those banners? That'll be the military post, brother!"

Ma Joong jumped up and shouted an order at the helmsman. Then he went to shorten the sail. Half an hour later the junk was lying alongside the quay.

Ma Joong handed Judge Dee's letter to the corporal in charge of the post. He reported that he was bringing in four robbers of Three Oaks Island, and one of their junks. "I don't know what she is carrying," he added, "but it's plenty heavy!" They went to have a look at the cargo together with four soldiers. Just as the corporal, the soldiers had their helmets strapped on tightly, they wore iron shoulder and arm plates over their mail coats, and next to their swords they carried on their belts heavy battle-axes.

"Why do you fellows drag along all that ironware?" Ma Joong inquired, astonished.

The corporal gave him a worried look. He replied curtly:

"There are rumors about skirmishes with armed bands downriver. These four men are all I have left here; the rest have gone with my captain to Liu-chiang."

In the meantime the soldiers had broken open one of the boxes. It was packed with iron helmets, leather jackets, swords, crossbows, arrows and other military goods. The helmets were marked in front with a small white lotus flower, and there was a bag with hundreds of small silver models of the same emblem. Chiao Tai put a handful of those in his sleeve. He said to the corporal:

"This junk was bound for Liu-chiang, and also a second one with forty armed robbers on board. But that one foundered upstream."

"That's good news!" the corporal exclaimed. "Else my captain would have been in trouble in Liu-chiang; he has only thirty men with him down there. Well, what can I do for you? Across the river there is the military post that guards the southern tip of your district, Han-yuan."

"Have us ferried over there quick!" Ma Joong said.

Back in their own territory, Ma Joong requisitioned four horses. The sergeant in charge told them that if they rounded the lake they could be in the city in two or three hours.

Chiao Tai removed the gag from Mao Loo's mouth. He wanted to start cursing but his tongue was swollen and he could only bring out a few hoarse croaks. While Ma Joong tied Mao Loo's feet to the saddle girth he asked Mrs. Djang:

"Can you ride?"

"I'll manage!" she said. "But I am a bit sore. Lend me your jacket!"

She placed his folded jacket on the saddle, then swung herself on the horse.

The cavalcade set out on the way back to the city.

Seventeenth Chapter

AN EYEWITNESS REPORTS ON THE MURDER IN THE TEMPLE; JUDGE DEE FINDS THE SOLUTION OF AN ANCIENT RIDDLE

WHILE MA JOONG AND CHIAO TAI, TOGETHER WITH MRS. Djang and their prisoner, were riding back to Han-yuan, Judge Dee was presiding over the afternoon session of the tribunal.

It was very hot and the judge felt clammy in his thick brocade dress. He was tired and in an irritable temper, having spent the preceding night and that entire morning with Sergent Hoong and Tao Gan looking into the antecedents and manner of living of every single member of the personnel, without discovering a clue. None of the constables or clerks spent more money than he could afford; none of them was frequently absent or seemed in any other way suspect. The judge had the murder of Wan I-fan officially announced as suicide. The body had been put in a temporary coffin and placed in a cell of the jail, pending the autopsy.

The session dragged on, with a large number of routine matters. None of them was particularly important, yet if not dealt with at once there would result stagnation in the administration. The judge was assisted only by Sergeant Hoong. He had ordered Tao Gan to go downtown that afternoon and get an impression of the situation in the city.

Judge Dee heaved a sigh of relief when he could close the session. While Hoong was assisting him to change in his private office, Tao Gan came back. He said in a worried tone:

"There's something brewing downtown, Your Honor. I sat around a bit in the teahouses. People are expecting trouble, but nobody knows what it's all about. There are vague rumors about robber bands assembling in our neighbor district Chiang-pei. Some people whisper that armed robbers are planning to cross the river and come here to Han-yuan. When I walked back here, the shopkeepers were already putting up their shutters. Their closing shop so early is always a bad sign."

The judge pulled at his mustache. He said slowly to his two helpers:

"It started a few weeks ago. I felt it directly after my arrival here, but now it is taking a more definite shape."

"I noticed that I was being followed," Tao Gan resumed. "That was only to be expected; I know many people downtown, and the fact that I was concerned in the arrest of the monk is, of course, being talked about."

"Did you know the man who followed you?" Judge Dee asked.

"No, Your Honor. It was a powerfully built, tall fellow with a red face and a ring beard."

"Did you have the guards arrest him when you arrived at the gate here?" the judge asked eagerly.

"No, Your Honor," Tao Gan replied sadly. "I couldn't manage that. Another fellow joined him when I was passing through a back street near the Temple, and they were closing in on me. I halted in front of an oil shop, next to a large vat that was standing on the sidewalk. When the big fellow came for me I tripped him up so that he fell against the oil vat, which toppled over. The oil ran all over the street, and four sturdy millers came rushing out of the shop. The ruffian said it was all my fault because I had attacked him, but after one look at the two of us the oil millers decided he was fooling them and fell on him. The last I saw was," Tao Gan concluded contentedly, "that they were breaking a stone jar to pieces on the head of the tall fellow, while the other rascal was running off like a hare."

Judge Dee gave the thin man a searching look. He remembered what Ma Joong had told him about Tao Gan luring the monk to the inn. He reflected that this innocent-looking scarecrow apparently could be a very nasty opponent.

Suddenly the door opened, and Ma Joong and Chiao Tai came in, with Mrs. Djang between them.

"Mao Loo has been put in jail, Your Honor!" Ma Joong announced triumphantly. "This girl is the missing bride!"

"Well done!" Judge Dee said with a broad smile. Motioning the girl to be seated, he addressed her kindly: "You are doubtless eager to go home, madam. In due time you'll deliver testimony in the tribunal. Now I only want you to give me an account of what happened after

177

you had been placed in the Buddhist Temple, so that I can check on a murder that was committed there. The unfortunate occurrence that brought you in your predicament is already known to me."

Moon Fairy's cheeks went scarlet. After a while she mastered herself and began:

"For one horrible moment I thought that the coffin had been buried already. Then I noticed a faint whiff of air that came through the cracks between the boards. I tried to push up the lid with all my force, but it didn't budge. Shouting for help, I started kicking and beating the boards till my hands and feet bled. The air had become very close and I was afraid that I would suffocate. I don't know how long I was in this terrible state.

"Then I suddenly heard sounds of laughter. I shouted as loud as I could and again kicked the boards. The laughter stopped abruptly. 'There's someone inside,' a hoarse voice exclaimed. 'It's a ghost, let's run!' I shouted frantically: 'I am no ghost! I have been encoffined alive, help me!' Soon the coffin resounded with hammer blows. The lid was lifted and at last I could breathe fresh air again.

"I saw two men who looked like laborers. The elder one had a kind, wrinkled face; the other looked sullen. I could tell from their flushed faces that both had been drinking heavily. But the unexpected discovery sobered them up. With their help I got out of the coffin, and they took me outside to the Temple garden and made me sit down on the stone bench next to the lotus pond. The old man scooped water from the pond and let me moisten my face; the younger one made me drink some potent liquor from a calabash he was carrying. When I felt somewhat better I told them who I was and what had happened. The elder one then said he was the carpenter Mao Yuan who had worked in Dr. Djang's house that very afternoon. He had met his cousin in the city; they had eaten together and since it had become very late they had decided to pass the night in the deserted temple. 'We'll now take you home,' the carpenter said. 'Then Dr. Djang will tell you everything.' "

Moon Fairy hesitated a moment. Then she went on in a steady voice:

"His cousin had been staring at me silently all the time. Now he said: 'Let's not act rashly, cousin! Fate has decided that this woman should be considered as dead.

Who are we to interfere with the decrees from on high?'
I knew the man desired me and all my fears came back.
I implored the old man to protect me and take me home.
The carpenter scolded his cousin severely. The other flew
in a terrible rage, and a violent quarrel started. Suddenly
the cousin raised his ax and hit the old man a fearful
blow on his head.''

Her face had become pale. Judge Dee gave a sign to the
sergeant, who quickly offered her a cup of hot tea. When
she had drunk that she cried out:

"That horrible sight was too much for me! I fell
down in a faint. When I came to, Mao Loo was standing
over me with an evil leer on his cruel face. 'You'll come
with me!' he growled. 'And keep your mouth shut! One
sound and I'll kill you!' We left the garden by the back
door and he bound me to a pine tree in the forest behind
the temple. When he came back he didn't have the toolbox
and that ax with him any more. He took me through the
dark streets to what seemed to be a low-class inn. We
were received by a horrid woman who took us to a small,
dirty room upstairs. 'Here we'll pass the wedding night!'
Mao Loo said. I turned to the woman and begged her
not to leave me alone. She seemed to understand a little.
'Leave the chicken alone,' she said gruffly to Mao Loo.
'I'll see to it that tomorrow she's ready for you!' Mao Loo
went away without another word. The woman gave me
an old robe so that I could throw that horrible shroud
away. She brought me a bowl of gruel and I slept till
noon of the following day.

"Then I felt much better and wanted to leave that
place as soon as possible. But the door was locked. I
kicked and shouted till the woman appeared. I told her
who I was, that Mao Loo had kidnaped me, and that she
should let me go. But she just laughed and shouted, 'That's
what they all say! Tonight you'll be Mao Loo's bride!' I
became angry and scolded her, saying that I would report
her and Mao Loo to the tribunal. The woman called me a
vile name. She tore down my robe and stripped me naked.
I am rather strong, so when I saw her taking a roll of rope
from her sleeve to tie me up I gave her a push, trying to
get past her to the door. But I was no match for her.
She suddenly hit me a hard blow in my stomach. While
I doubled up gasping she pulled my arms back and in a
moment had tied them behind my back. She grabbed me

by my hair and forced me down on my knees with my head bent to the floor."

Moon Fairy swallowed; an angry blush colored her cheeks as she went on:

"She gave me a vicious lash across my hips with the loose ends of the rope. I cried out in pain and anger and wanted to crawl away, but that horrible woman planted her bony knee on my back, pulled my head up with her left hand and, swinging the rope in the other, began to beat me cruelly. Crying frantically for mercy, I had to submit to that humiliating punishment till the blood trickled down my thighs.

"Then the woman left off. Panting, she pulled me up and made me stand against the bedpost. When she had tied me to it the foul creature left, locking the door behind her. I was left standing there, groaning in agony, for what seemed an interminable time. At last Mao Loo came in, followed by the woman. He seemed to take pity on me; muttering something under his breath he cut my ropes. My swollen legs would not support me; he had to help me onto the bed. He gave me a wet towel, then threw my robe over me. 'Sleep!' he said. 'Tomorrow we'll go traveling!' Soon after they had gone I fell asleep from sheer exhaustion.

"When, the next morning, I woke up I found that every movement caused me a searing pain. To my horror the woman came again. But now she was in a friendly mood. 'For a crook,' she remarked, 'I must say Mao Loo paid handsomely!' She gave me a cup of tea and put ointment on my sores. Then Mao Loo came and made me put on a jacket and trousers. Downstairs a one-eyed man was waiting for us. When they took me outside every step hurt me but the two men kept me moving by hissing horrible threats at me. I didn't dare to accost people in the street. We had an awful journey through the plain in a farmer's cart, then went by boat to the island. Mao Loo wanted to possess me the first night, but I said I was ill. Then two of those robbers came for me, but Mao Loo fought them off till the guards came and took them away. The next day these two officers came—"

"That'll do, madam!" Judge Dee said. "The rest I'll hear from my two lieutenants." He gave Hoong a sign to pour another cup of tea for her; then he continued gravely: "You have shown great constancy in the most trying circumstances, Mrs. Djang! Both you and your husband have, in the brief space of a few days, gone through the most fearful mental and physical anguish. But both of you have shown your undaunted spirit. Now all your troubles are over. Since you two have passed this severe test, I feel certain that a long and happy future lies before you.

"I must inform you that your father, Liu Fei-po, has suddenly left under suspect circumstances. Have you any idea what could have been the reason for his sudden departure?"

Moon Fairy looked worried. She said slowly:

"Father never told me about his affairs, Your Honor. I always thought he did very well in business; we never had any financial worries. He is a rather proud and self-willed man, Your Honor, and not easy to get along with. I know that my mother and father's other women aren't too happy; they seem— But for me he was always so kind. I really can't imagine—"

"Well," the judge interrupted her, "we'll find out in due time." To Hoong he said: "Take Mrs. Djang to the gatehouse, and order a closed palanquin. Send the headman ahead on horseback to inform the professor and Candidate Djang of her impending arrival."

Moon Fairy knelt and thanked the judge; then Sergeant Hoong led her away.

Judge Dee leaned back in his chair and told Ma Joong and Chiao Tai to report.

Ma Joong gave a detailed account of their adventure, stressing the courage and resourcefulness of Mrs. Djang. When he told about the second junk with the armed men, and the cargo of weapons, the judge sat up straight. Then Ma Joong went on to quote the corporal about the unrest in Liu-chiang. He didn't mention the lotus emblem on the helmets, for the simple reason that he didn't know its significance. But when he had finished, Chiao Tai laid a few of the silver White Lotus emblems on the table and said worriedly:

"The helmets we found were also marked with this same emblem, Your Honor. I have heard that many years ago there was a dangerous uprising of a secret political society that called itself the White Lotus. It would seem that the robbers in Chiang-pei now use that old, dreaded symbol in order to intimidate the population."

Judge Dee cast one glance at the silver tokens. Then he jumped up and began pacing the floor, muttering angrily.

His assistants exchanged frightened looks; they had never seen the judge in such a state.

Suddenly he took hold of himself. Standing still in front of them he said with a wan smile:

"I have a problem I must think over quietly. You people go and seek a bit of diversion; all of you deserve some rest!"

Ma Joong, Chiao Tai and Tao Gan went silently to the door. Hoong stood for a few moments undecided, but when he saw his master's haggard face he also followed the others. All the happy excitement over the successful mission of Chiang-pei had left them; they knew that more and very serious trouble lay ahead.

When all had left Judge Dee slowly sat down again. He folded his arms and let his chin rest on his breast. Thus his worst fears had come true. The White Lotus Society had been revived, and it was preparing for action. And one of their centers was located in Han-yuan, his own district, where the Emperor had appointed him, and he had proved unable to discover it. A sanguinary civil war was about to break out; innocent people would be killed, flourishing cities destroyed. Of course, he was powerless to prevent a national disaster; the society would have ramifications all over the Empire and Han-yuan was but one of their many centers. But Han-yuan was close to the capital, and every important point that could be denied to the rebels was an asset for the Imperial Army. But he hadn't even warned the government of what was going on in Han-yuan. He had failed, failed when faced with the most important task of his entire career! He covered his face with his hands in utter despair.

But soon he mastered himself. Perhaps there was still time. The fighting in Liu-chiang was probably a first attempt of the rebels, to gauge the reaction of the Imperial forces. Through the excellent work of Ma Joong and Chiao Tai, the reinforcements for the rebels in Liu-chiang had not arrived. It would take a day or two until the conspirators would have organized another probing attack elsewhere. The local commander in Liu-chiang would inform the higher authorities, and they would institute an investigation. But all that would take too much time! It was the duty of him, the magistrate of Han-yuan, to warn the government that the uprising in Liu-chiang was much more than a local affair, that it was part of a larger campaign, a nationwide conspiracy organized by the revived

White Lotus. He had to prove that to the authorities, prove it that very night, and backed with irrefutable evidence. But he didn't have that evidence!

Liu Fei-po had disappeared, but Han Yung-han was still available. He would arrest Han now, and question him under torture. There was insufficient evidence for such an extreme measure, but in this case the security of the State was at stake. And the chess problem pointed straight at Han. Doubtless his ancestor, Hermit Han, had in the olden days made some important discovery, found some ingenious device, and hidden its key in the chess problem—a discovery that was now being utilized by the Hermit's depraved descendant for his own nefarious scheme. But what could that discovery have been? Besides being a philosopher and chess expert, Hermit Han had also been a good architect; the Buddhist Chapel had been built under his personal supervision. He had also been extraordinarily clever with his hands: he had engraved the inscription of the jade plaque in the altar with his own hands.

Suddenly the judge sat up straight in his chair. He gripped the edge of the table tightly with both hands. Closing his eyes, he visualized the conversation in the Buddhist Chapel, in the deep of night. He called up before his mind's eye that beautiful girl as she stood there opposite him, pointing at the inscription on the altar with her slender hand. The inscription occupied a perfect square, that he remembered clearly. And Willow Down had said that every word had been engraved on a separate piece of jade. The inscription was therefore a square, divided into smaller squares. And the other relic of the old Hermit, the chess problem, consisted also of a square divided into squares. . . .

He pulled out a drawer. Throwing the papers inside carelessly on the floor, he searched with feverish haste for the traced copy of the inscription that Willow Down had given to him.

He found it rolled up in the back of the drawer. He quickly unrolled it on his desk and placed a paperweight on either end. Then he took the printed sheet with the chess problem and laid it next to the text. He carefully compared the two.

The Buddhist text consisted of exactly sixty-four words, arranged in eight columns of eight words each. It was indeed a perfect square. Judge Dee knitted his bushy eyebrows. The chess problem also was a square, but here the surface was divided into eighteen columns of eighteen squares each. And even if the similarity in design had a special meaning, what could be the connection between a Buddhist text and a chess problem?

The judge forced himself to think calmly. The text was taken verbatim from a famous old Buddhist book. It could hardly be used for concealing a hidden meaning without substantial alterations in the wording. Therefore the clue to the relation of the two, if any, was evidently contained in the chess problem.

He slowly tugged at his whiskers. It had been established without doubt that the chess problem was in reality no problem at all. Chiao Tai had observed that the white and black men seemed to be distributed over the board at random; especially, black's position didn't make any sense at all. Judge Dee's eyes narrowed. What if the clue were contained in the black position, the white men being added afterward, merely as camouflage?

He quickly counted the points occupied by the black men. They were spread over an area eight by eight square. The sixty-four words of the Buddhist text were arranged in exactly the same way!

The judge grabbed his writing brush. Consulting the chess problem, he drew circles round seventeen words in the Buddhist text, occurring on the places indicated by the black men. He heaved a deep sigh. The seventeen words read together made a sentence that could have but one meaning. The riddle was solved!

He threw the brush down and wiped the perspiration from his forehead. Now he knew where the headquarters of the White Lotus sect were located.

He rose and walked briskly to the door. His four assistants were standing huddled together in a corner of the corridor outside, unhappily discussing in whispers the possible causes for Judge Dee's despair. He motioned them to come inside.

When they entered his office they immediately saw that the crisis had been tided over. Judge Dee was standing very straight in front of the desk, his arms folded in his wide sleeves. Fixing them with burning eyes, he spoke.

"Tonight I shall clear up the case of the strangled courtesan. I have now finally understood her last message!"

184

Eighteenth Chapter

A CURIOUS ACCIDENT DESTROYS PART OF A MANSION; THE JUDGE DISCOVERS AT LAST A LONG-SOUGHT ROOM

GATHERING HIS FOUR ASSISTANTS ROUND HIM, JUDGE DEE unfolded his plan in a hurried whisper. "Be very careful!" he concluded. "There's treason here in this tribunal; the walls have ears!"

When Ma Joong and Chiao Tai had rushed outside, the judge said to Sergeant Hoong:

"Go to the guardhouse, Hoong, and keep an eye on the guards and constables there. As soon as you see that one of them is approached by someone from outside, you have both of them arrested at once!"

Then the judge left his office, and ascended together with Tao Gan the staircase to the second floor of the tribunal. They went out on the marble terrace.

Judge Dee anxiously looked up at the sky. There was a brilliant moon and the air was hot and still. He held up his hand. There was not the slightest breeze. With a sigh of relief he sat down near the balustrade.

Resting his chin in his cupped hands, the judge looked out over the dark city. It was past the first night watch; people were putting out the lights. Tao Gan remained standing behind Judge Dee's chair. Fingering the long hairs that sprouted from his cheek, he stared into the distance.

They remained there in silence for a long time. From the street below came the sound of a clapper. The night watch was making his rounds.

Judge Dee rose abruptly.

"It's getting late!" he remarked.

"It's not an easy job, Your Honor!" Tao Gan said reassuringly. "It may take more time than we thought!"

Suddenly the judge clutched Tao Gan's sleeve.

"Look!" he exclaimed. "It's starting!"

In eastern direction a column of gray smoke was rising above the rooftops. A thin flame shot up.

"Come along!" Judge Dee called out. He ran down the stairs.

As they arrived in the courtyard below the large gong at the gate of the tribunal raised its bronze voice. Two stalwart guards were beating it with heavy wooden clubs. The fire had been spotted.

Constables and guards came running out of their quarters fastening the straps of their helmets.

"All of you go to the fire!" Judge Dee commanded. "Two guards stay behind here at the gate!"

Then he ran out into the street, followed by Tao Gan.

They found the large gate of the Han mansion wide open. The last servants came running out carrying their belongings in hastily made bundles. The flames were licking at the roof of the storeroom at the back of the house. A crowd of citizens had assembled in the street outside. Under the direction of the warden of that quarter they were forming a chain, handing on buckets of water to the constables standing on the garden wall.

Judge Dee stood himself in front of the gate. He called out in a stentorious voice:

"Two constables will stand guard here! Let no thieves or marauders slip inside! I'll go and see whether anyone is left behind!"

He rushed with Tao Gan into the deserted compound. They went straight to the Buddhist Chapel.

Standing in front of the altar, Judge Dee took the traced copy of the Buddhist text from his sleeve and quickly pointed at the seventeen words he had marked with his brush.

"Look!" he said, "this sentence is the key to the letter lock of the jade panel: 'If ye understand My Message and depress these words ye shall enter this Gate and find peace.' That can only mean that the jade panel is a door that gives access to a secret room. You hold the paper!"

The judge pressed his index on the jade square with the word "if" in the first line. The square receded a little. He pressed harder, using both thumbs. The square receded half an inch; then it would go no farther. The judge went on to the word "ye" in the next line. That square also could be pressed down. When he had pressed the word "peace" in the last line, he suddenly heard a faint click. He pushed the panel and it slowly swung inward, revealing a dark opening of four feet square.

Judge Dee took over the lantern from Tao Gan and crept inside.

When Tao Gan had followed his example, he noticed that the door slowly closed again. He quickly grabbed the knob on its inside and turned it round. He found to his relief that thus he could pull the door open again.

The judge had gone ahead through the low tunnel. After about ten steps it became higher and he could stand upright. The light of the lantern revealed a flight of steep steps leading down into the darkness below. The judge descended, counting twenty steps. He stood in a crypt of about fifteen feet square, hewn from the solid rock. Along the wall on his right stood a dozen large earthware jars, their mouths sealed with thick parchment. One of the covers was torn. Judge Dee put his hand inside and brought out a handful of dried rice. On the left they saw an iron door; ahead there was a dark archway, giving access to another tunnel. Judge Dee turned the knob of the door. It swung inside noiselessly on well-oiled hinges. He stood stock-still.

He saw a small, hexagonal room, lighted by a single wall candle. At the square table in the center a man sat reading a document roll. He only saw his broad back and hunched shoulders.

As the judge tiptoed inside with Tao Gan on his heels the man suddenly looked round. It was Guildmaster Wang.

Wang jumped up and threw his chair backward against Judge Dee's legs. When the judge had scrambled up Wang had run around the table and drawn a long sword. As Judge Dee looked at his face distorted with rage something whizzed past his shoulder. Wang ducked with a quickness amazing in so ponderous a man. The knife landed with a thud in the door of the cupboard against the back wall.

Judge Dee grabbed the heavy marble paperweight from the table. Turning half-aside to avoid the sword thrust that Wang was aiming at his breast, he overturned the table with a powerful push. Wang had quickly retreated a step, but the edge of the table struck his knees. He toppled forward, but at the same time thrust his sword at the judge. As the sharp blade cut through Judge Dee's sleeve he crashed the paperweight on the back of Wang's head. He fell over the tilted table, blood oozing from his crushed skull.

"My knife just missed him!" Tao Gan said ruefully.

"Sht!" Judge Dee hissed. "There may be others about!"

He stooped and examined Wang's head. "That paper-weight was heavier than I thought," he remarked. "The man is dead."

When he righted himself his eye fell on two high stacks of black leather boxes that were piled up against the wall on either side of the door. There were more than two dozen of them, each provided with a copper padlock and a carrying strap.

"That's the kind of box our ancestors used for storing gold bars!" the judge remarked, astonished. "But all seem to be empty." He quickly surveyed the room and continued: "Han Yung-han knows that one lies best if one mixes his lies with the largest possible quantum of truth. When he told me the tale about his alleged abduction, he described these secret headquarters of the White Lotus under his own house! Han must be the leader; he sent Liu Fei-po away to transmit his last instructions to the local heads of the conspiracy. Also, Wang must have held a high position in the society. His head is bleeding heavily, Tao Gan! Wipe the blood up with your neckcloth, then wind it tightly round his head. Presently we shall hide his dead body; we mustn't leave any traces of our visit here!"

He picked up the document roll Wang had been engrossed in. He held it near the candle; it was covered with small, neat handwriting.

Tao Gan wiped the blood from the table and the paperweight, then wrapped the cloth round the dead man's head and deposited the body on the floor. As he was righting the table, Judge Dee said excitedly:

"This is the complete plan for the rebellion of the White Lotus! But unfortunately, all the names of persons and places are written in code characters! There must be a key to this. Look in that cabinet against the back wall over there!"

Tao Gan pulled his knife from the door and looked into the cabinet. On the lower shelf stood a row of large seal stones, all engraved with slogans of the White Lotus. He took the small document box of carved sandalwood from the upper shelf and handed it to the judge. It was empty, but there was place for two small document rolls. Judge Dee rolled up the document he had picked up from the floor. The outside of the protecting flap consisted of purple brocade. The roll fitted exactly into the box; next to it there was just enough space for a second roll of the same size.

"We must find that second roll!" Judge Dee said in an agitated voice. "That must contain the key! See whether there is a secret wall safe!"

While he himself lifted the carpet and scrutinized the stone floor, Tao Gan pulled the half-decayed wall hangings aside and examined the walls.

"Nothing but solid rock!" he reported. "Up there are a few apertures; I feel air coming through."

"Those are ventilation shafts," the judge said impatiently. "They'll come out somewhere on the roof of the house. Let's inspect the leather boxes!"

They shook every one of them, but all were empty.

"Now we go on to the the other tunnel!" the judge said. Tao Gan took up his lantern, and they stepped out into the crypt. Pointing at a square hole in the floor by the side of the dark archway, Tao Gan remarked:

"That'll be a well!"

Judge Dee gave it a casual look. He nodded and said:

"Yes, Hermit Han thought of everything! This crypt was evidently meant as a hiding place for his family in times of trouble. Here they had his entire treasure of gold, dried rice to eat and water to drink. Give me a light!"

Tao Gan held the lantern high so that its light shone through the archway.

"This second tunnel must have been made much later, Your Honor!" he remarked. "The rock stops here, the tunnel has earthen walls, and the wooden shorings look quite new!"

Judge Dee took the lantern from Tao Gan's hand and let its light fall on an oblong, narrow box on the floor of the tunnel, close to the wall. "Open that box!" he ordered.

Tao Gan squatted and inserted his knife under the lid. When he raised it he quickly averted his face. A nauseating smell rose from the box. Judge Dee pulled his neckcloth up over his mouth and nose. He saw the decaying corpse of a man stretched out in the box. The head had been reduced to a grinning skull; frightened insects crawled over the tattered robe that clung to the rotting carcass.

"Put the lid back!" he said curtly. "In due time we shall examine this corpse. We have no time for that now!"

He went down ten steps. About twenty yards farther

on he found his progress barred by a high and narrow iron door. He turned the knob and pushed it open. He looked out into a moonlit garden. Right in front of him he saw an arbor, overgrown with ivy.

"That's Liu Fei-po's garden!" Tao Gan whispered behind him. He poked his head round the corner and went on: "The outside of this door is covered with fragments of rock, luted onto its surface. The door forms part of a large artificial rock. In that arbor over there Liu was wont to take his siesta."

"This secret door explains Liu's vanishing tricks!" Judge Dee remarked. "Let's go back!"

But Tao Gan seemed reluctant to go. He looked at the door with undisguised admiration. They heard in the distance the shouts of the men who were trying to extinguish the fire in the Han mansion.

"Close that door!" Judge Dee whispered.

"Superior workmanship!" Tao Gan said regretfully as he pulled the door closed. When he followed the judge back through the tunnel the light of his lantern fell on a recess in the wall. He grabbed the judge's sleeve and pointed silently at the dry bones in the recess. There were four skulls, which the judge examined. He said:

"The White Lotus apparently killed its victims in the crypt. These bones must have lain here for some time already. The body in the box was their most recent victim."

He quickly went up the flight of steps, entered the hexagonal room and said:

"Help me to get Wang's body to the well!"

They carried the limp corpse into the crypt, and dropped it into the dark hole. Far below they heard a splash.

Judge Dee again entered the room, blew out the candle and pulled the door to behind him. They crossed the crypt and climbed the steep stairs to the altar tunnel. When they were standing in the chapel again, the jade panel closed noiselessly.

Standing in front of it, Tao Gan depressed at randon a few words of the inscription. But as soon as he had pressed down one square, and started on a second, the first rose and resumed its position level with the surface.

"What a fine craftsman that Hermit Han was!" Tao Gan sighed. "If one doesn't know the key sentence, one can press down these squares till one's hair goes gray!"

"Later!" Judge Dee whispered. He dragged Tao Gan by his sleeve to the door of the chapel.

In the courtyard they met a group of servants who were coming back from the town.

"The fire has been put out!" they shouted.

Out in the street they met Han Yung-han, clad in a house robe. He said gratefully to Judge Dee:

"Thanks to the prompt action of your men the fire hasn't done much damage, Your Honor! The greater part of the roof of the storeroom is gone, and all my rice bales have been damaged by the water, but that's all. I think that the hay under the roof got heated, and caused the fire. Two of your officers were on the roof in a remarkably short time and thus could prevent the fire from spreading. Fortunately, there was no breeze; that's what I had been afraid of most!"

"So had I!" the judge said wholeheartedly.

They exchanged a few polite phrases; then Judge Dee and Tao Gan went back to the tribunal.

The judge found two weird figures waiting for him in his private office. Their robes were in tatters and their faces smeared with soot.

"The worst is," Ma Joong said with a scowl, "that my nose and throat are scorched by that accursed smoke! We have found out now that it's much easier to start a fire than to put it out!"

Judge Dee smiled bleakly. When he was seated behind his desk he said to the two men:

"Again you did an excellent job! I regret that I can't yet let you go and take the rest you so well deserve. The biggest task still lies ahead!"

"Nothing like variety!" Ma Joong said cheerfully.

"You and Chiao Tai had better go and wash yourselves," the judge continued, "and have a quick snack. Then put on your mail jackets and helmets, and come back here." To Tao Gan he added: "Call Sergeant Hoong!"

When he was alone Judge Dee moistened his writing brush and selected a long roll of blank paper. Then he took from his sleeve the document roll he had found in the crypt, and started to read it through.

When Hoong and Tao Gan came in the judge looked up and said:

"Get all documents relating to the case of the dead dancer together on the table here, so that you can read out for me those passages I shall ask for!"

While the two men set to work, Judge Dee began to write. He covered the roll with the quick, cursive hand-writing at which he was expert, his brush seeming to fly over the paper. He paused only now and then to ask his assistants to read aloud passages from the records which he wanted to quote verbatim in his report.

At last he put down his writing brush, with a deep sigh. He rolled up his report tightly, together with the document found in the crypt, wrapped them up in oilpaper and told Hoong to seal the roll with the large seal of the tribunal.

Ma Joong and Chiao Tai came in. Clad in heavy mail jackets with iron shoulder pieces and with their pointed helmets, they looked taller than ever.

Judge Dee handed each of them thirty silver pieces. Then, looking at them intently, he spoke.

"You two will ride to the capital at once. Change horses frequently. If there should be none in the post stations, rent them; this silver should be sufficient for that. If there are no accidents, you'll be in the capital before dawn.

"Go straight to the palace of the President of the Metropolitan Court. A silver gong is suspended at the gate there. Every citizen in the Empire is entitled to beat that gong in the first hour after dawn and bring his grievance before the President. You'll beat that gong. Tell the palace chamberlain that you have come from afar to report a grievous wrong done to you. When you are kneeling before the President, give him this roll! No further explanation is necessary."

As Judge Dee handed the sealed roll to him Ma Joong said with a smile:

"That sounds easy! Wouldn't it be better if we wore a light hunting dress? All this ironware is hard on the horses!"

Judge Dee looked gravely at his two lieutenants. Then he said slowly:

"It may prove easy, or it may prove very difficult. It is not impossible that people will try to waylay you on the road. Therefore it's better that you go as you are. Don't ask help from any officials; you are completely on your own. If anyone tries to stop you, cut him down. If one of you should be killed or wounded, the other will go on and bring the roll to the capital. Hand it to the President and to no one else."

Chiao Tai tightened his sword belt. He said quietly:

"That must be a very important document, Your Honor!"

Judge Dee folded his arms in his sleeves. He replied in a tense voice:

"It concerns the Mandate of Heaven!"

Chiao Tai understood. He squared his shoulders and exclaimed:

"Ten thousand years to the Imperial House!"

Ma Joong gave his friend a bewildered look. But he automatically completed the time-honored formula:

"And long live the Emperor!"

Nineteenth Chapter

JUDGE DEE IS VISITED BY A DREADED PERSON; A DANGEROUS CRIMINAL IS FINALLY EXPOSED

THE NEXT MORNING HELD THE PROMISE OF AN EXCEPtionally fine summer day. Overnight a cool mist had come down from the mountains, its freshness lingered on in the sunny morning air.

Sergeant Hoong expected to find Judge Dee out on the terrace. But as he was about to climb the stairs leading up to the second floor, he met a clerk who told him that the judge was in his private office.

Hoong was startled when he saw him. He was sitting hunched over his desk, staring ahead of him with red-rimmed eyes. The stale air in the room, and Judge Dee's rumpled robe, indicated that he hadn't gone to bed at all but had passed the entire night at his desk. Noticing the sergeant's disconcerted look, Judge Dee said with a wan smile:

"Last night, after I had sent our two braves to the capital, I found I couldn't sleep at all. Therefore I stayed at my desk here, and again went over the entire situation as we have it now. Our discovery of the secret headquarters of Han Yung-han, and the subterranean connection thereof with Liu Fei-po's garden, have proved that both Han and Liu play an important role in a criminal complot. I can tell you now, Hoong, that it is a conspiracy directed against our Imperial House, and with ramifications all over the Empire. The situation is serious but, as I have reason to hope, not yet beyond remedy. I suppose that by now my report is in the hands of the President of the Metropolitan Court, and no doubt the government will instantly take all necessary measures."

The judge took a sip from his tea, then continued:

"Last night one link was still missing. I vaguely remembered that in the course of the last few days I had once noticed a small incongruity. It had struck me momentarily, but thereafter I clean forgot it. It had been a trifling thing, yet last night I suddenly felt that it was very

194

important, and that it would prove to supply the missing part of my puzzle, if I could only remember it!"

"Did Your Honor find it?" the sergeant asked eagerly.

"Yes," the judge replied, "I did! This morning, just before dawn, it suddenly came to my mind—but only when the cocks started crowing! Did you ever pause to think, Hoong, that the cocks crow even before the first rays of dawn make their appearance? Animals have sharp senses, Hoong! Well, open the window, and tell the clerk to bring me a bowl of rice, with some pickled green pepper and salted fish; I feel like eating something appetizing. And make me a large pot of strong tea!"

"Will there be a session of the tribunal this morning, Your Honor?" Hoong asked.

"No," replied the judge. "As soon as Ma Joong and Chiao Tai are back, we shall go and visit Han Yung-han and Councilor Liang. I would like to do so right now, for time presses. But inasmuch as the murder of the courtesan has proved to be an affair of national importance, I, a mere district magistrate, am no longer competent to deal with it as I see fit. I can't take further steps without instructions from the capital. We can only hope that Ma Joong and Chiao Tai will come back soon!"

After he had finished his breakfast Judge Dee sent Sergeant Hoong to the chancery to supervise there, together with Tao Gan, the routine business. He himself went upstairs to the terrace.

He stood for a while at the marble balustrade, surveying the peaceful scene at his feet. Countless small fishing craft crowded alongside the quay, and on the road along the lead-gray lake there was a busy traffic of farmers carrying meat and vegetables to the city. As usual, the industrious countryfolk went quietly about their business; even an impending insurrection could not interrupt their ceaseless toil for their daily bowl of rice.

The judge dragged an armchair into a shadowy corner of the terrace and sat down. Soon his lack of sleep asserted itself: he dozed off.

He didn't wake up until Sergeant Hoong came, carrying a tray with his noon meal. Judge Dee got up, walked over to the balustrade and gazed into the distance, shading his eyes with his fan. But there was no sign of Ma Joong and Chiao Tai. He said, disappointed:

"They ought to be back by now, Hoong!"

"Perhaps the authorities wanted to question them, Your Honor," the sergeant said reassuringly.

Judge Dee shook his head with a worried look. He quickly ate his rice, then went down to his private office. Hoong and Tao Gan sat down opposite him, and together they set to work on the papers that had come in that morning.

After they had been at it for half an hour, heavy footsteps resounded in the corridor. Ma Joong and Chiao Tai entered, looking hot and tired.

"Heaven be thanked that you are back!" Judge Dee exclaimed. "Did you see the President?"

"We did, Your Honor," Ma Joong said in a hoarse voice. "We handed him the document roll, and he glanced it through in our presence."

"What did he say?" the judge asked tensely.

Ma Joong shrugged his shoulders. He replied:

"He rolled the documents up, put them in his sleeve and ordered us to tell Your Honor that he would study them in due time."

Judge Dee's face fell. This was bad news. He had, of course, not expected that the President would discuss the matter with his assistants, but neither had he expected so casual a reaction. After some reflection he said:

"Well, I am glad anyway that nothing happened to you two!"

Ma Joong pushed the heavy iron helmet back from his perspiring brow. He said dejectedly:

"No, nothing really happened, but I still think that things don't look too good, Your Honor! This morning, when we had passed through the west gate of the capital, two men on horseback overtook us, both elderly men. They said they were tea merchants on their way to the western provinces, and asked whether they might join us as far as Han-yuan. They spoke civilly enough, and they carried no arms, so what could we do but say yes? But the elder one had such a thoroughly mean look that I felt shivers up my spine every time I caught his eye! They didn't make any trouble, however, although they were remarkably silent all the way."

"You were tired," Judge Dee remarked. "Probably you were a bit oversuspicious."

"That wasn't all, Your Honor!" Chiao Tai now said. "Half an hour later a group of about thirty horsemen emerged from a side road. Their leader said they also were merchants, and also on their way to the western provinces! Well, if those were merchants, then I am a nursemaid! I seldom saw such a fine collection of assorted ruffians, and I am certain they carried swords concealed under their robes. However, since they took the lead and went to ride in front of us, it didn't look too bad. But when after another half hour or so another thirty self-styled merchants came and joined us, and brought up the rear of our cavalcade, Brother Ma and I thought that we were in for trouble."

The judge had straightened in his chair. He looked fixedly at Chiao Tai as he continued:

"Since we had delivered the document, we didn't worry. We thought that if the feast started, at least one of us should be able to fight his way through to the roadside, take to the field and fetch help from a military post. But what makes it look so bad is that the fellows didn't attack us at all. They were completely sure of themselves; they evidently had larger things in mind than killing two messengers! Their only aim was apparently to prevent us from raising the alarm. But we could hardly have raised any alarm, for all the guard posts we passed were deserted! Not a soldier in sight, all along the road! When we were rounding the lake, the men started to melt away in groups of five or six, and when we entered the town we had only those two elderly fellows with us. We told them they were arrested, and took them here to the tribunal. But they didn't seem to mind that at all; the insolent rascals said they would like to speak to Your Honor!"

"Those sixty scoundrels who rode with us are but one column of the rebels, Your Honor!" Ma Joong added. "When we were approaching the town I saw in the distance two long files of horsemen riding through the mountains, heading for the city. They probably think they can take us by surprise! But our tribunal is solidly built and occupies a strategic position; we can easily defend it!"

Judge Dee crashed his fist on the table.

"Heaven knows why the government didn't take any action on my report!" he exclaimed angrily. "But whatever happens, those despicable rebels won't be able to take my town so easily! They haven't got battering rams, and we can dispose of about thirty able men. How are we standing with our stores of arms, Chiao Tai?"

"There are plenty of arrows in the armory, Your Honor!" Chiao Tai said with enthusiasm. "I think we can hold them off at least one day or so, and give them a bad time too!"

"Bring those two miserable traitors here!" Judge Dee ordered Ma Joong. "They think they can make a deal with me! Han-yuan is their headquarters; they hope I'll hand the town over to them without a fight. We'll show them how wrong they are! But first we'll make those two scoundrels tell us how many men the rebels have, and where their positions are! Get them here!"

Ma Joong left the room with a happy grin.

He came back with two gentlemen in long blue robes and wearing black skullcaps. The elder one was tall; he had a cold, expressionless face with a thin, ragged ring beard. His heavy-lidded eyes were half-closed. The other was a thickset man with a sharp, sardonic face. He had a jet-black mustache and a stiff, short beard. He looked at the judge and his four lieutenants with watchful, very bright eyes.

But Judge Dee stared only at the elder man, speechless with astonishment. A few years earlier, when he was serving in the Cabinet Archives in the capital, he had once seen this dreaded person, from a distance. Someone had then told him his name, in a frightened whisper.

The tall man raised his head and let his queer, slate-colored eyes rest for a while on the judge. Then he made a move with his head in the direction of Judge Dee's assistants. The judge motioned the four men peremptorily to leave them alone.

Ma Joong and Chiao Tai looked dumfoundedly at the judge, but as he nodded impatiently they shuffled to the door, followed by Sergeant Hoong and Tao Gan.

The two newcomers sat down in the pair of high-backed armchairs that stood against the side wall, reserved for important visitors. Judge Dee knelt down in front of them, and touched the floor three times with his forehead.

The elder man took a fan from his sleeve. Leisurely fanning himself, he said in a curious, flat voice to his companion:

"This is the Magistrate Dee. It took him two months to discover that here in Han-yuan, in his own district, in his own town, a treacherous conspiracy had its headquarters. Apparently, he is unaware of the fact that a magistrate is supposed to know what is going on in his district."

"He doesn't even know what is going on in his own tribunal, sir!" the other said. "He blithely states in his

198

report that the rebels have a spy among his personnel. Criminal negligence, sir!"

The elder man heaved a resigned sigh.

"As soon as these young officials get appointed outside the capital," he remarked dryly, "they at once start to take things easy. Lack of control by their immediate superiors, I suppose. Remind me that we summon the Prefect of this region; I'll have to speak to him about this disgraceful affair."

There was a pause. Judge Dee remained silent. One spoke to this exalted person only when asked to. And it was his duty to blame and criticize. For the elder man, although officially ranking as an Imperial Censor, was in reality the Grand Inquisitor, the formidable Chief of the Imperial Secret Service. He was called Meng Kee, a name that made the highest metropolitan officials shiver in their gold-embroidered robes. Fiercely loyal, completely incorruptible, of inhuman, detached cruelty, this man was invested with practically unlimited authority. He represented in his person the final check, the ultimate control on the colossal apparatus of the Imperial civil and military service.

"Fortunately, you were, as always, diligent, sir!" the bearded man said. "When ten days ago our agents reported rumors about the White Lotus being revived in the provinces, the Generalissimo was informed and immediately took all necessary measures. And when this Magistrate Dee at last woke up from his comfortable slumber and reported that the headquarters were located here in Han-yuan, the Imperial Guards took up positions in the mountains and around the lake. They never yet have caught you napping, sir!"

"We do the little we can!" the Censor said. "It's the local officials that are the weakest link in our administration. The rebellion will be crushed, but with considerable bloodshed. If this man Dee had been more diligent about his duties, we could have immediately arrested the leaders, and crushed the insurrection in the bud." Suddenly his voice rang out with a metallic ring as he directly addressed the judge: "You made at least four inexcusable mistakes, Dee! First, you let Liu Fei-po escape, although you yourself state that you suspected him. Second, you allow one of the rebel agents to be murdered in your own jail, before you extract information from him. Third, you kill Wang when you should have captured him alive so as to

199

question him. And fourth, you send an incomplete report to the capital, with the key missing. Speak up, Dee, where is that key document?"

"This person confesses his guilt!" Judge Dee said. "He doesn't have the document, but he assumes that——"

"Spare me your theories, Dee!" the Censor cut him short. "I repeat, where is that document?"

"In the house of Councilor Liang, Excellency!" Judge Dee answered.

The Censor jumped up.

"Have you taken leave of your senses, Dee?" he asked angrily. "You shall not cast doubt on Councilor Liang's integrity!"

"This person confesses his guilt!" the judge repeated, giving the formula required by etiquette. "The Councilor was unaware of what went on in his house."

"He tries to gain time, sir!" the bearded man said disgustedly. "Let's arrest him and throw him in his own jail!"

The Grand Inquisitor made no response. He started walking up and down, angrily swinging his long sleeves. Then he halted in front of the kneeling judge. He asked curtly:

"How did that document come to be in the Councilor's house?"

"It was removed to there by the leader of the White Lotus, Excellency, for greater safety," Judge Dee replied. "This person proposes respectfully that Your Excellency's men occupy the Councilor's mansion and arrest everybody they find there, without the Councilor himself or anyone outside knowing it. Then I wanted to send a messenger to Han Yung-han and Kang Choong, pretending to come from the Councilor, and informing them that the Councilor wishes to see them immediately on an urgent matter. I propose that then Your Excellency proceed there too, allowing me to act as Your Honor's attendant."

"Why all the tomfoolery, Dee?" the Censor asked. "The town is in the hands of my men; I shall have Han Yung-han and Kang Choong arrested at once. Then we shall go all together to the Councilor's house. I shall explain to the Councilor, and you shall show us where the document is!"

"This person wanted to make certain," Judge Dee said, "that the leader of the White Lotus didn't escape. I suspect

Han Yung-han, Liu Fei-po and Kang Choong, but I don't know what role they play in the conspiracy. Perhaps the leader is quite a different person, so far unknown to us. The arrest of the others might warn him, and he might flee."

The Censor thought for a while, slowly pulling at the thin fringe round his chin. Then he said to the other:

"Let our men bring Han and Kang to the Councilor's house. See to it that it's done in complete secrecy!"

The bearded man frowned; he didn't seem to agree. But as the Censor made an impatient gesture, he quickly got up and left the room without a word.

"You may rise, Dee!" the Censor said. He resumed his seat, pulled a roll of documents from his sleeve and started to read.

Judge Dee made a gesture toward the tea table. He said diffidently:

"May this person have the honor of offering Your Excellency a cup of tea?"

The Censor looked up from his papers with an annoyed air. He said haughtily:

"You may not. I eat and drink only what has been prepared by my own men."

He resumed his reading. The judge remained standing, his arms straight at his sides, as prescribed by Court rules. He never knew how long he stood there. His initial feeling of relief when he knew that the Imperial Government had taken instant and adequate measures against the rebellion now made place for an increasing anxiety about the correctness of his theories. With feverish haste he tried again to survey all possibilities, searching for a clue that he might have overlooked, for a conclusion that was not completely justified.

A dry cough roused him from his thoughts. The Censor put the documents back in his sleeve, stood up and said:

"It's time, Dee. How far is the Liang mansion from here?"

"Only a short walk, Your Excellency."

"Then we shall go there on foot so as not to attract attention," the Censor decided.

Outside in the corridor Ma Joong and Chiao Tai gave the judge an unhappy look. The judge smiled at them reassuringly and said quickly:

"I am going out. You two will guard the front gate, and Hoong and Tao Gan shall keep an eye on the back

201

door. Don't let anybody go in or out until I am back."

In the street there was the usual bustle of the crowd going about its business. Judge Dee was not astonished. He knew the terrible efficiency of the secret service; no one would have noticed that the town was in their hands. He strode along quickly, the Censor close behind him. No one paid any attention to these two men in their plain blue robes.

The door of the Liang mansion was opened by a thin man with an impassive face. The judge had not seen him before; evidently the Inquisitor's men had taken over the house. The man said respectfully to the Censor:

"The members of this household have been arrested. The two guests have arrived; they are with the Councilor in his library."

Then he led them silently through the semiobscure corridors.

When Judge Dee entered the dim library he saw the old Councilor sitting in the armchair behind the red-lacquered desk in front of the window. In the armchairs against the wall opposite he saw Han Yung-han and Kang Choong, sitting very straight.

The old Councilor lifted his heavy head. Pushing his eyeshade up a little, he looked in the direction of the door.

"More visitors!" he mumbled.

Judge Dee stepped up to the desk and made a deep bow. The Censor remained standing by the door.

"I am the magistrate, Excellency," the judge said. "Please excuse this abrupt visit. By Your Excellency's leave I only wanted—"

"Be brief, Dee!" The old man spoke wearily. "It's time that I retire for taking my medicine." His heavy head sagged forward.

The judge had put his hand in the goldfish basin. He quickly felt under the water the pedestal of the small statue. The goldfish swam round excitedly, their cool, small bodies slipping past his hand. He felt that the upper part of the pedestal could be turned round. It was a lid; the statue of the Flower Fairy was its handle. He lifted it up; a copper cylinder became visible, its rim just above the water. He put his hand inside, and took from it a small document roll, its protecting flap consisted of purple brocade.

The Councilor, Han and Kang Choong sat very still. "Sit

down!" the myna bird in the silver cage screeched suddenly.

Judge Dee went over to the door and handed the roll to the Censor. He whispered:

"This is the key document!"

The Grand Inquisitor unrolled it, and quickly read through the beginning. Judge Dee turned round and surveyed the room. The old Councilor sat still as a graven image, looking at the goldfish basin. Han and Kang Choong stared at the tall men by the door.

The Censor gave a sign with his hand. Suddenly the corridor was crowded with Imperial Guards in their shining gold armor. He pointed at Han Yung-han and Kang Choong, saying:

"Seize me those men!" As the soldiers poured inside, the Censor continued to Judge Dee: "Han Yung-han does not occur on this list, but we'll arrest him anyway. Follow me; I shall offer our apologies to His Excellency."

The judge held him back. He quickly went up to the desk himself. Bending over the table, he ripped the eyeshade from the Councilor's forehead. Then he said sternly:

"Rise, Liu Fei-po! I accuse you of having foully murdered the Imperial Councilor Liang Meng-kwang!"

The man behind the table slowly got up. He righted himself and squared his broad shoulders. Despite the false beard and whiskers, and the paint, it was easy to recognize the imperious face of Liu Fei-po. He didn't look at his accuser; his burning eyes were fixed on Han Yung-han, who was being put in chains by the soldiers.

"I have killed your paramour, Han!" Liu called out to him in a sneering voice. With his left hand he lifted up his beard in a taunting gesture.

"Arrest the man!" the Censor barked at the soldiers.

Judge Dee stood aside as four men came to the table, the one in front swinging a rope. Liu stepped up to them with folded arms.

Suddenly Liu Fei-po's right hand shot from his sleeve. There was a flash of a knife, then blood spurted from his throat. He swayed on his feet; then his tall shape collapsed on the floor.

The leader of the White Lotus, the pretender to the Dragon Throne, had himself put an end to his life.

Twentieth Chapter

**THE JUDGE GOES OUT FISHING WITH HIS ASSIST-
ANTS; HE REVEALS THE MYSTERY OF THE LAKE OF
HAN-YUAN**

DURING THE ENSUING DAYS THE EMPEROR'S HAND WAS
heavy on the White Lotus Society.

In the capital and in the provinces numerous higher and
lower officials and several wealthy civilians were apprehended, heard and summarily executed. With the sudden
arrest of the central and local leaders, the backbone of the
revolt had been broken; there was nowhere any organized
attempt at large-scale rebellion. There were minor upris-
ings in some distant districts, but those were quelled by
the local troops with little losses.

In Han-yuan the men of the Grand Inquisitor had temporarily taken over the entire administration from Judge
Dee. The Censor himself had hurried back to the capital
directly after Liu Fei-po's suicide. The sardonic man with
the black beard was in charge; he employed Judge Dee
as handyman and general adviser. The district was cleaned
thoroughly of subversive elements. Kang Choong confessed, and informed against the clerk who had been the
agent of the White Lotus inside the tribunal. Besides,
there were also some henchmen of Guildmaster Wang,
and a dozen or so ruffians whom Liu Fei-po had employed
to do the rough work for him. All these criminals were
forwarded to the capital.

Since Judge Dee had been suspended from his duties,
to his relief he did not have to be present at the execution
of Mao Loo. The higher authorities had originally decided
that Mao was to be flogged to death. But the judge succeeded in having the sentence mitigated to simple decapita-
tion, pointing out that Mao Loo had not raped Mrs.
Djang, and had even defended her when the two robbers
on Three Oaks Island wanted to ravish her. The monk
was sentenced to ten years' hard labor on the northern
frontier.

On the morning that Mao Loo was beheaded there fell
a torrential rain. The citizens of Han-yuan said that their

tutelary deity wished to wash away the blood that had been shed in his territory. The rain stopped as suddenly as it had begun and the afternoon was cool and sunny.

That evening all executive powers would be officially restored to Judge Dee. Therefore this was his last free afternoon. He decided to go out fishing on the lake.

Ma Joong and Chiao Tai went down to the quay and rented a small, flat-bottomed boat. When they had brought it along the landing stage, Judge Dee arrived on foot, wearing a large round sun hat on his head. He was accompanied by Sergeant Hoong and Tao Gan; the latter carried the fishing tackle.

When all had entered the boat, Ma Joong stood himself in the stern and took hold of the oar. Slowly the boat moved out over the rippling waves. They all silently enjoyed for some time the fresh breeze over the water.

Suddenly Judge Dee spoke.

"I found it quite interesting this last week to watch how our secret service men operate. That fellow with the short beard—I still don't know who or what he really is!—was rather reserved at first, but later he thawed somewhat, and allowed me to see the more important documents. He is an excellent investigator, thorough and systematic. I have learned much from him. But he has been keeping me so busy that now is the first time that I can have a quiet chat with all of you!"

The judge let his hand hang into the cool water. He pursued:

"Yesterday I went to see Han Yung-han; he was still upset about the severe questioning he underwent, but even more about the fact that Han-yuan, his own city, had been the center of a treacherous plot! He never knew about the crypt his ancestor had built under the house, but our bearded friend refused to believe that. He questioned Han two days in succession and was becoming quite nasty over it. At last, however, Han was set free because I pointed out that he had immediately reported to me his having been abducted by the White Lotus, despite their dire threats. Han was very grateful and I therefore took the opportunity of informing him that Liang Fen and his daughter were in love with each other. First Han said indignantly that Liang Fen was not good enough for his daughter, but later he gave in and said he would not object to their betrothal. Liang Fen is an honest, serious young fellow, and Willow Down a charming girl, so I think that it'll be a successful marriage."

"But didn't Han have an affair with the courtesan Almond Blossom?" the sergeant asked.

Judge Dee smiled ruefully.

"I must frankly confess," he said, "that I have judged Han wrongly all through. He is a very old-fashioned, slightly bigoted and rather narrow-minded man, good at heart but not too bright. In fact, not a very impressive personality. No, he never had an affair with the dead dancer. She, however, was a great personality! Great in her love—and in her hate. Look; you can just see in the distance over there, among the green trees of the Willow Quarter, the white marble pillars of the memorial arch that they are erecting there on His Majesty's august command. The inscription will read: 'Example of loyalty to State and Family.' "

They were well out on the lake now. The judge cast out his line. Suddenly he quickly drew it in again. Ma Joong cursed. He also had seen the large, dark shadow that passed through the green water, just underneath the boat. There was a flash of two small, glowing eyes.

"Here we shan't catch anything!" Judge Dee remarked testily. "Those brutes will have chased away all the fish! Look, there goes another one!" Noticing the frightened look of his four companions, he went on: "I had surmised all along that it was those huge tortoises that explained the disappearance of the bodies of those unfortunate people who drowned in the lake. Once those animals have acquired a taste for human flesh . . . But don't be afraid, they'll never attack live people. Take her farther out, Ma Joong; ahead we'll have a better chance."

Ma Joong started to scull vigorously. The judge folded his arms in his sleeves, and looked pensively at the town on the distant bank.

"When did Your Honor discover that Liu Fei-po had murdered the old Councilor and usurped his place?" Sergeant Hoong asked.

"Only at the very last moment," Judge Dee replied. "I mean that night I passed without sleep at my desk, after I had sent Ma Joong and Chiao Tai to the capital. The case of the spendthrift Councilor, however, was but a side issue; the central problem was that of the dead dancer. And that case really started several years back, with Liu Fei-po's thwarted ambitions. But during the last phase, which we witnessed here in Han-yuan, the political plans of Liu were relegated to the background by his emotional relation to two women, namely his daughter, Moon Fairy, and his paramour, Almond Blossom. That relation is the kernel of this case: when I had understood that point, all the rest at once became crystal clear.

"Liu Fei-po was a man of extraordinary talents, courageous, resourceful, energetic, a born leader. But his failing to pass the literary examination wounded his pride, and his subsequent great success in the business world could never heal that wound. It festered on, and culminated in a bitter resentment against our government.

"An accidental occurrence roused his ambition to revive the old White Lotus movement, in order to overthrow our Imperial House and found himself a new dynasty. Once he happened to purchase in a curio shop in the capital an old manuscript, written by Hermit Han, which contained his plan for the secret crypt. The Grand Inquisitor discovered this manuscript among Liu's papers, in his residence in the capital. Hermit Han states there that he planned to build such a crypt, as a haven of refuge for his descendants in turbulent times. He says he planned to hide there his entire treasure, twenty boxes with gold bars; to dig there a well, and to store there dried foodstuffs. The manuscript ends with a design for the letter lock of the entrance to the crypt, in the altar in the Buddhist Chapel. And the Hermit appended a note to the effect that the secret should be transmitted in the Han family, from father to eldest son.

"When he had read this, Liu probably began by assuming it only represented the vagaries of an old man's mind. But he decided that it might be worthwhile to visit Han-yuan, in order to verify whether Hermit Han perhaps actually executed his plan. Liu arranged for Han Yung-han to invite him to stay in his house for a week or so. Then Liu found out that Han knew nothing about his ancestor's plans. Han only knew about Hermit Han's instruction that the Buddhist Chapel should never be closed, and that a lamp should be kept burning there always. Han thought that this was a proof of his ancestor's piety, but of course the Hermit's real intention was that his descendants should have access to the secret entrance at all times of day and night, to cope with any sudden emergency. One night Liu must have paid a secret visit to the chapel. Then he found that the crypt and everything else really existed, just as the Hermit had described. Liu must have realized that the sudden demise of the old Hermit had prevented him from divulging the secret to his eldest son, Han Yunghan's grandfather. But the printer of the chess handbook published the manuscript exactly according to Hermit Han's draft, including the last page with the enigmatical chess problem. No one except Liu Fei-po, and probably the dead dancer, ever knew that the problem was nothing but the key to the letter lock in the Buddhist Chapel."

"The Hermit was an exceedingly clever man!" Tao Gan exclaimed. "The fact that the chess problem was published guaranteed that this key would never be lost; yet no un-initiated person could ever guess its real meaning!"

"Indeed," Judge Dee said, "Hermit Han was a wise and very learned man, a man I would have liked to have met! But to continue. Now Liu Fei-po had in the Han treasure the enormous capital needed for organizing a nationwide conspiracy, and at the same time he had at his disposal an ideal place to serve as secret headquarters and council room of the movement. He built a villa on the empty lot in between the Han mansion and the residence of Councilor Liang, and had four workmen make the subterranean passage connecting the crypt with his own garden. I assume that thereafter Lieu himself killed the four unfortunate workmen, since we found the bones of four men in the secret passage.

"However, as the plot expanded, Liu's expenses increased. He had to send substantial bribes to corrupt officials; he had to pay bandit leaders and supply them and their men with arms. Liu's own capital and the Hermit's treasure melted away, and he had to look for other sources of income. Then he conceived the plan to appropriate the wealth of Councilor Liang. He used to walk with the old man in his garden, and it was easy for Liu to make himself familiar with the Councilor's habits and those of his small household. About half a year ago he must have lured the old man into the secret passage, and there murdered him. He placed the body in a coffin there, where Tao Gan and I found it. From that time on the 'Councilor' became ill, his eyes grew worse, he became forgetful, and began to pass the greater part of his time in his bedroom. All this camouflage enabled Liu Fei-po to play his double role. He must have disguised himself in the crypt, then crept through his own garden into the Councilor's house. The rooms occupied by the secretary, Liang Fen, were located at the other end of the compound, and the old couple who acted as servants were really in their dotage; thus everything was favorable for his impersonation. Sometimes, however, unforeseen circumstances obliged him to act his part longer than anticipated. This, together with Liu's attending meetings of the White Lotus council in the crypt, explain his 'vanishing tricks,' which began to attract the attention of the members of his household—as related by the palanquin bearer to Sergeant Hoong.

"Together with his henchman Wan I-fan, Liu made a careful study of the Councilor's properties, and then they began to sell out his estates. In this manner Liu obtained the funds he needed for completing the preparations for the insurrection. Everything went well. He began to consult with his confederates about a suitable time for action. Just then, however, there came trouble. It started in Liu's private life. This brings us to the courtesan Almond Blossom, or, to call her by her real name, Miss Fan Ho-i."

The boat was lying still now. Ma Joong had seated himself, cross-legged, in the stern. He and the three others listened intently to the judge. Judge Dee pushed the sun hat back from his forehead. Then he spoke.

"The conspiracy had spread also to Shansi Province. A landowner in Ping-yang, called Fan, became a member. But later he repented, and decided to denounce the plot to the authorities. The White Lotus came to know about his plan. He was forced to commit suicide, after they had compelled him to sign a forged document in which he confessed to having commited a crime against the State. All his possessions fell into the hands of the White Lotus; his widow, his daughter, Ho-i, and his infant son were reduced to the state of beggars. His daughter thereupon sold herself as a courtesan. With the money thus obtained her mother could purchase a small farm in Ping-yang, and later Almond Blossom sent her regularly the greater part of her earnings, for the education of her small brother. These data I found in the report which the secret agents sent in yesterday from Ping-yang, after they had apprehended and questioned the local leaders of the White Lotus.

"The rest of her story can be easily reconstructed. Before her father died he must have told her something about the plot, including that the headquarters were located in Han-yuan, and that Liu Fei-po was the chief. The courageous and loyal girl then resolved to avenge her father, and to expose the conspiracy. That is evidently why she insisted upon being resold in Han-yuan, and why she accepted Liu Fei-po as her lover. Her aim was to extract from him the secrets of the White Lotus, then to denounce him and his fellow plotters to the authorities.

"She was a woman of a strange, haunting beauty, and she had an exceptionally strong personality. I think that her family was one of those for which Ping-yang is well known, where there are transmitted from mother to daughter abstruse secrets regarding the exercise of occult powers. Yet I doubt whether she would have succeeded in binding such an utterly egoistic and ambitious man as Liu Fei-po to her, were it not that she bore a striking resemblance to Moon Fairy, Liu's own daughter.

"I don't pretend, my friends, to be able to understand and analyze the dark vagaries of human passion. I confine myself to stating that Liu's love for his daughter was mingled with a feeling that, according to our sacred social order, a man may harbor only for a woman not related to him by the ties of blood. Liu's passionate love for his daughter was the only vulnerable spot in his cruel, cold soul. He must have fought his guilty passion with all his might; his daughter never knew about it. I don't know how much this passion affected his relation with his wives, but I wouldn't be surprised if his home life had been a very strained and unhappy one. However this may be, his love affair with the courtesan must have afforded Liu an escape from the conflict that was raging in his soul, and that gave the liaison a depth of passion that Liu could probably never have experienced with any other woman.

"During their secret meetings—it has now transpired that these took place in a pavilion in the garden of Guild-master Wang—Almond Blossom learned from her lover several facts about the White Lotus, including the secret meaning of the chess problem. Liu wrote her love letters. He had to give vent to his obsessing passion, even in writing. But he was sufficiently clever not to write those letters in his own hand. He imitated that of Liang Fen, the Councilor's secretary, with which he had become familiar through his study of the Councilor's financial documents. Heaven knows what perverse whim made Liu sign those love letters with the pen name of Candidate Djang, his daughter's lover. I repeat, those dark impulses are beyond my comprehension.

"Liu had never intended his daughter to marry. He couldn't bear the thought that she would ever leave him and be possessed by another man. When she fell in love with Candidate Djang, Liu violently opposed the match and ordered his henchman Wan I-fan to slander Dr. Djang, to give him a valid reason for withholding his permission. But then Moon Fairy fell into a decline. Liu couldn't bear to see her so unhappy so, with what must have been a tremendous effort, he gave his consent. We may safely assume that the impending separation from Moon Fairy distressed Liu greatly. Moreover, his love letters to the dancer show that at the same time he began to suspect her real intentions, because of her eagerness to obtain information on the White Lotus. He decided to break off their liaison. Since he was thus about to lose the two women he loved, we can easily imagine his perturbed state of mind. On top of that, his financial worries increased daily. In his role of 'Councilor' he had sold the greater part of the Liang estates, and the day set for the outbreak of the rebellion was approaching. He needed money, much money, and he needed it quickly. Therefore he took the capital of his confederate, Guildmaster Wang, and he ordered Kang Choong to persuade his elder brother to extend a substantial loan to Wan I-fan. I think this about sums up the situation as it existed about two months ago, shortly after our arrival here in Han-yuan."

Judge Dee paused a moment. Tao Gan asked:

"How did Your Honor discover that Kang Choong was a member of the White Lotus?"

"Only because he had gone to so much trouble to secure the loan," the judge answered. "It had at once struck me as strange that an experienced businessman such as Kang Choong should advise giving a large loan to such a dubious small promoter as Wan I-fan. As soon as I had understood that Wan I-fan must be a member of the conspiracy, I knew that Kang Choong must be concerned in it also. Liu Fei-po's last, frantic efforts to obtain ready cash supplied me with an important clue, which, together with Liu's 'disappearances' and the sudden illness of Councilor Liang, led me to the discovery of the impersonation. I connected the queer thirst for gold of the old Councilor with the need for money of the White

Lotus member Wang. Since the Councilor, also because of his advanced age, was above suspicion, there was but one possible conclusion."

Tao Gan nodded. He pulled slowly at the three hairs that sprouted from his left cheek. Judge Dee continued:

"Now I come to the murder of the courtesan—a most complicated affair that became clear to me only at the very last moment. Moon Fairy was married to Candidate Djang, and the next day the banquet on the flower boat took place. Since Liu suspected the dancer, he watched her all the time that night. When she, standing between Han and me, spoke to me about the plot, Liu read the words from her lips. But he wrongly thought that she was addressing Han."

"But we had agreed that such a mistake was impossible," Sergeant Hoong interrupted. "She addressed you as Your Honor!"

"I ought to have seen through that sooner!" Judge Dee said with a wan smile. "Remember that she wasn't looking at me when she spoke, and that she spoke fast. Therefore Liu Fei-po misread 'Your Honor' as 'Yung-han,' Han's personal name! This must have put Liu in a cold rage: his mistress not only planned to betray him, but she wanted to do so to a secret rival in love, Han Yung-han! For how could he explain her addressing Han by his personal name otherwise than that she had intimate relations with him? That explains the nasty way Liu employed the next day to close Han's mouth by abducting and threatening him. And it also explains why Liu's very last words before he plunged the dagger in his throat were a sneer at the expense of his supposed rival in love. Fortunately, the dancer's remark on chess had escaped Liu, for at that moment Anemone returned to our table and obstructed Liu's line of vision. If Liu had caught that second remark too, he would doubtless have evacuated his secret headquarters in the crypt at once!

"Since the dancer wanted to betray him, Liu had to kill her instantly. I could have read the truth in Liu's eyes when he was watching her dance. He had to kill her, and he knew it was the last time he would see her in her dazzling, breath-taking beauty. There was hate in his eyes, the hate of the betrayed lover, but at the same time the deep despair of the man who is going to lose the woman he loves.

"Guildmaster Peng's sickness gives Liu a good pretext

for leaving the dining room. He accompanies Peng to the starboard deck. While Peng is standing there at the railing, very ill, Liu walks over to port, beckons Almond Blossom through the window, and leads her to the cabin. He knocks her unconscious, places the bronze incense burner in her sleeve, and lets her down into the water. Then he joins Peng, who by then is feeling better, and returns together with him to the dining room. You can imagine Liu's state of mind when he heard that the body had not sunk down to the bottom of the lake, and that the murder had been discovered.

"However, worse things were still to come for Liu. The following morning he learns that his beloved daughter, Moon Fairy, has been found dead on her bridal couch. He had lost the two women who dominated his emotional life. His maniacal hatred does not turn against Candidate Djang, but toward his father. Liu's own forbidden passion makes him assume at once that the professor too is guilty of desire for Moon Fairy. This is, at least as far as I can see, the only explanation for Liu's fantastic accusation of Dr. Djang. Moon Fairy's death is a fearful shock for Liu. When her dead body unaccountably disappears, Liu at last loses his self-control completely. From then on Liu is as a man possessed, hardly responsible for his actions.

"His henchman Kang Choong has stated in his confession that Liu at once ordered all his men to search for his daughter's body. He then behaved so strangely that Kang Choong, Guildmaster Wang and Wan I-fan began to worry over their leader. They strongly disapproved of Liu's abducting Han Yung-han; they said it was much too risky, and that the murder of the courtesan would be sufficient warning to Han not to talk about what she had told him. But Liu refused to listen; he had to hurt his rival in love. Thus Han was put in a closed palanquin by Liu's underlings, carried round in Liu's garden, then brought into the secret room under his own house! Han described to me the hexagonal room correctly, and he remembered that he was carried up the ten steps that lead from Liu's secret passage up to the crypt. The man with the white mask was Liu himself, who would not forego this opportunity for humiliating and maltreating the man with whom he thought Almond Blossom had been deceiving him.

"We now approach the end of this somber tale. Moon

213

Fairy's body is not found; Liu is hard pressed for money, and he also fears that I am beginning to suspect him. In this tight corner he decides to disappear as Liu Fei-po, and to direct the final phase of the conspiracy in his role of Councilor Liang.

"I arrest Wan I-fan before Liu has apprised him of his planned disappearance. When I tell Wan that Liu has fled, Wan is convinced that Liu has abandoned his ambitious scheme, and he decides to tell me everything, in order to save his own skin. But the clerk of the court, Liu's agent in our tribunal, warns Liu, and Liu has him hand Wan the poisoned cake. The lotus emblem on the cake was not intended for Wan—remember that it was dark in his cell!—it was meant for me, in order to frighten and confuse me so that I would not interfere those last days before the revolt.

"That same night Liu lets Wang and Kang Choong be informed that henceforward they must contact him in the Councilor's residence. Wang and Kang hold council together; they agree that Liu is losing his head, and that Wang shall take over. Wang goes to the crypt to appropriate the secret-key document, which will give him power over the entire organization. But Liu had already transferred that document to the hiding place in the goldfish bowl. Tao Gan and I surprise Wang in the hexagonal room, and he is killed."

"How did Your Honor know that the document was concealed in the goldfish basin?" Chiao Tai asked eagerly.

Judge Dee smiled. He said:

"When I visited the so-called Councilor, and was kept waiting in his library, the goldfish first behaved in a perfectly natural manner. As soon as they saw me standing over the bowl, they came to the surface, expecting to be fed. But when I stretched out my hand to the statue, they suddenly became very excited. That astonished me, but I didn't stop to think about the possible cause. However, after I had reached the conclusion that Liu was acting the part of the old Councilor, I suddenly remembered the incident. I knew that those fish are hypersensitive, like all animals of breeding; they do not like people dipping their hands in their water. I realized that they must have had a previous experience of a hand doing something under the water and thus disturbing their small, quiet world. Thus I deduced that the pedestal probably was a secret hiding place. And since the most important

214

possession of Liu was a small document roll, I assumed that he had hidden it there. That's all!"

Judge Dee took up his angling rod and started to put the line in order.

"This important case," Sergeant Hoong said with satisfaction, "will doubtless bring quick promotion for Your Honor!"

"For me?" the judge asked, astonished. "Goodness, no! I am very glad that I wasn't summarily dismissed from the service! The Grand Inquisitor has reprimanded me severely for my belated discovery of the plot, and the official document about my being reinstated in my function as magistrate here repeated that remark in black and white, and in no uncertain terms! There was added to it a note from the Board of Personnel, which said that it was only my last-moment finding of the key document to the conspiracy that had moved the authorities to clemency. A magistrate, my friends, is supposed to know what is going on in his district!"

"Well," Hoong resumed, "anyway, this is the end of the case of the murdered courtesan!"

Judge Dee remained silent. He put down his rod and looked pensively out over the water for a while. Then he slowly shook his head and said:

"No, I have a feeling that this case is not yet ended, Hoong; not quite. The courtesan was possessed by such an implacable hatred that I fear that Liu's suicide has not appeased her. There are passions so intense, of such an inhuman violence, that they gain, as it were, a life of their own, and retain their power to harm even long after those who harbored them have died. It is even said that those dark powers will sometimes possess themselves of a dead body and then use it for their sinister aims." Noticing the disconcerted look on the faces of his four companions, he hastily added: "However, strong as they are, those ghostly forces can only harm a man who raises them himself by his own dark deeds."

The judge bent over the gunwale and looked into the water. Did he see again, deep down below, that still face staring up at him with unseeing eyes, as on that fateful night on the flower boat? He shivered. Looking up, he spoke, half to himself.

"I think that a man whose mind is bent on evil had better not roam alone at night on the banks of this lake."